CLOSE TO THE BONE

The Theresa MacLean series by Lisa Black

* *available from Severn House*

CLOSE TO THE BONE

Lisa Black

This first world edition published 2014
in Great Britain and in the USA by
SEVERN HOUSE PUBLISHERS LTD of
19 Cedar Road, Sutton, Surrey, England, SM2 5DA.
Trade paperback edition first published
in Great Britain and the USA 2014 by
SEVERN HOUSE PUBLISHERS LTD.

British Library Cataloguing in Publication Data

Black, Lisa, 1963- author.
    Close to the Bone.
    1. MacLean, Theresa (Fictitious character)–Fiction.
    2. Women forensic scientists–Ohio–Cleveland–Fiction.
    3. Murder–Investigation–Fiction. 4. Detective and
    mystery stories.
    I. Title
    813.6-dc23

ISBN-13: 978-0-7278-8402-2 (cased)
ISBN-13: 978-1-84751-520-9 (trade paper)

All Severn House titles are printed on acid-free paper.

Severn House Publishers support the Forest Stewardship Council™ [FSC™],
the leading international forest certification organisation. All our titles that
are printed on FSC certified paper carry the FSC logo.

Typeset by Palimpsest Book Production Ltd.,
Falkirk, Stirlingshire, Scotland.
Printed and bound in Great Britain by
TJ International, Padstow, Cornwall.

ONE

T he blood didn't worry her, not at first. A few drops of blood at a morgue are like a coffee stain or an errant paper clip in a sea of cubicles. The dead are often not tidy, and any person overly concerned with biohazards quickly chooses another line of work.

Theresa MacLean was not overly concerned with biohazards, so she ignored the red smear on the ancient tiled wall as she crossed to the elevator, just as she ignored the lone occupant of the receiving dock, a large figure lying lifeless beneath a white sheet on a rolling steel gurney. Theresa carried no less than ten small paper bags, clutched in both hands, containing bits of windshield glass and amber brake lights from a hit-and-run, for which Dispatch had ripped her from her warm bed in the wee hours of the morning. The clock now gained on three a.m., placing her in that awful limbo in which she had to decide whether 'tis nobler to go home and try to eke out, by the time she finally got between the sheets, perhaps another hour of sleep before the morning began, or to just give up and stay at work. Even after a dozen years in forensic work this particular debate never failed to stymie her and, getting a firmer grip on the bags, she spared one finger to punch the 'Up' button with a touch more force than strictly necessary. The corpse under the sheet left her to it. The dead are courteous that way.

Then she noticed the rest of the blood.

A tiny smear on the floor in front of the elevator, underneath the hand-like print on the wall. Another near the door to the front area, which contained the deskmen's office, Property, and Reception.

Theresa glanced up the long hallway of the back half of the building, to the autopsy suite and teaching amphitheater. Nothing. The rooms were dark, as would be expected in these early hours. Cleveland's death rate remained robust, but the county budget had never allowed for a night shift.

There should have been no one present in the three-story building except two deskmen with their feet up, watching television and venturing out to the dock only when the body-snatchers brought in an after-hours victim. The deskmen would transfer the deceased to a gurney, accept the paperwork, wheel the body into cold storage and return to the small flat-screen. Now Theresa realized that she did not hear the television. No gunshots or canned laughter. Nothing.

Walking away from the elevator now, she managed to pull open the door without dropping the ten small bags and move into the front hallway.

Property was closed, of course, and only a nightlight glowed out in the lobby, next to the reception desk. The Property officer worked banker's hours but would be available for call-back if a corpse rolled in with a few bricks of gold or a briefcase of cash. Anything smaller went into a drop box. Through large glass windows Theresa could see into the desk-men's office; it looked messy, but then it always did. She stepped into the doorway of this, the only brightly lit room in the entire building, and promptly wished she hadn't.

She let the ten small paper bags slip to the counter. Some landed in dark flecks of dried blood – terrific, nothing like contaminating one set of evidence by disturbing another set. She pulled her cellphone from a pocket. Theresa had no intention of plucking her way through the puddles to use the office phone, off its hook and lying in a tangle of wire next to the body. Her fingers began to shake as she called the only number that doesn't mind answering in the middle of the night.

Dispatch answered; specifically, a recent transplant who had left her former life in Manhattan but kept the accent.

Theresa identified herself, which the dispatcher probably already knew from the caller ID. Then she told the dispatcher where she called from. Then she told the dispatcher that their deskman, Darryl Johnson, now lay on the floor in front of Theresa, covered in blood and not moving, eyeglasses lying unbroken in a nearby puddle.

'Can you find a pulse?' the dispatcher asked.

Theresa picked her way through the red swipes on the floor – she could see from the color that they had largely dried and only the thicker pools still glistened with wet centers – and put two fingers to the fleshy, blood-covered neck, wondering how callous she would seem if she stopped first to pull on a pair of gloves. She had them right in her pocket . . . perhaps she'd been a bit hasty to dismiss the dangers of biohazards.

But she didn't, and her fingers slid against his skin with a sickening ease. She couldn't find a pulse, but that might not mean anything . . . Theresa could barely find her own pulse in a calm moment, much less anyone else's. The people she usually worked with no longer *had* pulses, or else they'd be heading next door to University instead of the Medical Examiner's Office.

'No pulse,' Theresa said into the phone.

'Are you sure?'

'No.'

'Can you turn him on his back? We can try CPR.'

Theresa looked around the small room. 'I don't think you understand. The floor looks like a kid's finger painting, and the desks and ledgers and stacks of paper are all flecked with red spots, beginning to turn brown. It got on the glass windows, some of it. One eye is swelling, and I'm pretty sure his nose is broken. He's bleeding from the mouth, and there's a tooth on the floor—'

'Okay,' the dispatcher said, 'but we need to get some oxygen to his brain. You say he's on the floor – just turn him so his back is flat.'

Theresa said nothing for a moment, then stammered: 'Move the body? Before I photograph the scene?'

She'd sooner cut off a finger.

But even ex-New Yorkers can still sound tough when they want to. 'He's not a body yet! Now shove him on to his back!'

Theresa shoved. She tucked the phone between ear and shoulder and shoved, getting both hands bloody now. Biohazards be damned.

The voice on the phone walked her through an awkward and completely ungraceful attempt at CPR, her hands pressing down with all the weight she could muster while balancing in a crouch to avoid soaking her pants or disturbing the blood pools around the body any more than she already had. Darryl spewed out a few droplets at first as Theresa worked his lungs, and she looked down at his ruined face and tried to muster up a sense of urgency. She had said goodnight to him only seven or so hours before, abandoning her shift as he came on for his. He had waved a hand and she had smiled, the routine for the past eleven or twelve years. But Theresa's urgency went straight to grief. He was gone, his eyes clouding, his flesh cooling, his black skin coated with a red sheen of blood, and she could only marshal counter arguments for the dispatcher in case she even mentioned mouth-to-mouth. Sirens howled in the distance.

'There's a word,' Theresa said, in between tiny puffs of exertion.

'What?'

'A word. Written on the cabinet door. Just above the body.' She added: 'Written in blood.'

This distracted the dispatcher from the revival efforts. 'What does it say?'

'*Confess.*' The sirens sounded closer now. 'It says "confess".'

'Are you alone in the building?' the dispatcher asked.

'I have no idea. There should be a second guy here – Justin Warner, I think. They always work in pairs. I need to look for him. He might still be alive.' And then she guiltily abandoned Darryl, who certainly wasn't. None of the compressions had produced a pulse or affected him in any way. Sightless eyes continued to stare, and not so much as a knuckle hair moved. Theresa turned her back on him and used her elbows to hit push bars until she could open the loading dock door for the EMTs. She pointed with bloody hands and they went to work, and for the second time that night Theresa violated crime scene protocol by abandoning her crime scene to non-forensic personnel. She didn't even stay to observe their disturbances but made her way up the darkened back hallway to the autopsy suite.

The lights from the parking lot illuminated the room sufficiently for her to find a path to the sink, the orangey rays glinting off steel tables with their own drains and the implements from a cheesy horror movie which hung on the wall. She went through half a stack of folded paper towels getting the blood off her hands, then left them in a pile in a corner of the dissecting counter; she didn't want to use the sink or the garbage cans in case the killer had done the same – though, to judge from the smears he left in the loading dock on his way out, she bet he hadn't.

Then she could finally remove the phone from under her neck before the extreme angle became a permanent crick.

'EMTs are with the victim,' she said to the voice on the phone, hoping to sound crisp and professional and, she felt certain, failing. Instead her voice trembled and cracked. 'I have to go now.'

'You can stay on the phone with us until the police arrive,' the dispatcher said in equal parts suggestion, order, and attempted comfort. 'ETA is sixty seconds.'

But Theresa had had enough of a victim's job; time to get back to her own. 'No. I'm going to find Justin.'

'Who?'

'The other deskman,' she said, and hung up.

TWO

Moving faster now that she didn't have to risk contaminating surfaces or balance a cellphone on her shoulder, Theresa pulled on gloves (finally!) and flicked on the lights in the autopsy suite, small teaching amphitheater, and X-ray room, and pulled the chain to open the mechanical sliding door to the cooler. No drops of blood, no scrawled messages, and no signs of the missing deskman. The bodies in the refrigerated chamber lined up in a neat row, fatally cold within their zipped-up white bags, the abattoir smell leaching from the stainless steel walls.

Next she stepped into the all-black room with the charcoal-gray paper backdrop and the lights with umbrellas over them – a standard photography studio, except that instead of happy couples and adorable babies the cameras here flashed on bloodied clothing and weapons of destruction. Through a rotating door sat a three-by-six-foot darkroom, no longer needed in these days of digital technology, but the photographers had left it in place (largely to discourage visitors, Theresa suspected). To pass through it required stepping into the rounded spot and staying a moment in complete blackness while pulling the cylinder around oneself, an experience Theresa avoided at the best of times. It wasn't the darkness she minded but the close quarters, large enough for only one person. She stood in the exact center, found the handle, and rolled the recalcitrant cardboard cylinder to one side, wondering if she would be able to tell when the opening appeared in front of her, or if she'd have to push a hand through the space to know it was there.

Or if someone would reach in for her instead.

But the opening did come into view, near as she could tell, as a shade of less than total dark against inky blackness. She thrust first her hand, then her body into the unknown, its deep hues pulsing around her like a living thing.

But one advantage to the digital age is the ubiquitous ready light. No room is truly dark any more – each one has a few, or an array, of tiny red, blue or green lights indicating the presence of a monitor, a tower, a battery back-up, a cellphone dock, a charging station, until the area glows with a faint but usable ambience. Theresa used this to find a light switch.

Once the overhead fluorescents came on – no worries of overexposing a photo, the room hadn't seen a strip of film in seven years – the cavern appeared as simply the messy, cramped work space of some very busy technicians rather than the lair of a bloody murderer. Unless he had wedged himself into one of the overfull cabinets, and Theresa wasn't about to embarrass herself by checking. She flicked out the light and subjected herself to the claustrophobic cylinder. Her bravado clicked off as soon as the overhead bulbs did, and she hoped no one would be waiting to greet her on the other side.

No one did, and she moved on, making her way back up the rear hallway.

Truthfully, she might not even be looking for Justin. She hadn't seen a second person in the deskmen's office when she'd left that night; in a normal rotation it should have been Justin paired with Darryl, but for all Theresa knew he could have called in sick and someone else had taken his shift, or Darryl had toughed it out solo. Unusual, but not unheard of.

The ME's office consisted of three floors built in the early fifties, and neither the ventilation nor the decor had been improved since that time. Plans had been finalized for a gleaming new center, but after the housing market imploded and the economy went to hell the project had become lost in budget limbo. Theresa complained along with everyone else but secretly expected to weep the day they had to leave this battered piece of history behind. She spent most of her waking hours here, now with Rachael off at college, and felt as comfortable on this worn linoleum as she did puttering around her own house – so stalking alone around an empty building possibly inhabited by a bloody killer did not strike her as insane. This was not a crime scene or an unsecured area. This was her home.

She heard the EMTs working in the front, destroying the

sanctity of her scene while trying to save an already lost life, but still Theresa did not return. The remainder of the first floor consisted of three spaces. The first – the viewing room, a tiled chamber just large enough for a single gurney and large windows, through which the family could identify a loved one – sat empty. The second – the separate autopsy suite for decomposed cases – also appeared undisturbed. Though rarely used, the air there had long since festered into that of a slaughterhouse with even more disgusting overtones; without thinking she held her breath, and not from apprehension. Theresa moved on to the third and final space, the decomp autopsy suite's accompanying 'deep freeze' cooler, kept at minus seventy degrees Fahrenheit. She flicked on the light. Nothing.

She checked in on Darryl and the EMTs on her way back through the front hallway. They were crouching on her bloodied floor – she would have to get exemplars of their shoe prints, though most of the blood had dried and would not stick – and while one had his fingers pressed to the deskman's neck, the other had clearly given up and was gazing at the word scrawled on the cabinet door. He jumped when Theresa spoke. 'You're not planning to transport, are you?'

'Nah. He's gone.'

'Then please don't move him any more than you can help until I can photograph. And don't let the cops come in.'

'What? Hey—' he began to protest, but she had already moved on.

The Property Department could have housed half a dozen killers lying in wait, but there was nothing Theresa could do about it. She didn't have keys to the door; no one did, save the Property officer and probably the Medical Examiner himself, in order to protect the personal items, money, jewelry and prescription meds of their temporary residents. She hit the light switch in the reception area: boring furniture that appeared to have been there since the mid-'70s, a Formica-clad countertop and sliding window to the secretary's desk, a double set of glass doors leading to the visitor parking lot. She checked them. Still locked, deadbolts in place.

Theresa ignored the elevator. It moved only slightly faster than molasses in Antarctica, and any woman over forty needed to work off every possible calorie, so instead she always took the stairs to the upper floors where she spent most of her working hours. Second landing, Records and Customer Services to the right, doctors' offices and Histology to the left.

No one lay bleeding in the hallway. Theresa even checked the two restrooms, in case Justin had escaped the attacker and run up here to hide – not as silly an idea as it sounded, she consoled herself as she peered through the glass windows of dark offices. If he couldn't get past the killer to the back hallway and its loading dock door to the outside, and the front doors had been locked with their keyed deadbolt, he would have nowhere else to go but up.

But then he would have nowhere to hide. Unless both Justin and the attacker had the advanced degrees in science necessary to work in one of the labs or were Janice, Queen of the Secretaries, they would not be able to open any of the doors. None were broken, and no drops or smears of blood dotted the carpet. Same for the third floor.

Out of habit or some sort of homing instinct, Theresa pulled her keys from her back pocket and let herself in to the Trace Evidence Department. Once the lights flicked on she could see that nothing had been disturbed. The microscopes waited, shielded by soft plastic coverings; washed glassware dried in a dish rack that Theresa had bought at Walmart; a stack of Manila files needing additions or revisions had fallen over on her desk as if to express annoyance at her inattention; and the whole place smelled of disinfectant, dried blood and burnt coffee. Her home away from home, her corner of the world, her fortress and prison in one, but now she glanced around its cluttered space as if she'd never seen it before, its expanse turned alien and unfamiliar.

More sirens outside the building now. Theresa wondered if the police would search the lot and neighboring buildings, check for the blood trail which Justin or whoever might have left as he ran away. She should probably do that. But the twins of fear and worry pushed her to circle the entire lab, to make sure the floors were clean of blood drops and check the rear two rooms where Don performed his DNA magic.

Nothing.

Finally satisfied, she pulled the rear lab door shut behind her and started down the back staircase, which would let her out between the cooler and the autopsy room.

Except that a man with a gun blocked her path.

He said: 'Freeze. Police.'

'I gathered that,' Theresa told him, 'from the badge around your neck.'

THREE

He seemed to take her outward serenity as something of an affront, but was professional enough to let it go, and within ten minutes Theresa had told him everything she knew. The sergeant – his nameplate said 'L. Shephard' – and his crew had cleared the building without locating the missing deskman. They had even checked the basement, a greenish-looking young man reported to Shephard. If the autopsy room could appear in a horror movie then the basement could provide the entire setting for a fifties drive-in. But though the four-inch thick wooden doors with the heavy steel latches appeared intimidating, nothing sat behind them but supplies and old paperwork. Same for the crypts, the individual openings with smaller versions of the same heavy doors where bodies used to be stored on slide-out platforms. All empty now, but still plenty creepy-looking.

The only nightmare-inducing items in the morgue's basement were the plastic quart containers which looked like take-out soup but which were actually tissue sections of past victims. They would be kept for five years and then destroyed, and were harmless unless someone opened the lids and poured the irritating formalin solution over their skin. Nevertheless the intrepid officers checked each area except the large storage room, unable to get its door open. Theresa had a key but didn't offer it. The Trace Evidence Department kept the clothing from past victims and evidence from past cases in there and she couldn't have unauthorized people trooping through and if a cop couldn't get in then a killer, or Justin, could not possibly have entered.

Theresa sat on the ancient vinyl couches in the reception area while the men roamed the building, upstairs, downstairs, all talking and radioing and sometimes shouting. She found herself flexing her fingers and gritting her teeth, no matter how often Shephard assured her that the deskmen's office had been undisturbed since the EMTs pronounced Darryl. A cop had been posted at the door to keep all his co-workers out until the scene could be properly processed.

'Which is me,' Theresa couldn't help pointing out to the sergeant for the second time during the past ten minutes. 'I process. I need to photograph, and then sketch. Please don't let your men touch anything, including the doors, walls, banisters, because I will have to fingerprint all that and I don't want to have to eliminate any more than—'

'I understand,' Shephard said with what might be mistaken as patience by someone who hadn't spent as much time around cops as Theresa had. 'We're just securing the scene.'

'You already *have* secured the scene. No killer on premises, guards on the entrances. Secured.'

His eyes narrowed, but not, apparently, at her contrariness. His eye lingered on Theresa's left pant leg where she had not been able to avoid dipping the cuff in some of Darryl's blood. 'Can't wait to get to work, can you?'

'I have a lot to do.' Her voice trembled a bit. Some sort of reaction setting in? Ridiculous . . . Theresa had no idea how many dead bodies she had encountered by then, but it had to be halfway to five digits.

Just not when she wasn't expecting to encounter one.

Not when it was someone she *knew*.

He continued to study her, taking in her rumpled BDU pants and heavy sweatshirt, mud-splashed steel-toe boots and braid of mostly reddish hair, messy because she hadn't redone it after getting out of bed. The only advantage to outdoor night-time scenes was that they took place in the dark, so she hadn't bothered with the make-up that would have made her forty-four-year-old face look better than just tolerable. But Shephard said only: 'Darryl Johnson doesn't summon up a lot of grief from you?'

'I – um – yes, of course. I just – don't know what to say.' Though she did, and it was that Darryl had been kind of a jerk. One of those men who never outgrew the class clown persona. The type that finds it hilarious to be sarcastic, cutting, leering, bigoted and misogynistic every minute of every day. A trial to be around for more than three minutes at a stretch.

But, other than that, not a bad guy . . . He entered each deceased's information with reasonable accuracy, built up muscles hefting dead weights from one gurney to another, went home with blood splashed on his own shoes from hanging up the fluid-soaked shirts and pants of victims dead from homicide or accident. He showed up when scheduled, as he had that prior evening. By the time Theresa had sidled out, not more than ten seconds after quitting time, he had already rocked back in his desk chair, observing the evening exodus through a pair of smudged glasses. He'd refrained from the more risqué comments he sometimes tossed her way and simply waved, a comfortable grin on his face. In return she had given only her standard tight-lipped, patently insincere smile, designed to maintain office cordiality without promising even the slightest friendly feeling.

And now he lay in his own blood, not ten feet from where she sat, in a government-operated building dedicated to the pursuit of justice, with locks on the doors. 'He's been working here a long time,' she said, and now her voice really did tremble, enough to make Shephard change the subject. Or maybe he got to what *was* the subject.

'What can you tell me about the suspect?'

She blinked at him. 'Nothing. I have no idea who did this.'

'I meant the other deskman. Justin Warner, you said?'

'I'm guessing Justin should have been working tonight, but I don't know that for sure.'

'According to the schedule by the lockers, it should have been Justin.'

'But still, he's not a *suspect* – why would you think Justin did this?'

He gave her a look which might have been pity. 'We started with two guys, and now one's dead and the other is not present. It's a math thing.'

'So they've been working on the same shift together for six weeks without a problem, and suddenly Justin takes it in his head to beat the guy to death?'

'How long have you been working here?'

The change in topics made her head swim. 'Twelve years. Almost thirteen.'

'And what's the motive for most murders?'

She shifted her weight, which sent the vinyl creaking. 'Anger.'

'Exactly.'

'But Justin never struck me as short-tempered. Darryl, maybe, but not Justin.'

'Fine. So maybe Darryl attacked Justin and it was self-defense. He panics and runs away. When we find him, we can ask him. What does the word "confess" mean to you?'

'What I expect it means to everybody else.'

'Did Justin Warner believe that the victim was keeping something from him? Did he mention any conspiracy-type theories? Believe that the ME's office had covered something up? Ever express distrust of your administration?'

'Never.' Though how would she know? The most likely candidate for those sorts of heart-to-hearts now lay in his own blood on their linoleum.

'What about someone else? A grieving family member who thinks there's more to their loved one's death?'

'And might want to hold Justin hostage until we reveal the truth? There certainly could be – many families have a hard time accepting certain facts. But I don't know of any such situations myself.'

Shephard kept asking questions, most of which Theresa could not answer. Justin Warner stood over six feet tall, perhaps weighed two-fifty, was a light-skinned black man of about thirty or thirty-five. Some tattoos on his neck, but she'd never looked closely enough to be able to describe them. He seemed cheerful enough but, now that she thought about it, never said much of anything beyond the weather, the state of the victim, or what he might have for lunch. No political commentaries, no complaints of a spouse or girlfriend or children, not even the strengths of the Indians' starting line-up. Theresa didn't know where he lived or what he drove. She had no idea if he lived alone, but had heard that he spent time flirting with one of the secretaries up in Records. She could contribute only one useful fact, that his cellphone number would be posted in the deskmen's office, scrawled on a curling piece of paper taped to the glass.

Meanwhile, other cops poked their heads in once in a while to give Shephard updates. No blood had been located on the outside loading dock or in the parking lot, at least so far as they could establish under the tungsten street lights. They had also checked DMV information. Justin Warner drove a seven-year-old brown Chevy Cavalier, which did not, currently, reside in the parking lot.

Shephard didn't say a word, but obviously young Justin's absence made him appear guiltier with each passing moment.

'Maybe he didn't even work tonight,' Theresa pointed out.

'Is there another deskman who would make a more likely suspect for you?'

She thought of the four other deskmen. The office had only six total, two each on rotating twelve-hour shifts. 'No.'

'Easy way to find out for sure – your cameras? Can you cue up the tape for me?'

She gave him her baffled blink again, so he pointed out that he had seen a camera outside the loading dock entrance. Were there more cameras, where were they, and could she operate the system so they could review what had happened?

Theresa hated to tell him that the one he had seen was the only one they had.

She didn't add that the county had tried to add more, specifically in the deskmen's office and the Property Department – a much criticized move, since these were two of the lowest-paid occupations in the building and did not attract college graduates or Shaker Heights residents. But the county's thinking didn't stem from simple bigotry; these were the only two areas with access to victims' cash and jewelry. No one thought of adding cameras to other floors because there was virtually nothing in the building worth stealing. And though the paperwork could be considered confidential, there wasn't much of a black market for autopsy reports and toxicology read-outs. No one in Cleveland warranted that kind of interest. Lacking a bit of wealth also kept the city from having the problems of LA or DC.

But in any case the first-floor interior cameras hadn't lasted long. They encountered an endless string of bad luck, mysterious power surges that melted their circuits, moisture somehow seeping into their wiring, condensation fogging their lenses, until the county gave up.

'Fine, the one camera, then,' Shephard sighed. 'Can you cue up the tape? Or – well, it's probably digital, right?'

'It's nothing,' she told him gently. 'It doesn't record. It's just a monitor.'

His face darkened so much that Theresa thought he might yell at her, an experience she had planned to leave behind after signing divorce papers. 'What?' he said.

'The purpose of the camera is to let the deskman see who's knocking at their door in the middle of the night, that's all. They'll either open the door or they won't. There's no need for it to record.'

Under the razor stubble his skin flushed. 'And you call that *security*?'

I don't call it anything, Theresa thought but didn't say. 'It's not my job' never sounded like a mature, responsible thing to express, even when it truly wasn't. 'This is a morgue. We're not a bank, and we're not the NSA. No one wants to break in here. Why would they?'

'Maybe to kill your deskman – assuming, just for the sake of argument, that he wasn't killed by your *other* deskman. Maybe they wanted to break into your property room, or wherever valuables are stored.'

'Then they changed their minds, because there's no damage to the door and the keys are not stored on site.' Something else occurred to her as her brain ping-ponged all over the place. 'What are you doing here?'

This confused him into speechlessness.

'I mean,' she went on, gesturing at the stripes on his sleeve, 'what are *you* doing here? Why is a sergeant the first responder?'

It was his turn to blink. 'The call came in, and – an ME's office employee killed *at* the ME's office? I—'

'Wouldn't miss it for the world?' She didn't intend it as criticism. She'd have felt the same way in his shoes.

'—thought I should supervise in person as a professional courtesy,' he finished. 'I came here enough times when I worked homicide.'

He *did* look vaguely familiar – dark hair, dark eyes, could use a shave, tall and solid. And now he was back in uniform as a sergeant. A promotion, a bigger paycheck and more regular hours, but Theresa wondered if he missed the unpredictability of the murder beat. 'You know Frank?'

'Yes,' he said, with a complete absence of inflection. Sometimes that happened when people spoke of her cousin. 'You don't need to call him, you know. I mean, the case will be assigned to the on-call detective. Though if you need some moral support I suppose there's nothing actually wrong with it—'

She put him out of the misery of worrying that another cop might interfere in his case. 'I would love to, but I can't. He's on a Royal Caribbean ship somewhere in the Panama Canal.' She didn't add that Frank had gone on his first real vacation in about a decade with his partner, detective Angela Sanchez. Her cousin subscribed to the *don't ask, don't tell* policy with his own department.

Shephard looked relieved, and Theresa made a mental note to ask her cousin how he got along with his co-workers. 'Has this ever happened before?' he asked. 'Someone actually killed here?'

She thought, which seemed to require way more effort than it should. 'Never, that I know of. We haven't even had a staff member *die*, here or anywhere . . . not since Diana, I don't think. That was ten years ago.'

'She died here?'

'No, in her home. She was—'

Polished shoes clacked against the floor as Medical Examiner Stone strode into the lobby, trench coat swirling around his calves in a way that would have looked much more impressive on a foggy bridge instead of sixty-year-old linoleum. 'What the hell is going on?'

His gaze fell from Shephard to Theresa. He didn't actually *say*, 'I might have known,' but it was a close thing. He'd never quite forgiven her for accidentally bringing an unstable explosive back to the lab, which had required an evacuation of the entire building. Make one mistake . . .

'Darryl's dead,' she said, 'and someone's kidnapped Justin.'

His scowl merely deepened, and Theresa couldn't really blame him. She had never mastered the art of concise summary. At the same time she noticed that his shirt had a few uncharacteristic wrinkles and his usual aroma of too much Axe had been replaced by old-fashioned sweat, so either he was wearing the previous day's clothing or he had never been home. Perhaps his wife had gone out of town again—

Shephard began to fill him in, and Theresa grabbed the opportunity. Mumbling something about needing the ladies room and holding a hand to her mouth as if she were about to lose her last meal, she stumbled up the hallway and went to check on her crime scene.

FOUR

The cop standing in the doorway to the deskmen's office looked at Theresa curiously but said nothing. He also didn't move, but that was all right – she didn't want to go in, not just yet. She simply glanced through the windows, to see that Darryl's body had been moved slightly from where she'd left it, probably by those pesky do-gooder EMTs, and someone's foot had slid through one of the larger puddles of blood since she had been in there. It could have even been her on her way out – she checked her shoes, but the soles seemed relatively clean. Most of the stains had already been dry upon her arrival – no wonder Darryl's body had grown cool. He must have been killed at least an hour earlier, probably two, with the chilly linoleum sucking out his body heat as quickly as his dead cells could give it up.

Theresa's camera bag and the small paper bags from the hit-and-run remained where she'd dumped them on the counter. Great. Now her equipment was part of the crime scene.

Theresa went up the rear staircase and let herself into the lab.

They had a spare camera, and she grabbed some swabs and a few other supplies before returning to the loading dock area. The smear of blood on the wall next to the elevator might not have suggested a hand to anyone else, but Theresa had seen a lot of brownish-red impressions left by hands and feet over the years and could make out three fingers and the outer edge of a palm. The outer edge – it was a right hand – had heavier staining in the upper interdigital area, right below the little finger.

Theresa applied scaled tape to the periphery of the pattern and took some photos. Then she took a closer look with a jeweler's loupe, but couldn't make out any discernible ridges. That didn't necessarily mean they weren't there, or that any pattern had been smudged beyond recognition – they might

simply be too faint to see. Amido black stain could bring
nearly invisible blood prints to life.

Theresa moved over to the other stain, at the edge of the
doorway into the front hallway area. A small blot that didn't
give her much to go on – it could be from the left hand of
someone walking toward the front, or the right hand of someone
walking toward the loading dock, but something about the
curve of what could be a finger above the most visible part
of the stain made her think of a right hand. Given that it
contained less blood than the other stain, she made a guess
that might be educated or wild depending on one's level of
conservatism: that it came from a wound on the right palm
instead of a palm stained with Darryl's blood. Otherwise there
would be more blood on the more interior stain, with some
wiped off by the time he made the second stain by the elevator.
But a wound would make the palm *more* bloody as time went
on. A handy piece of logic, with no guarantee of accuracy.

Theresa dampened a swab with a vial of sterile water and
collected a sample from the very edge of the badly smeared
spot. The swab went into a tiny paper box. The cop at the door
to the deskmen's office watched her curiously but said nothing.
It seemed remarkable to her how much easier it was to breathe
with someone else in the building, other people who were tall
and armed and tasked with protecting civilians like herself. Of
course, under normal circumstances she would be counting,
except for the armed part, on the deskmen to fill that role.

She went through the same process with the stain next to
the elevator.

It wasn't that she didn't trust the cops or her own co-workers;
it was simply that the building was awash in biohazards. At
any moment another deceased person could be brought in, wet
and wild, to contaminate any existing stains.

Speaking of which—

Theresa turned around. The gurney that had been against
the wall when she first arrived had not moved.

But there was no longer a body on it, just a rumpled, deflated
white sheet.

Theresa felt almost afraid to tell Sergeant Shephard.

*   *   *

She reached him just as Stone finished their confab and went off to make phone calls. He would have to make quite a number, Theresa knew. Almost all the staff would be given the day off, as much to keep them out of the crime scene as in sympathy for any grief they may feel at the death of a co-worker. One or two pathologists would need to come in to do Darryl's autopsy – one to do the autopsy, and one to act as their diener, or assistant. If the deskmen were at the bottom of the totem pole, the dieners were only one step above; plus both groups spent all their time on the first floor and got to know each other pretty well. Not even perpetually cash-strapped Cuyahoga County would ask someone to make a Y-incision into someone they considered a friend.

'*What*?' was Shephard's response when Theresa told him about the gurney. As they hurried to the loading dock he asked if she had looked under the sheet. How big was the person? How tall? Weight? Of course, she couldn't answer. This was a *morgue*. She had barely glanced at the body – or person, as the case appeared to be.

He strode up to the gurney, vacant except for a single pristine sheet. As he reached out toward the gleaming metal she cried: 'Don't touch it!'

He glared at her.

Theresa shrugged. She couldn't help it. She would have to process the gurney for fingerprints, and that officers would keep that in mind is not something she could take for granted.

He picked up the very edge of the sheet with finger and thumb, as delicately as Queen Victoria's maiden aunt, and peeked underneath. Nothing.

Then he pointed out that he might have a picture of who had emerged from underneath the sheet – if the building had cameras.

'Do you have cameras in your office?' Theresa asked, and he shut up.

She took a closer look at the metal surface – gleaming and clean except for a few smears. Fresh gurneys were always left in the loading dock, to be front and center for any new arrivals, but unless someone had gotten very sloppy in the hosing area . . . 'He left some blood here. Just a few swipes – it's either from

Darryl or himself.' Theresa explained her 'small wound in the right palm' theory. Shephard went off to relay the narrowed timeline to his men, and Theresa slipped to the front again in search of Justin Warner's locker.

In between the deskmen's office and the viewing chamber sat a row of metal cabinets. The doors had become decorated over the years with peeling stickers of rock bands, refrigerator magnets and the occasional political comment, but above this din each had been labeled with an old-fashioned punch-style label maker, and finding Justin's proved easy. Theresa pulled on fresh gloves and lifted the latch, careful to use only the tip of one finger should they want to process for prints later. None of the lockers had a lock on them – perhaps the deskmen felt it would show a lack of trust, and besides, lunches were the only thing subject to theft at the ME's office and the deskman had a refrigerator in their office, where they could keep an eye on theirs. Theresa had to use the general staff lunchroom and had lost a number of candy bars and leftover stromboli over the years. Not even injecting some decoy mini Milky Ways with Tabasco sauce seemed to help.

Justin's locker seemed as unremarkable as he had been. With a mini flashlight she took a closer look, but found only a hairbrush, a windbreaker with nothing in the pockets but (hopefully) clean tissues and a quarter, expired bus passes (county employees got them at a discount), two front page sections of the *Plain Dealer* from two and two-and-a-half months previously, and three loose but unopened foil Pop-Tarts packages, no doubt reserved for dire emergencies and of sufficiently low value to risk losing to the lunch thief. When Theresa moved the *Plain Dealers* – none of the stories suggested a connection to Darryl – a piece of paper fell out. The three-by-four white square had a series of numbers on it in distressing penmanship: *1432, 1433, 1555, 1830.* They were two digits too short for case numbers and one digit too short for evidence numbers. They might be bets of some type for his bookie, but she wouldn't know, sports so not being her thing.

Theresa pulled two Manila envelopes out of yet another of her pockets and scribbled down the numbers on one, then collected a bundle of hairs from the brush into the other. She had wondered all along if the police would decide to handle the entire investigation or even call in the state, shut the ME's office out entirely. That would be more or less standard procedure – if a cop is involved in an on-duty car crash resulting in injury, cops had the state Highway Patrol do the report. But the Medical Examiner's staff fell into a sort of gray area. Technically, they weren't an investigative agency. Theresa examined and processed crime scenes only when asked to by the police agencies, and had no authority of her own. On the other hand, the Medical Examiner was the highest official in the county, outranking even the Sheriff, so if Stone decided to dig in his heels there could be no telling what might happen.

In any event, if the cops needed a DNA sample there were plenty more hairs in the brush, and the paper remained unmolested.

The uniformed officer appeared at Theresa's shoulder, and she nearly dropped both her envelopes. 'Ma'am? Someone wants to see you.'

'Uh . . . yeah, okay.' His set of handcuffs remained clipped to his belt. Maybe he thought it was *her* locker.

It turned out that Stone had issued the summons, and he led the way from the first floor to his office on the second with Theresa and Shephard in tow. Apparently, they were going to powwow. They could have powwowed in the lobby, but then Stone wouldn't have been able to show off his office, and Theresa figured he felt more secure inside it. Medical Examiner Stone didn't believe in the austerity and stripped-down professionalism of other county offices and had enough of his own and his wife's money that he didn't have to. His workspace, while small, had been outfitted with suitably crammed bookshelves in deep cherry, a desk with just enough clutter to look authentic but not enough to hide the granite inlay, leather wing chairs and a beige alpaca-fur rug. Theresa didn't know people actually bought those. Next to this opulence, a glass shelf holding specimen jars of hearts and spleens seemed discordant, but perhaps it maintained his autopsy-room street cred.

Stone moved behind his desk but did not sit, giving them the benefit of his six-four frame, broad chest and hair with its perfect combination of wave for the ladies and gray for the jurors, and got right to it. 'I'll put out a press release but I don't want to publish Johnson's name for another day, maybe two, and certainly not Warner's. Is that understood, Sergeant?'

Shephard gave him a look, one of those alpha-dog-circling-the-other looks, each deciding how much of the marked territory they really wanted. Only on TV do police agencies fight to control a case. In real life if a case looks like it will develop into a pain in the butt, they're just as happy to let the other guy have it. But Shephard hadn't made up his mind about this one yet.

Theresa left them to it. She worked for Stone, and for once she actually agreed with him.

'That's fine with me,' Shephard said.

'What were you doing here?' Stone then demanded of Theresa, as if she had somehow invited bloody murder into the building by trying to pad her overtime.

'Hit-skip,' she said.

'And you didn't see anyone else in the building besides Johnson?'

'No.'

'And you think Justin hid under a sheet while you entered the building?'

'Someone did.' Though this didn't make a lot of sense to her. Darryl had been practically cold, and most of the blood had dried, implying that at least an hour or more had elapsed since the murder. Why was Justin or whoever still hanging around?

'All right. Despite being a witness in the case, you're still acting supervisor for Trace.'

Ever since the previous supervisor had covered up a homicide and then tried to kill her, yes. The temporary promotion – which, incidentally, did not come with a raise in salary – could not be taken to indicate any particular confidence in Theresa's abilities or sympathy for her near-death experience. Stone simply didn't have a lot to choose from. Since the county's budget had been whittling departments by attrition for years, Trace Evidence now consisted of Theresa, DNA analyst Don Delgado, a part-time intern from Case Western and the secretary, Neenah – and not one of them wanted the supervisor job. At least, Theresa didn't *think* she wanted the job.

And the county, or Stone, seemed in no hurry to fill it. The work still got done, and the funds budgeted for the salary Leo no longer drew went – where, exactly? An excellent question, and not one she would likely ever learn the answer to.

'The Police Department will need to process this crime scene,' Shephard said, with a nice balance of firmness and impartiality. 'That's standard practice in such cases—'

Theresa blurted: 'I'll want to look at the blood spatter. Other than that I'm all right with it.'

Stone glared at her, certainly for presuming that her opinion had been asked for in any way, but Theresa wanted to be clear. Normally, she hated to give up any control of a crime scene, but she also wasn't eager to spend a day swabbing up pieces of Darryl's dried cells. However, this was her own co-worker in her own workspace – of *course* she wanted to wrap her fingers around every aspect of the crime and never let go until she understood every blood drop and timeline and trajectory. But time would always be a luxury denied. Nothing happened in a vacuum. In short, nothing about this situation would be as she preferred, and everything would be awkward, uncomfortable and just plain bad.

But she didn't have much choice about the bloodstain pattern analysis, being the only expert in the county. Blood spatter can be the picture that's worth a thousand words, and Theresa *did* want to see it, comfort be damned.

The two men continued to argue oh-so-politely, a stance that did not come naturally to either of them. Shephard plopped himself into one of the leather chairs without waiting for an invitation, but Theresa browsed in the less luxe and more familiar territory of the specimen jars. Some organs do not look like an anatomy diagram, and some do. A set of lungs from April 2007, for example, did not look gray and puffy but wetly, deeply red, more like a liver. A spleen removed during the second month of 2011 resembled a red amoeba. But a uterus from 9/23/04 while soaking in its formalin bath appeared as expected, a pink, rounded triangle. It had some sort of cancer on it that looked like a cigarette burn and made her wince.

'Fine,' Stone said at last. 'CPD can process the crime scene. I trust you'll have it wrapped up by lunchtime so we won't have to lose the entire day. In the meantime two of my pathologists are coming in to do the autopsy. CPD won't be able to do *that*, will they?'

Shephard could have insisted that they send the body to another county, but must have assumed that immediate results trumped any possible conflict of interest.

The conference broke up, and Theresa went to process the gurney. Assuming that Sergeant Shephard would consider the deskmen's office the crime scene, then the gurney sat outside CPD's purview. Fingerprint powder brought up a nice palm print.

Before moving on to the bloody handprints on the walls she made herself a badly needed cup of coffee and checked her watch. Five a.m. – too early to call Don and go over recent events with him, especially since he had been told to stay home. Theresa would let him sleep.

Amido black is a dark, watery liquid that turns blood to a dark purplish black color, throwing a faint fingerprint or shoe print into startling relief. The process is easy enough – just dump on the stain, wait a few seconds, then rinse gently with distilled water. However, sloshing all that liquid around on a large, immovable object such as a wall is messy and, since the stain is dissolved in methanol, smelly. A few more ridges came into view, but still not enough to be able to compare to someone's hand. One of the CPD crime scene techs, Jen, came in while Theresa finished rinsing, gray-colored water coursing down the tile to be collected by a few soggy paper towels. Jen carried three separate metal cases and hadn't bothered to put on make-up, either.

Caught red-handed, Theresa said, 'I did the amido black staining,' as if she were being helpful instead of interfering.

'Oh good. I hate working with that stuff.'

Crime-scene techs don't bother with jurisdictional jealousy. They leave that kind of crap to the cops.

FIVE

B y seven thirty a.m. Theresa stood in the autopsy suite watching two doctors putter around and get their instruments in order before beginning the procedure. She had spent the previous two hours watching Jen process the crime scene. The CPD tech had collected all the samples and would write the report, but chain of custody would not be affected if Theresa watched over her shoulder, and besides, Jen did need to confer with her on what the bloodstain patterns could tell them. Their conclusion: not much.

The struggle apparently began in one corner, where a stack of papers had fallen from the top of a desk and a stapler had been knocked off the edge of the counter – signs of activity, perhaps from the first few blows. Apparently, the blood did not start flowing until the fight had moved to the floor and stayed there. They found no sign of a weapon nor any cast-off from one, and from the splashing patterns found near the largest pools they suspected that the floor had been used to cave in Darryl's head rather than any blunt instrument. They found patterns left by the men's pants, sleeves, knees and hair, but not a single usable handprint. Prints left by hands, yes, but nothing with a sufficient amount of discernible ridges. The hands had been *too* wet with blood, and the marks were just smears left by slippery flesh.

Shoe prints, however, were clearer. A few belonged to Darryl, mostly from the toe area as he struggled to right himself and push off the increasingly bloody floor. He wore Nikes, and the circle over the ball of the sole made the pattern easy to recognize. The other set, obviously the killer's, had a plain zigzag pattern and continued right out the door. Some were Theresa's, right next to where the body had been. There were a few pieces of something with a heavy tread next to the largest pool, which hadn't completely dried by the time the medics had arrived to confirm Theresa's initial diagnosis. Jen tried to

wager a buck that those prints belonged to the EMT, but
Theresa didn't take sucker bets no matter how small.

They also checked the sinks, the autopsy room, and the tiny
first-floor lavatory, but if the killer had cleaned his hands he
had cleaned the basins just as well. Theresa made a copy of
the palm print from the gurney for Jen.

The nineteen-inch, black and white monitor continued to
beam images of the rear loading-dock as cops stalked back
and forth, smoked, chatted and turned up their collars. The
April temperature hovered around a mild fifty degrees, but it
always felt colder in the small hours. The unmolested camera
and monitor bothered Theresa. Either an extremely unob-
servant killer had somehow made entry, murdered Darryl and
kidnapped Justin without noticing or caring that the camera
might be able to record, or the killer had been someone who
worked at or was sufficiently familiar with the ME's and *knew*
it wouldn't record. The idea of this someone kidnapping a
strapping young man like Justin seemed ridiculous, but then
the same someone had been strong enough to crush Darryl.
And that one-word warning: *Confess.* This person wanted
something. They didn't get it from Darryl, so maybe they
took Justin with a plan to force the agency to hand it over as
ransom. A strange plan, but killers often do very strange things
for very strange reasons.

After finishing with the floor, Theresa had stood around
with Jen in that nerve-wracking, soul-sucking indecision that
always comes when deciding to let a crime scene go. Had
they missed anything? Should they collect one more bloodstain? Take one more photograph? Fingerprint the tops of the
file cabinets? The instant they 'cleared' the scene, Stone
intended to call in the county HazMat team and have the room
sterilized. All HazMat really needed to do was mop the floor
with some bleach, but Stone wasn't going to ask the janitor
to handle it. Appearances often to the contrary, he really did
have a heart.

But finally Jen admitted that she had done all that could
reasonably be expected and took her dozens of samples
and hundreds of photos back to CPD in time for Theresa to
attend the autopsy.

Theresa had changed into another pair of pants that she kept in the closet for emergencies and given her beat-up BDUs to Jen as evidence, on the extremely slim chance the pool of blood next to Darryl's body might belong to someone else. Now, tugging at the waistband – how long had these khakis been hanging in that closet? – she went to the autopsy suite. She didn't particularly want to see Darryl gutted like a deer, but cops still monitored the front and back doors, and she feared that if she left, she might not be allowed back in. As long as Theresa utilized the classic technique of looking busy, no one bothered her.

Now little Dr Banachek pulled the sheet off Darryl without further ado, and Theresa saw more of her ex-co-worker than she had ever wanted to.

'This is terrible,' Dr Banachek clucked, shaking strands of gray loose from his comb-over.

The other pathologist, Dr Harris, said: 'It sure is. I have more seniority than Reese. How come I'm not home in bed and he's here instead?'

Theresa tried not to roll her eyes. The first words Harris spoke to her on her first day at the ME's office had been to complain about the fit of his lab coat, and every word since had kept to a similar vein. A dozen years later he still had no other form of conversation. Tall, skinny, with a grayish pallor to his skin, his cheeks had begun to sink as if the eternal negativity was eating him up from the inside out. He went on: 'You know why? I'll tell you why. Because I had the courtesy to answer my phone! Why couldn't they get an actual diener to work as diener? Why not Causer?'

'The county's trying to show a little compassion,' Theresa explained, unnecessarily. Harris knew perfectly well why he had been pressed into service. He just didn't care.

'Because they were friends? As if. The last friend Causer had came with a screw cap. And he was the wrong color to make Johnson feel warm and fuzzy. Causer could have made the incision while eating a muffin.'

As fed up as she felt toward the general boorishness of Harris, Causer *and* the dead Johnson, Theresa couldn't help a quick, slightly hysterical giggle at the image of Mitchell

Causer plunging a scalpel into Darryl's chest while holding a breakfast pastry in his other hand, a plastic apron over his flannel shirt with a beer gut barely held in check by a scratched WWF belt buckle. She choked it off as the other doctor spoke.

'Looks like some bruising starting over the abdomen. Someone slugged him in more than just the head.' Banachek hesitated, holding the scalpel over the dead man's chest, still trying to comprehend the depth of their collective violation. 'How could anyone be killed *here*? And who'd want to kill Darryl?'

'Besides his wife?' Theresa couldn't help saying. 'His comments about her always sounded so – violent.'

Harris said, 'Nah. She crashed the Christmas party here once, and I'm pretty sure that if he had ever hit her, she'd have flattened him. And she wouldn't have waited until he was at work to do it. Face it, it was Justin.'

'No,' Banachek said, dragging the scalpel from Darryl's shoulder to groin.

'No,' Theresa said. 'Justin hardly seemed like some hair-trigger maniac to me.'

'How would you know?' Harris fixed her with a suspicious gaze, ready to verbally pounce if she had been secretly dating one of the deskmen, and not because it would have been inter-racial or cougar-like or against county policy. He would care only that a piece of gossip existed without his knowledge.

Despite that, it was a valid question. Theresa saw Justin in passing, long enough to get a quick patient history that usually consisted of abbreviations or phrases: MVA (motor vehicle accident), GSW (gunshot wound), suicide – hanging, suicide GSW, decomp, stabbing, or industrial (meaning an accident at work). Occasionally, there might be an addendum, such as: 'This guy owned the car dealership at Euclid and Fifty-fifth, you know, next to the restaurant that used to be the BirdHouse?' They had not had in-depth conversations about politics or their personal lives or even their preferred sports teams. Theresa couldn't claim to know the man just because he had beautiful eyes and a certain gravity to his aura.

But she protested anyway. 'This is a morgue. We attract very strange people. We've had estranged family members who thought we hid a victim's body because they weren't invited to the funeral and thus it didn't happen. We've had abusive spouses or parents who thought we framed them by pointing out that the victim died of blunt impact trauma instead of falling down the basement steps. We've had self-styled psychics who thought this building bulged with trapped souls trying to cross over to the light. Remember? They stood outside with picket signs.'

'Then where's Justin?' Harris asked, picking up the long-handled clippers. Most people used them to trim trees; pathologists use them to snap ribs, two of which, Dr Banachek pointed out, had been cracked during the struggle. Theresa kept her kidnapping/ransom theory to herself as he freed up the thoracic cavity a little more with each sickening crunch and the smell of offal and clotting blood filled the room.

Instead, she took a closer look at Darryl's mashed face, now that the blood had been hosed away. The nose looked broken, left cheek flattened where it had been pressed to the floor as he died. He had nearly matching cuts over both eyebrows and another on the right temple. These had coated his face in blood, but from the sheer volume of it on the office floor she felt sure he had more gashes on the back of his skull, under the hair. Theresa thought she'd been getting used to the idea, but it still felt strange to realize this had been a person she'd interacted with regularly for more than a dozen years. She expected his clouding eyes to pop fully open as he shouted, 'Gotcha!' with that rumbling, Barry White laugh.

Dr Banachek had peeled back the skin from the Y-incision, clearing the way to examine the organs. Lemon-yellow, bubbling fat bulged outward.

'He should have left off some of those cheeseburgers,' Harris said.

'Definitely a lot of bruising here,' Banachek said, peering at the spider-like red tendrils of blood vessels broken by a blow to the area.

Harris excavated the skin on his side, finding more of the same kind of damage, prodding at the subcutaneous fat with an expression of distaste. 'And here I am, reduced to a friggin' diener. How could Reese not be home at four in the morning?'

'His wife's out of town,' Banachek said absently.

'So what, he's at his mistress's? Hah. No, he had the sense to look at his caller ID before picking up. Not like me.'

'It's not like this happens often,' Theresa said in an attempt to shut him up, though she'd never been able to get him to see the bright side of anything.

Banachek removed the lungs, slapping them on to the polypropylene cutting board next to the sink. As usual, they just looked like raw meat to Theresa. 'Not since Diana, and that was, what – ten years ago?'

'At least,' Theresa said, feeling a residual pang much more deeply than she would ever be able to for Darryl Johnson. She and Diana had been friends of sorts, sharing plenty of lunch hours together. Until her husband had strangled her with a jump rope and left her body on their kitchen floor.

'I remember that,' Harris said. 'The pretty one from Records. They emptied the building for the whole day for her, no talk of a half-day. And they called in Reese – why? Because I have more seniority!'

He and Dr Reese had had a friendly rivalry for as long as Theresa could remember. Friendly on Reese's part, anyway – Harris, she couldn't be sure about.

Banachek sectioned the lungs with a large bread knife, slicing off tiny bits he found interesting and dropping them into the plastic quart container filled with formalin, murmuring the occasional comment, such as: 'Too many cigarettes. They would have begun to haunt him in another decade.'

The stomach was largely empty, unsurprising if death occurred five or six hours after dinner time. From Darryl's gut she would have pegged him for a snacker, though, and indeed, some tough yellowish flecks bobbed here and there in the red-brown purée that emptied out of his digestive sac. Banachek helpfully retained most of it in a fifty ml plastic tube and labeled it to be sent to Theresa's department, where she would have to rinse off the acids and bile and put the remaining solids under the stereomicroscope. Oh joy. Theresa would rather run her hands through a bucket of blood than deal with two tablespoons of gastric contents.

Harris photographed the hands, after taking four minutes to

figure out how to turn the camera on. Another advantage of the digital era, making photography fairly simple even for laymen. Simply point and click. Now that the hands were clean, Theresa could easily see the damage – both sets of knuckles were scraped and bruising. 'He put up a fight.'

'I'm sure losing came as a shock to him,' Harris said. 'He's bigger than Justin. Probably wasn't worried at first.'

Dr Banachek examined the heart, exposing the coronary arteries with dozens of shallow slices. 'Don't understand that. They never even had an argument, that I heard of. Hasn't been a feud in this building since old Doc Brewster was the head of histology and took over that supply closet in the hallway. Arteriosclerosis, getting pretty bad.'

'Cheeseburgers,' Harris said darkly.

'Wonder what mine looks like,' Banachek muttered, and cut open the heart to measure the walls. When the heart had to work harder to pump the blood out it tended to bulk up, like any other muscle. Thickened walls could indicate high blood pressure, arrhythmia, or heart valve problems. Circulation fascinated Theresa, and she watched over his shoulder.

Harris withstood their abandonment for about four seconds before peeling back the skin on the top of Darryl's head to comment on the skull. 'Shattered,' he pronounced.

Theresa wandered back to him. Her career as a cardiologist would have to wait.

Fracture lines criss-crossed Darryl's parietal bone, and as Harris pulled the brain out of the way with a soft, sucking sound, a piece actually fell out. Theresa felt bad for looking at it, the broken bone, the severed brain stem, the now-empty torso. The victim had been laid as bare as he could be. This was someone she knew. Someone she worked with on a daily basis for over a decade. *And we just ripped out his brain.*

'Looks like Justin bounced his head off the floor a couple of times,' Harris said, with a bit too much glee to his voice. It set Theresa's teeth on edge.

'How many times?' a voice behind them said. Shephard stood in the doorway, more out than in, and Theresa wondered how long he'd been there.

'You can come in, Sergeant,' she told him, honestly trying to be nice instead of screwing with him, but his eyes narrowed and he moved another half-inch back instead of forward. Obviously, the sergeant did not care for autopsies – but then, that was the normal response. Hanging over the doctor's shoulder while he carved a heart into little pieces was, perhaps, not.

Harris and Banachek traced the tracks in the skull with their gloved fingers as if reading a road map. 'At least five,' Banachek said at last.

'Is that what killed him?' Shephard asked.

'Oh, yes. The edges of the fracture cut open the hematomas that formed from the concussions. Those swellings put pressure on the brain that would have killed him eventually, but this one—' he held up the loose piece – 'actually broke through the skin from the inside, letting the hematomas vent.'

'In other words,' Harris said, 'his brain started oozing out of his head.'

'Thank you, doctor,' Theresa said severely. He managed to look hurt.

Banachek continued, talking either to them or to himself: 'In a best-case scenario, bleeding to the outside might have relieved the pressure and saved him. But this was worst-case, and he bled to death.'

Shephard looked at Theresa. 'So our killer should have this man's blood on him?'

Had he *looked* at the deskmen's office? 'Covered in it.'

He nodded to himself.

'Who's doing the scene?' Harris demanded of the cop.

'We are.' He meant CPD.

'And how long are you going to tie up the building for?'

What, now he couldn't wait to get back to work?

'No longer than absolutely necessary, Doctor,' Shephard said with exaggerated courtesy. 'Your ME made that stipulation clear.'

Harris snorted. 'As if he minds. Lock out the county auditor along with the rest of the employees and Stone will let you have the run of the place for weeks.'

'Auditor?' Theresa asked.

'Didn't you know that?' the man reported with unabashed glee. 'Our new manager hasn't quite finished cleaning house.'

Cuyahoga County managers and employees had conducted shady deals for decades, mostly involving jobs and contracts but also utilizing bribes from gift cards to televisions, free labor, lowered property appraisals and some really good steaks. The populace had finally decided they couldn't afford that kind of nonsense any more and had thrown out the county commissioners and their entire system of government, opting to replace them with a county manager and a brand-new, never before done Department of Inspector General, to make sure that the forty-odd crooks sent to jail weren't simply replaced with a new set.

'No wonder he seems stressed,' Theresa said.

Shephard, to whom, surely, county corruption hardly came as breaking news, thanked them and moved away.

Theresa wanted to leave herself, go up to her locked lab with its inanimate specimens and microscopes and computer monitors; she could make another cup of coffee and finally take a moment to, as the guru said on her yoga tape, 'assimilate all that has occurred'. But she would feel like a coward if she bailed. She hadn't liked Darryl, but now she would stay with him until the end, until they zipped that white plastic body bag over his face. She would wheel his gurney into the cooler herself, save Harris that one last chore. That ought to make the old whiner happy.

Fifteen minutes later she pulled the cord that closed the sliding door to the cooler, abandoning Darryl Johnson to the company of the other corpses. It was a final goodbye, and Theresa felt guilty for saying it; it felt as if, having received the last bit of physical attention he would in this world, Darryl had now crossed the line from an actual person to just a memory, his body now simply an inconvenient chunk of decomposing meat. Theresa could only console herself by realizing that he and the rest of his new colleagues didn't care. They had moved on to another plane where the disposition of their used flesh weighed no more on their mind than a lost button off an old sweater.

Theresa went back up the rear staircase and into the lab.

As soon as she entered she knew she was not alone behind those locked doors. Someone else had penetrated her stronghold.

And more than that, he'd made coffee.

SIX

DNA analyst Don sat on the edge of Leo's abandoned desk. Half African-American and half Spanish, he had enviably smooth amber skin, an enviably slender frame, and enviably huge brown eyes. He also appeared enviably well-rested.

'You angel,' Theresa said with an embarrassing amount of fervor.

'I admit that I am naught but Sweetness and Light, but do you mention it specifically for a reason?'

She rinsed out her porcelain Cleveland FBI mug and filled it by way of an answer. Then she told him of the events during the previous seven hours. Her voice apparently hadn't learned to stop doing that trembling thing, because at one point he got up and gave her a hug. Don was sweet that way.

What Theresa didn't think he knew was how it made her heart pound and her skin sweat; she tightened her arms around him in a way that pushed some of the air out of his lungs, and she knew it was too tight but couldn't make herself let go; she pushed her nose into his shoulder and inhaled Ivory soap and Gain laundry detergent; she wished the world would freeze forever at that one moment in time so that she'd never have to remind herself that she was an adult, a professional, and eleven years too old for this nice boy who should date a nice kindergarten teacher and then settle down to raise two or three children of his own.

But the world didn't stop, and she stepped away and went back to her coffee with cheeks burning, knowing Don would chalk it up to grief and shock. Well, shock. He would know she felt no more grief for Darryl than he did.

He gave her a moment to collect herself, then asked: 'So, Temporary Acting Supervisor, what do we do now?'

'Glad you asked.' Theresa pulled several envelopes out of her pockets.

He groaned.

'Hair samples, presumably Justin's. Blood sample from the wall by the elevator. Ditto from the wall by the hallway. Blood sample from the deskmen's office floor. Blood sample from Darryl's autopsy.'

'I thought you said CPD was handling this scene.'

'They are. And they have plenty of samples of their own.'

'All right. What else?'

'A few other tasks, but for yours truly. I'm going to need Justin's fingerprints from his personnel file.'

'Good luck with that,' he said.

HazMat had responded for the unhappy task of wiping up her co-worker's spilled blood, and the disinfectant smell permeated the entire first floor. On the plus side, Theresa guessed that the deskmen's office hadn't smelled that fresh since long before her tenure at the ME's. They bundled all the soiled cleaning materials into three large red biohazard bags, and then finally stripped off the isolation suits they had to wear. Those Tyvek suits serve their purpose admirably, protecting both the worker and the crime scene from contaminating each other, but they're hotter than hell, and the day Theresa had to wear one to each scene she would begin to think about retiring.

But on the second floor the staff had begun to trickle back in, reluctantly, disappointed at not getting the entire day off. Many comments were made as to the efficiency of coming in for only half a day; the staff were convinced that the county would be more cost-effective if it had left them home enjoying a third cup of coffee in front of the midday talk shows. The county, of course, couldn't have cared less.

The center of the room consisted of empty space for citizens to wait in line at the counter to obtain autopsy reports or death certificates. To the right sat the copy machine, protected behind a low swinging door that only employees could enter, and then the glass wall and door to Stone's office. To the left sat the vault, a storage room with file cabinets going back to the seventies. Small windows lined the room, filling the space with a grayish light as the sun filtered through the usual late winter clouds and reflected off the buff-colored Formica and faded carpeting.

Janice, Queen of the Secretaries, stood in her usual spot behind the counter, directing the day's chaos from underneath her helmet of shellacked brown hair, armed with a gel pen and a cordless phone she'd bought herself in order to have more range of motion. Like most queens, she could be quite gracious as long as one followed court protocol and showed the proper amount of respect. Theresa waited as she finished explaining to their histologist over the phone that, yes, she really did have to come in or the entire afternoon would have to come out of her vacation pay. Period.

Then she hung up. 'You poor thing. You walked in on his body?'

'Yep.'

'But CPD did the crime scene?' Stone might have been okay with allowing others into their territory, but Janice certainly hadn't signed that off.

'Yep.'

Janice said nothing, but punched a number into her handset with an angry thumb.

'I have a few prints that I need to compare, though. I'm going to need Justin Warner's print card from his personnel file.' Theresa spoke gently, respectfully, while knowing that it might not do any good. Couldn't hurt, though.

Janice put the receiver to her ear. 'I can't give you anything out of a personnel file.'

'He's missing and possibly dead. Either that, or he's a murder suspect. In any case, I have prints I need to eliminate.'

She scowled, either at Theresa or at whoever was at the other end of her line and not picking up their phone. Theresa could hear the relentless buzzing from across the counter.

'You don't have access to personnel files,' she said, putting a very delicate emphasis on *you.*

'I don't want his personnel file. Just the fingerprint card. I *am* the fingerprint examiner.'

She terminated the unanswered call with an impatient stab to the 'End' button. 'Reese won't pick up. We're going to be short a pathologist, and there are six already scheduled for today.' She meant six autopsies, plus any other traffic accidents or heart attacks which occurred between now and the early afternoon. 'You'll have to get the ME's permission.'

'Fine,' Theresa said. 'But any minute now CPD is going to come up here and ask for it, and you'll have to give it to them. I don't even need the original. Just let me make a copy of it.'

She considered this.

'I mean—' Theresa tried to carefully prod, though subtlety had never been her strong point – 'our own guy was murdered, in our own building.'

Janice walked away without another word. Theresa crossed her fingers and waited, worrying about Reese. He lived not ten minutes away in one of the vast brick mansions that lined Fairmount Boulevard. She had been there a few times for parties; he and his wife liked to entertain, though only the upper echelons. Theresa could not recall him ever being late to the morning viewing, much less blowing off an entire day. Despite their funds, they didn't even seem to vacation very often. And from his growing potbelly, she didn't think he'd be out jogging.

Janice returned, holding out a square piece of stiff white paper.

'Thank you.' Theresa went off to the copy machine behind its swinging door before Janice could change her mind. When Theresa returned it, she asked the woman, 'Where do you suppose Dr Reese is?'

'The man may be a bit of a snob,' she said, while Theresa clamped her tongue down on a comment about elitism, pots and kettles, 'but in twenty years here I have never had him not answer his phone.'

Theresa said, 'If anyone needs me, I'm going on a short break.'

Calling the homes on Fairmount Boulevard mansions was not an exaggeration. Gorgeous English country houses outfitted in hardwood and surrounded by greenery, where anything that sold for less than half a million or had fewer than five thousand square feet under truss would be considered on the small side.

Theresa had second-guessed herself through every inch of

the winding, wooded boulevard, asking herself just what the hell she thought she was doing. So an older, professional man had decided to sleep in? So his cellphone had gone dead? Maybe they had a family emergency, one of the grandchildren broke an arm or something, and the Reeses had rushed to whatever junior mansion their doctor offspring lived in, in whatever equally gorgeous suburb of whatever city. Or maybe Dr Hubert Reese had awoken in the night in the grip of a homicidal rage, driven to work, murdered one deskman and brought the other one back there to lock in his cellar for future use. No matter which scenario might be most likely, none were any responsibility of Theresa's. None at all.

She kept driving.

Maybe she simply needed to take a break, to get some fresh air, a moment away from the horrific scene she'd encountered this morning, even though it wasn't really that horrific, not for Theresa, who had waded through such scenes at least a couple of hundred times before.

Just not when personally acquainted with the victim. Not usually, anyway.

With the sun up, albeit hidden behind the sky's usual carpet of gray haze, Theresa found the house without any trouble. She'd last seen it at some sort of summer barbecue. Fourth of July, she thought. Rachael had been out on a date, and Frank had gone to the ball game, so Theresa had shown up with only a plate of deviled eggs as company. Now, the grass, though soggy with the spring rains, looked just as neat as she remembered it, the driveway perfectly clear of last fall's dead leaves. No cars were in the long drive, but then any present would reside in the four-car detached garage behind the house. Both buildings were made entirely of brick, of course.

Theresa got out of the car, sucking in the smell of clean air and damp tree bark, listening to the chirps of birds filtering back from the southern states. Aside from the tail end of the morning commute along Fairmount, she seemed to be the only human in the area.

The driveway curved around to the back; she left her car there and didn't bother walking around to the front. The three stone steps up to the rear door were as clean as the driveway.

The very ordinary-looking screen door seemed a little out of place, but behind it sat a heavy, dark wood barrier with an ornate brass handle.

Which hung open about six inches.

Maybe he'd just been leaving, preparing to go to work.

Through the screen she could see the kitchen, cherry cabinets, granite countertops, a coffee cup sitting on the island in the middle. No blood, no bodies. But still, reaching out to rap on the aluminum frame made her heart pound and her throat go dry. Something, somewhere, was bad. Very bad.

Her knock rattled the screen door, and she called Reese's name. She had to force herself to give it proper volume. He would probably appear in the doorway any second, himself startled at her unexpected presence and scaring the friggin' life out of Theresa.

Nothing.

She couldn't make herself knock again.

Time for the next step. She pulled out her cellphone and called CPD. Theresa wasn't stupid.

After a few minutes she got Dispatch to route her through to Shephard. Theresa told him where she was and why.

'What's this doctor's connection to Johnson?' he asked.

'Other than working in the same building? None that I know of.'

'Why do you think he may be in danger?'

'He's not answering his phone, and his back door is open.'

'That's it?'

Theresa said, 'With this guy, that's enough.'

He paused to think, no doubt weighing manpower concerns over the risks of blowing off even a minor anomaly in light of that morning's events. 'Okay, I'll send a car. Stay where you are.'

'No,' she said. 'I'm going in.'

'Excuse me?'

'What if he's bleeding to death, like Darryl? A few minutes could save his life.'

'*No.* Stay out of that house! That's an order.'

Theresa felt sorry for the guy – he'd had a busy morning, too – but she was already in the kitchen. It did not appear any more ominous without the intervening screen. Some dishes in the sink, crumbs on the shiny granite counter, and nothing else of note. 'I understand, Sergeant, I do. But I don't work for you, and I have valid reason to be concerned for Dr Reese's safety, so I'm going to look for him. It's on me. Is this a recorded line?'

She moved into the hallway. A paneled dining room with a table long enough to seat twelve comfortably and original, though uninteresting, paintings on the walls . . . but no blood, and no doctor.

'This is my cellphone, so no, it's not a recorded line!'

'Oh, sorry. I was just trying to give you an out – I mean . . . you know what I mean.'

'*I* mean get out of that house! Wait in the driveway.'

'No can do. Stay on the phone with me?' she asked. Okay, begged, but she hoped that desperation would not translate through one or two cellphone towers.

'Yes, I will stay on the phone, but do not go into that house.'

'Too late. Kitchen and dining room clear. I'm going to call him again, maybe he's upstairs and I don't want to startle him.' She covered the receiver with her hand and shouted the doctor's name as loudly as she could. Waited. Nothing.

'No response. Here's a family room, puffy couches, big screen, leftover potato chips. Nothing – sinister. Small hallway bath, clear. Nice towels. I'm moving toward the front of the house. This must be the living room proper.'

'Do you hear anything? Any movement?'

She paused. 'No. Okay, living room, English chintz furniture, mahogany tables. Everything is too perfect, I bet they live in the family room. It's nippier in here, too, probably harder to heat with these large windows. They could put plastic over them in the winter, but that always ruins the look—'

'MacLean! I'm not interested in listing the place,' he protested finally. 'Just make sure there is no one else there – look for people, not decor.'

'Sorry,' she said. 'Foyer. Front door is closed and, let me check, locked. Moving into a . . . what would this be? Parlor? Rumpus room? Living Room Part B? There's a few couches and end tables and – oh.'

'MacLean?'

'There's blood here.'

She thought she sounded calm. More or less.

'There's a smear of something that looks like blood on an otherwise perfect fawn carpet. Maybe it's dirt. Next room – okay.'

'Theresa?'

'It's not dirt.'

SEVEN

Shephard found her in the library – an actual library, her dream room, with four walls of bookshelves in deep walnut, a matching desk, overstuffed leather armchairs and a window seat below leaded glass panes. Her dream room except for the body of Dr Reese, awkwardly sprawled between the front corner of the desk and a small round occasional table with an inlaid wood design.

The medics had taken him away, albeit with grim little shakes of their heads over his condition. Theresa had found a faint pulse and nearly indiscernible respiration, and he had lost a lot of blood.

He had been beaten, just like Darryl, his head coming to rest in a pool that the Persian rug could only partially contain. Eventually, it had spread to the edge, beyond the fringe, and formed a thin stream that ran across the hardwood planks to reach some unseen low spot beneath the radiator. The radiator had only come on once since she'd been there – even doctors have to watch those heating bills – and filled the room with the smell of warmed-up blood.

Dr Reese's face showed similar bruising and a small cut on the nose. He wore flannel men's pajamas, white with a blue pinstripe, which fit their surroundings as well as any sleep wear could have. The bottom edge of the loose top had flipped up as he fell, but Theresa couldn't really tell much from his fleshy abdomen – blows there might not have had enough time or blood flow to form their purplish markers. Aside from the abrasion on the nose, his only other wound seemed to be a gash in the back of the head. Theresa didn't feel qualified to go poking around in the man's skull, but could feel a rough indent where the bone had suffered a slight cave-in, most likely from the corner of his desk. She looked around for what could have been used as a weapon, but there were no loose candlesticks or bookends or golf trophies scattered nearby that would fit the bill, and the walnut desk felt hard as granite. Reese was a tall man, and that high center of gravity coupled with the lethally inflexible corner had apparently produced enough cerebral edema to depress his life functions to the point of nil.

The first thing she had done was to try to call Frank. Theresa had actually disconnected Sergeant Shephard without another word, selected her cousin's name in the contact list and had her thumb on the 'Call' button before she remembered. Cruise ship. No cellphone service. A hollow feeling froze her in place for a moment before she thawed and redialed Shephard.

Two patrol officers and the ambulance had arrived simultaneously, and quickly enough to scare the crap out of her. Shephard had dispatched them as soon as she'd called, just in case.

Now she and the sergeant stood looking at the book-lined room, the only area of the house that showed any signs of disturbance. A lamp on the desk had been overturned and two issues of *The Wall Street Journal* sent fluttering to the floor. A framed photo of Reese with two other men in front of Case Western Reserve University had fallen over. The desk drawers were all ajar, the contents stirred up, a few paper clips and pens spilled. A two-drawer filing cabinet, built into the bookshelves and nearly invisible behind the desk, had been thoroughly rifled – each and every hanging folder removed and stacked in a slanting pile to the left. Crime scene tech Jen, looking weary, had snapped a number of pictures before moving on to the rest of the house.

Shephard floated the idea that Reese had surprised a burglar, but she didn't even throw the idea a follow-up question. Unless someone had begun a rampage in University Circle that left a trail of bodies to Shaker Square – and no such reports had come in – then Reese's attack somehow related to Darryl Johnson's murder.

'Did he say anything?' Shephard had asked Theresa immediately upon arrival.

'One eyelid fluttered,' she said. 'That was the most response I got. It doesn't look good.'

'What did the EMTs say?'

'That it doesn't look good.'

He had scanned the house himself, with Theresa trailing in his wake. As the uniformed cops had reported, nothing seemed suspicious . . . except for Mrs Reese's jewelry box. A stand-alone miniature wardrobe with double doors, there seemed to be more pendants and rings on the floor than hanging from its hooks. She apparently liked diamonds, and a myriad of stones glinted with that deep twinkle that lets one know they're real. No cubic zirconium for the lady of this house. The bed was unmade, in keeping with the victim's attire.

'Plenty of jewelry,' Shephard had said, more to himself than to Theresa. What he meant was that it didn't look like there were any pieces missing, and to judge from the floor of Mrs Reese's closet, the clutter might just be a housekeeping issue.

He had done a quick check of the rest of the bedroom, drawers, walk-in closets, medicine cabinet in the bath. Nothing. If whoever attacked Reese had waded through Mrs Reese's jewelry, they had been looking for a specific item. It threw out the burglary-gone-bad theory.

Now Shephard sat on the hardwood floor next to the filing cabinet skimming over the contents, blue latex gloves on his hands, legs folded underneath him like a teenage girl. They would ache when he had to get up, Theresa thought. 'Were they friends? Reese and Johnson?'

Theresa snorted before she could help herself. 'Not likely.'

'Why not?'

She considered. 'I don't know for sure, of course, I can only tell you that I never saw them hanging out together, lunching together, or even saying anything more to each other than a comment on the football game or the weather or a particularly interesting victim history. On the flip side, there were no conflicts between the two that I know of. Darryl could be – irritating? But never any more than mildly irritating, and irritating to everyone equally.'

'What about Reese and Justin Warner? Any relationship?'

'That's even less likely. For one thing, Justin has only been here – at the office – three months.'

'And for another?'

She started to lean against the edge of the desk, thought of fingerprints, and rested her back against the bookcase instead.

'The ME's is like any workplace – there's a pecking order. At the summit is Stone, of course; then the pathologists. They're great people but they're doctors, which makes them gods, just like any other place on earth. Then there's the scientists – me, Don, the toxicologists, the histologists. The artists, our photographers. Then support staff, starting with Janice. Then the ones who really have to get their hands dirty – dieners, who end up with enough medical knowledge to open their own practice but still make peanuts because they don't have a degree. And then, pretty much at the bottom, are the deskmen.'

He continued to fan paper files – from what she could see over his shoulder, they seemed to be tax returns, home appliances warranties, medical records and a family tree. The same kind of stuff that most people have in their personal filing cabinets. Theresa didn't know if he was reading or digesting what she'd said, and she tilted her head back against a collection of world atlases and closed her eyes. The weariness that adrenalin had been holding back suddenly seeped into her body. She'd barely slept, and now she'd found two men – men she knew, men she worked with – lying in their own blood within the past eight hours.

She opened her eyes. 'I've got to call Stone. Has anyone called Stone? Or – Mrs Reese? Where *is* Mrs Reese, anyway?'

'According to a neighbor, she is in Minnesota helping out their daughter, who just had her second baby. A beautiful baby boy, she told us, seven pounds, six ounces. I never understand why people tell you how much the kid weighs. I'm happy for the happy happy parents, but really, what do I care how much the kid weighed?'

Theresa wondered what prompted this sudden burst of commentary . . . either he was getting punchy, staying up past his normal shift, or perhaps babies were a sore spot for him. Trying to conceive and not having any luck? No wedding ring, but that didn't mean much in this day and age. He had a rip in his sleeve near his right wrist and two old stains on the left leg of his pants. He needed a shave (not surprising, he should have gone home for the day hours before) and a haircut (just a half-inch) and maybe a little bit of sun. Aftershave had worn off earlier in his shift so she couldn't tell much from that.

Theresa guessed single, probably divorced (and probably more than once, being a cop) and not in a serious relationship with anyone except perhaps video games (pale and accustomed to sitting on the floor).

Theresa had been quiet too long, and he noticed her scrutiny, flushed a bit, and rose stiffly to a crouch high enough to plant his butt in Dr Reese's desk chair. Bent over, he continued to study the files.

Perhaps he was expecting a grandchild soon, and the idea made him nervous.

Perhaps he would never have grandchildren, and the idea made him unhappy.

Perhaps Theresa should get back to work. She asked again about ME Stone; Shephard said no one had called that he knew of and that she should. She knew she should, too, and did, and it wasn't fun. As usual the Medical Examiner managed to imply, with silence and a single expelled breath, that the blame for all the agency's recent misfortunes could be laid squarely at her door. Theresa kept it short.

She put the phone back in her pocket. 'So someone knocked Reese out in order to rifle through his old tax returns? And maybe his wife's lavalieres? You—'

He looked up. 'What?'

She'd been about to say *you didn't touch the file cabinet drawers, did you?* but thought better of it. It annoyed cops to constantly remind them of Principles of Crime Scene Management 101. 'You find anything interesting?'

'Other than wondering who would pay eighty-nine dollars for a wallet, no. He did have one file of clippings, though. Your past cases. It was on top.'

He flipped open a hanging folder, spreading some of the newspaper columns across the floor for her to see. A murder-suicide from six months before. A traffic accident in which three children died. A drive-by in Euclid. Just a fraction of the stories that pass through the medical examiner's office.

Shephard asked her, 'Any of those ring a bell? Stand out in your mind? A case that was controversial, that particularly involved Dr Reese? Any disgruntled customers?'

Theresa shook her head. 'I wouldn't have any idea. You

need to ask Stone – if there were complaints or threats, he would know. I wouldn't.'

'Pecking order, huh?'

'Exactly. Everything is need-to-know.'

'And you didn't have any beefs, arguments, or dramas with one or both of these two victims in recent memory?'

Theresa felt sure her eyes widened, which probably looked ridiculous.

He shrugged, all casual-like but with a piercing gaze. 'I have to ask. You've reported two brutally attacked victims in less than a full shift.'

'Well . . .' She swallowed. 'Yes. And no, no conflicts with either man.'

After a moment he shrugged again. 'Don't worry. My money's still on our missing Justin Warner.'

This time she didn't argue. She also felt guilty about not arguing.

'And,' he went on, 'there's a slim – very slim – chance that the two cases aren't related. This place was rifled, like a burglary gone bad or maybe a family member who needed cash right away. Your deskman still had on a nice watch and a diamond ring, wallet in his pocket. On the surface it looks like very different motivations.'

'That's true. But why just the office and the wife's jewelry box, and then not take half the jewelry? He didn't open another drawer or a closet; usually, they're looking for cash, guns and prescription meds – well, you know that. He might have been interrupted.'

'By what? The wife isn't home, the neighbors are two hundred feet away, the trees give plenty of cover. No one phoned.'

So he had checked the caller ID already. Theresa felt fairly impressed by Sergeant Shephard.

He went on: 'And if Dr Reese surprised him in here and he attacked the doctor, thought he killed him, why did he go upstairs and open the jewelry box before getting overcome by the heebie-jeebies and decide to run? It's possible, of course.'

Theresa knew it was *possible*. Criminals were human beings, fully capable of being as capricious, inexplicable and illogical as anyone else.

Something started to swell in the base of her brain, some vague wisp of an idea that melded into some faded scrap of memory.

She left Shephard to his tasks and exited the doctor's house. From the driveway she called Don. 'Are you still at the lab?'

'Of course I'm still at the lab. It's back to business as usual here, according to the county. Time to get our butts back into our task chairs.'

'Stay there,' she said – stupidly, in light of what he had just told her. 'I have a really funny idea.'

'Funny ha ha, or funny—'

'Funny scary,' she said. 'I think someone's hunting us.'

EIGHT

For the second time that morning she presented herself to Janice, Queen of the Secretaries, for consideration. She needed more than just a copy of a fingerprint card this time. She needed to get into the vault itself. Theresa needed to see a case file.

Case files were not like personnel files, though, and Janice let her in without hesitation.

Theresa had to look up his six-digit number but located the file for George Bain. Bain had been a cop in Euclid Heights for most of his life, but the moment he had his twenty years in he took the retirement and came to the Medical Examiner's office for the regular hours and (relatively) safe working conditions of Ambulance Crew Member, aka bodysnatcher. Within two weeks the regular hours and safe but sometimes back-straining conditions had him bored stiff and stiff as a board, and he spent the next fifteen years bemoaning his haste to bid his cop days adieu. Then eight months ago he bid the ME's adieu as well and retired completely.

That hadn't agreed with him, either; he'd barely made twelve weeks of leisure before his heart succumbed to despair. Or succumbed to too little exercise combined with too many chicken wings. Either way the result had been the same.

Theresa sat at a table in the center of the room. She could look at the file all she wanted, maybe even make a copy of some items, but couldn't leave with it. Janice always gave Theresa's lab coat a long look upon her exit, as if considering a quick frisk. Happily for both of them, Janice had never actually tried it.

Theresa skimmed the contents of the file. George Bain had been sixty-seven years old, divorced, overweight, a smoker, with cholesterol deposits and arteriosclerosis. Essentially, a heart attack waiting to happen, and the autopsy confirmed it. She had always wondered how, even with a partner, he managed to heft dead weights on to gurneys without becoming one himself.

His body had a few bruises to the arms and two to the ribs, one rather harsh one on the left clavicle, thought to have occurred as he stumbled around in pain or possibly looking for a phone, according to the scribbled notes of the responding officer. There were no signs of foul play; the door was unlocked but closed, victim's wallet still in his pocket. Cash and two guns were found in the bedroom, undisturbed. Neighbors had not seen or heard anything unusual that evening, though neighbors tended to keep their observations to themselves in that corner of town. Discretion being the better part of valor, and all that.

George had died on a Saturday night, so there had been no need to clear the building since there was only a skeleton staff present on Sunday anyway. The night-shift deskmen hadn't been particularly close to him since they worked at different times and so would have been expected to suck it up. Dr Harris had been assigned that weekend, probably complaining the entire time that a former employee should have known enough to die during business hours.

Theresa pulled out the source of her brain twinge, the crime scene photos. George had not been much of a housekeeper, and his home had many obstructions which could cause a fall – stacks of newspapers, empty boxes, an abandoned mop, spilled liquids and scattered shoes. It didn't *quite* qualify for an episode of *Hoarders*, however, and the clutter had some sort of order to it. The newspapers were stacked, and the boxes set parallel to the wall. George had probably considered the place rather tidy.

Except for the corner of the living room used as a home office, and the bedroom.

A cheap computer desk held a dusty monitor, yet more stacks of paper, three staplers and a coffee can brimming with pens and pencils. A clean end of the desk had a small mountain of sheets and notes on the floor underneath it, almost as if one stack had fallen over or had been gone through. Theresa could see a two-drawer file cabinet, similar to Dr Reese's, except that instead of glossy walnut, George had a cheap metal one with scratches and some deep dents. It had been emptied, its contents in one large heap next to it.

She studied the photos, then turned each over one by one. She wondered why they had even been printed – most scene photos weren't in this digital age, when doctors and other people with access could view them on their computers, zooming in and out at will. (Theresa had access only to cases with samples assigned to Trace Evidence; simply browsing through death scenes out of morbid curiosity was not allowed . . . The medical examiner's office really *did* try to preserve the privacy and the dignity of the deceased.)

Certain aspects of the scene sorted themselves out as she studied it. The living room coffee table had stacks of playing cards and magazines next to an array of remotes for the home entertainment system. Cardboard boxes had been stacked behind the sofa in a nearly perfect rectangle of bricks – apparently, George spent way too much time on the home shopping channels. But the file cabinet and the desk drawer had everything removed from them and put in a condensed but not neat pile.

The kitchen: the back half of the counter had cereal boxes, a blender, a toaster, a knife block, and so on and so forth packed into a continuous block from one wall to the next. The kitchen table had been similarly loaded up to three-quarters of its capacity, with the remaining quarter left as pristine as the front half of the counter.

The bathroom: medicine cabinet contents undisturbed (all over-the-counter, basic first-aid kind of stuff – no syringes, no industrial-sized jugs of sleeping pills, no worn bottles of expired Xanax such as addicts carry around to lend themselves legitimacy if searched). Enough toilet paper to stock a good-sized men's room lining the walls, but everything in its assigned though cluttered space.

The bedroom: bed made, albeit with more than a few wrinkles in the old-fashioned bedspread. No less than three dressers with their tops packed with the now-familiar boxes, cartons, and a stack of folded polo-type shirts. But on the lowest dresser this layer had been topped with smaller items: an open ring box, a loose tie, a bundle of letters held with a rubber band

and what looked like a tiny bowling trophy. A decorative bottle of cologne, which she hoped had been empty since it lay on its side on top of the polo shirts. A bunch of watches.

The next shot showed a more aerial view of this collection. Beneath the stuff, the top drawer jutted out about three inches and appeared to be empty except for some loose pieces of paper.

Theresa's mind made that immediate, instinctive leap: someone had emptied the first drawer out piece by piece, placing the items on top of the stuff that was on top of the dresser.

The other drawers were closed – not perfectly flush, but closed. Not a burglar, then; at least, not a professional one. Burglars didn't take the time to close drawers.

Maybe George had been cleaning out this drawer when overcome by his fatal heart attack? Or maybe George had a fatal heart attack because someone had attacked him, just as someone had attacked Dr Reese. Or someone attacked George because George walked in just as the attacker had been method-ically searching through the retired bodysnatcher's stuff.

Or maybe Theresa was now engaged in the all-too-human pursuit of seeing patterns that weren't really there simply because she felt convinced there must be a pattern in the first place.

The closet had a similar aura to it. The doors were open, clothes hanging, light on. But the top shelf had two blankets, a stack of jeans, and a stack of sweatshirts, leaving large spaces between these items – odd, considering that every inch of available space stayed filled throughout the rest of the house. Boxes and containers left on top of the shoes on the closet floor. She peered at the colored pixels, trying to sort their contents into specific items: smaller boxes, more envelopes in rubber bands, a baseball, a few books, a worn teddy bear—

'What are you doing in here?' Don asked at her elbow, scaring a few years off her life . . . annoying that they always came off at the wrong end and thus wouldn't make her any younger. She tended to think bitterly and a bit nonsensically about age whenever Don entered the room. Particularly when he was accompanied by Elena, who didn't look old enough to drive and was cute enough to make Miley Cyrus look like Leona Helmsley.

'Reviewing a file. How are you doing, Elena?'

'What an awful day,' she said, blonde hair glimmering to her shoulders, hot pink fingernails fluttering. Elena had a lot of awful days, her nerves consistently rubbed raw by the strain of living with two doctor parents who imagined their little girl doing her residency at Johns Hopkins or some such place; Elena herself had just enough intelligence and common sense to know that would never be an option for a girl who couldn't even pass high school biology. So she strode through life as a constant contradiction, an eternal disappointment and yet the envy of all who set eyes upon her. One couldn't *not* like the kid – for all her dewy beauty she looked as awkward as a shy seventh-grader standing in a clique-ridden school cafeteria. Theresa patted the table across from herself and suggested Elena sit down for a moment.

Don sat beside Theresa, gingerly. She thought he felt wary at her being sweet and mothering for no apparent reason to anyone other than, well, him, but it turned out he had something else on his mind.

Instead of looking past her at the spread-out file, he turned toward her, removed her right hand from the table and held it in both of his. 'I have to tell you something.'

She knew at once it would be bad. Solemn wasn't a common expression for either of them.

'Dr Reese died.'

'Oh,' she said, and nothing more, though her stomach plunged at least a foot deeper into her body, and she revisited the question of exactly how to feel about the death of a co-worker to whom one had not been especially close. In the next instant she moved on to less selfish concerns. 'His poor wife. And his daughter, with a new baby—'

Don simply held her hand, and when she could stand the silence no longer, Elena mercifully interrupted, asking: 'Did Justin really kill them?'

'I don't know. I can't believe he did, either.'

'Justin was always so nice to me,' the girl said, eyes as wide as the lake and twice as blue.

Theresa didn't point out that *all* men were nice to her and would continue to be until she hit forty or so. Then all that niceness and attention and helpfulness would drop off expo-nentially, and she would miss it, no matter how much she had always told herself that her looks weren't important to her. 'I heard that he tended to hang out here and talk to you a lot.'

Elena nodded earnestly. 'He used to, when he was on days for training. Of course, since he went to nights I hardly see him. Just in passing. But he bought me lunch once or twice – twice – because I had gone over to the medical school food court and he happened to be there too and bought me lunch even though I told him he didn't have to.'

'Uh-huh,' Theresa encouraged. 'What was he like?'

She nibbled one fingernail, chipping off some of the hot pink. 'Nice! Even when he would kind of flirt with me – I know everyone thought he wanted to ask me out, and he did once, but I kind of said no because . . .'

Because what? He was black? He had a gap between his front teeth? He snorted when he laughed? 'Because?'

'He was so much older than me.'

Justin couldn't have been more than thirty-five. But then Elena couldn't yet legally drink, so yes, that *was* a significant age difference.

'And I don't like to date people I work with,' the girl added.

'That is very sensible,' Theresa assured her. Without irony, even given the direction of her own thoughts at times.

'But Justin was even nice about *that*. I know people think he was all like, "Hey, baby," but he wasn't. We mostly talked about work. He really cared about his job.'

'That was my impression, too,' Theresa said. Don just listened. A formidable mother and adoring but chatty sisters had turned him into a very good listener.

'He told me that he needed to keep this job, that he had screwed up a few things in the past and didn't want to do that again. It sounded like drugs, but I didn't ask. He said he had goals now, and that once he found the right path to them then nothing could be allowed to stop him from reaching justice. That's how he got past the blood – when he first came here it really made him sick, but he told himself that blood is a

trail leading back to the person so that they could never really
get lost. In this life or the next, they could never be lost. I
thought that was sweet.' Her eyes filled with tears. 'That's
why I can't believe he'd kill Darryl.'

Theresa pressed her hand over the girl's for a moment. She
couldn't believe it either. Yet the talk of blood trails seemed
creepily prescient. 'Did he mention any problems with Darryl?
Did they get along?'

'No, but then he didn't even work with Darryl then. He was
still on the day shift when we would talk a lot.'

'Oh, right. Justin's only been on nights for, what, six weeks?'

'I guess.'

'Any problems with anyone else?'

'No. He seemed to really like it here. He wanted to know
everything, who everyone was, how long they'd been working
here, how the doctors divvy up the work, what kind of slides
they make in histology, everything. Even the paperwork, the
reports, the files, how we organize them, how we made the
switch from paper to the new digital system. He really seemed
interested in what I do. *That* was a first,' she added with a
surprisingly indelicate snort, and for an instant Theresa could
glimpse a spark of snarky intelligence. Elena might never
become a doctor, but she might yet become one hell of a
something else.

'Did he ever ask to look at some records? A case file, or
a personnel file?'

'No . . . um . . . well, sort of. He said once or twice that
he'd like to – what'd he say? – *browse* through the records.
Just to see how the other deskmen fill out their forms – even
though they don't have that many. The clothing form, the
personal property form, the main ledger. The release form—'

'He didn't ask for a particular person's file?' Don asked.

'No, no. Just wanted to look at some at random. But of
course Janice would never go for that.'

'Of course not,' Theresa agreed.

Elena thought a minute, her frown causing a furrow in her
perfect skin. 'But if he didn't kill Darryl, then what happened
to him? Do you think the real killer kidnapped him?'

'I suppose it's possible. But for what? Ransom?'

'Yes! They could make the county pay. That's what they do in Mexico all the time – families don't have any money, so they ask the victim's employers to pay up.'

'True, but—'

Elena's eyes had begun to glisten again. 'I hope he's okay. Even if he *did* kill Darryl – I still hope he's okay.'

'So do I.'

Janice appeared in the doorway, managing to express great displeasure using only one eyebrow, though whether it might be directed at her, Elena, their momentary lack of constructive labor, the current crisis or simply the disruption in the day's routine, Theresa couldn't guess.

Janice said, 'Elena, customers are lining up.'

The girl got up and left without another word. Janice gave Don and Theresa another sharp look – interlopers in her territory, which custom forced her to tolerate. Then she turned away, and Don asked Theresa what the hell she was doing, though not in so many words.

'Looking at our ex-Property-clerk's case file.'

He raised an eyebrow to express curiosity that she might choose this moment to revisit history when current events had overwhelmed them.

'His house is packed to the gills, but it's not messy. Not messy at all.'

Don leaned over the pictures. 'I'm not following you, kiddo.'

'Someone's looking for something. He's not interested in clothes, food, prescriptions or money. He's looking for some-*thing*.' Theresa looked into her friend's deep brown eyes, and for once they didn't make her feel better. 'And he's going to keep killing us until he finds it.'

NINE

They told Shephard. He had gone home and freshened up – to judge from the freshly (and hastily, leaving two tiny scabs at the back of his jaw) shaved face and the clean smell of Coast soap – and then come back, somehow assigning the case to himself. Apparently, he could do that. Two detectives had been put on it as well, of course, Williams and Conroy, called Ying and Yang both in and out of earshot. Williams' skin was dark enough to have been sprayed on with a can of paint only that morning, and Conroy was so pale that if he fell naked into a snow bank he might be lost forever. They had always been friendly to Theresa, and today were even more so after learning that her cousin Frank was currently floating around the Caribbean and so would not be available to peer over their shoulders and home in on their case simply because it involved Theresa. Then they had gone off to speak to Dr Banachek.

Now they were busy interviewing the other deskmen and the dieners, so Shephard alone got to hear her great theory. To wit: somehow George Bain, Hubert Reese and Darryl Johnson were connected, other than simply by working in the same building, and someone had attacked them for some reason, which might be because he wanted something.

'And that something would be?' Shephard asked drily, drinking a cup of coffee Theresa had graciously provided him. Neenah, the Trace Evidence secretary, had arrived as well and sat at her desk but with her chair turned toward them, watching their verbal volleys with wide eyes. (Her bet still rested on Mrs Johnson, Darryl's long-but-not-quietly-suffering wife. Neenah's verdict: 'Man had it coming for a long time now.')

'I have no idea,' Theresa told Shephard. 'But it's something small, maybe a piece of paper, since he – the attacker – gravitates toward file cabinets, jewelry boxes and dresser drawers.'

Shephard studied the photos from George Bain's death on their computer, since Janice wouldn't let her leave the file room with the prints. Just as well, because then she could use the zoom feature to make certain points such as: Bain's house might have been a wreck, but it was a neat wreck.

'But Bain died of a heart attack,' Shephard pointed out, his voice carefully neutral.

Theresa said, 'Yes, he did. But it might have been brought on by the stress of being punched in the stomach. And the areas of his home which were disturbed—'

'Given the condition of his home that's a complete guess, and you're making it entirely from photographs.'

'—are the same as Dr Reese's house. Nothing out of place, except for the home office and a jewelry box.

'Which could indicate an interrupted burglary.'

'Who looks for valuables in a filing cabinet?'

He didn't answer that.

'Who responded to Bain's house?' she asked.

Don said, 'Patrol officers. Detectives declined to respond.'

Shephard scowled, forming wrinkles across his forehead that pulled taut the skin over his cheekbones.

'That wasn't unreasonable,' she consoled him. 'With no signs of forced entry, no signs of a struggle and his valuables still in place, it looked like a heart attack.'

'Which it was,' he pointed out.

'Except that it looks like someone was looking for something.'

'And that couldn't have been the victim?'

Theresa stopped. Of course, George could have been searching through his own belongings for some item, getting frustrated when he couldn't find it, dumping more strain on an already overloaded heart. It began to seize up, and he stumbled around . . . 'Except that most self-inflicted stumbling injuries will be to the arms, elbows and shins. Not the ribs and the shoulder, unless he actually fell on to something.'

'Which he could easily have done.'

'But even so, three deaths with a workplace in common? That feels like way too much coincidence to me.'

Shephard went on: 'But why would the same person who attacked two men in their homes alone also attack two – if we assume Justin is not the killer – men in a workplace? There's no evidence of searching in the deskmen's office.'

Theresa couldn't tell if he was arguing, playing the devil's advocate, or simply brainstorming. 'No,' she admitted with reluctance.

'Which would indicate Justin *is* the killer. He didn't need to search the deskmen's office because he'd had access to it for months already. He knew they wouldn't be disturbed, that there were no bodies on the way, that he'd have all night to do what he wanted.'

So. He'd thought of that.

Theresa said, 'Do we know that Justin was even here and not home with the flu? Maybe he got sick or felt like taking the night off and nothing was happening, so Darryl told him to go ahead.' Though she couldn't picture Darryl covering for another employee without a few dozen phone calls, a hefty bribe and maybe a signed agreement.

Shephard told her, 'He was here at eleven when a heart attack victim came in. The driver from the hospital spoke with him. And we checked the apartment he's renting – his car isn't in the lot, and no one answers the door. We're getting a warrant to go in, but that will take a while.'

Theresa couldn't say why she felt so reluctant to believe that Justin was their killer. 'But George Bain retired before Justin was even hired. They never even met.'

'Because, as you say, he's looking for something.'

'What?'

'Don't ask me. It's your theory.'

Don said, 'Where does Dr Reese come in?'

But Shephard had moved on to something else. 'Since Justin did work here, though, and already had access to everything in the building he needed—'

Don and Theresa cocked their heads at him in unison, quizzical starlings that had encountered an oddly colored speck of birdseed.

'—then why would he still be here after most of the blood had dried? When he knew you would be coming back from the hit-and-run . . . or, at least, he should have known. All he had to do was check the CAD screen.'

He had thought of that, too.

'So maybe it isn't Justin,' Don said, taking the words out of her mouth. 'The killer got Darryl out of the way so he could search the rest of the building. But of course all the offices were locked and Darryl didn't have the keys. By the time the killer figures that out, Theresa is coming in the back door.' He put one hand on her arm, his lips pressed together. He had just realized how closely the killer and Theresa had passed in the night, and it scared him.

That would have warmed her to her toes, had she not been scared as well.

Shephard said, 'Except that the deskmen's office *wasn't* searched and there's no blood smears through the rest of the building. He didn't rattle the door knobs or check the drawers. So how did he know that what he wanted wasn't in there if he wasn't Justin?'

The man worked in challenging syntax, but she saw what he meant. 'If we're lucky we might be able to find out one way or the other.'

The two men and Neenah stared as she got up and went to her desk.

'The prints I lifted from the gurney. In the – event – of finding Dr Reese, I'd almost forgotten about them. Let's see if they belong to Justin, or not.'

Fingerprints are the second most important piece of forensic evidence (actually, the first, since even identical twins with identical DNA will have different fingerprints, but just get a DNA analyst to admit that) while ranking, quite possibly, the first most tedious. Fingerprint examiners spend most of their time sitting in front of a computer monitor looking at black lines on the screen, which is exactly as exciting and glamorous as it sounds. But it's the pattern of where those lines end and divide that distinguishes one finger from all the other fingers on earth. Or palms, or feet, as the case may be.

From a little fabric basket Theresa kept on her desk she pulled out two loupes, small magnifying glasses about two inches in diameter, with their own adjustable stands. Then two pointers, pen-like, evil-looking spikes with wooden handles. Examiners rest the tip against the ends or divisions in the ridges of the unknown print (these areas are called 'points of minutiae') to keep their place while their attention switches to the other, known fingerprint. If they find a corresponding 'point' in that print, they move on to another set of points, until they find one that doesn't correspond. Or if they don't find a set that doesn't correspond – in fact they don't find any significant differences at all – they can then be sure that those two prints, the known (collected at arrest or, as in Justin's case, employment) and the unknown (collected at a crime scene or from a piece of evidence), were made by the same finger.

It takes a couple years of practice and a lot of patience and attention to detail. It's also hard on the neck, Theresa reflected as she bent over Justin's finger and palm prints and the copy of the print she'd lifted from the gurney. Theresa wondered if she could get either Don or Shephard to rub it for her . . . after all, if they were going to hover over her like that, they might as well make themselves useful.

'You can sit at the table and wait, you know,' she pointed out. 'This isn't going to go any faster just because you're standing there.'

'But I love watching you work,' Don said.

'I'm good,' Shephard said.

There were times, certainly, when she could appreciate a little bit of attention – it didn't come her way that often any more, nothing like when she wore the skin of a twenty-four-year-old – but not while she worked. 'Seriously, this could take a while.'

'I didn't think you could work from a copy,' Shephard said. Theresa had given the original lifted print to Jen for the CPD case.

'Sure. As long as it's a one-to-one reproduction. A copy is fine, a scan is fine, as long as you don't change the scale by enlarging or shrinking it and the resolution is good enough. An emailed scan is fine. Anything except a fax.' She slid the loupe along Justin's fingerprint card.

Of course he asked, 'Why not a fax?'

'It sort of digitizes the image at one end and reassembles at the other. You can't be sure it reassembled it correctly.'

After another few minutes he said, 'I thought you did this by computer now.'

'We keep the database on a computer. All the arrestees' prints are entered, and the latent prints, from crime scenes and suchlike, are also entered. Then the computer looks to find the most closely matching pattern it's got. Unlike what you see on TV every day, the computer just comes up with the best it's got. It does not light up with a big banner that says '*Match!*'. Computers do not match people,' she added primly. 'Only people match people.'

'Same with DNA,' Don put in.

She continued: 'The computer is a tool to narrow down possibilities and point us in the right direction. But if we're already pointed in a direction, then there's no need to go through the extra and pointless work of involving the computer. Since I still have to go through the same process, it doesn't save any time.'

'Oh,' Shephard said, probably making a mental note not to ask any more questions.

Plus, it was a palm print. She liked working with palm prints because they were usually larger than fingerprints and therefore one had more information to work with. They were also easier to orient. Theresa had never quite gotten the hang of looking at a fingerprint and knowing right away which finger it probably came from. She could guess a little finger (examiners don't write *pinkie*) from a thumb based on size, and loops most often slant toward the outside of the hand so that the lines on a right-hand finger come in and go out toward the right and the left toward the left, but after that it became strictly a guess for her. But palms are chiral, or mirror images, and what with that and the permanent creases and the differences in the three main areas, it could be fairly easy to hone in on the right area of the corresponding print. And that's what she was trying to do while sandwiched in between the heat of the two men at each of her shoulders.

It wasn't going well.

Theresa sat up and rubbed her neck. Neither of them took the hint.

'Are you done?' Shephard asked. 'Is it him?'

Without looking at him she said, 'Go sit down. Over there. Both of you.'

Theresa gestured with the pointer, and they must have intuited how ready she felt to use it as a weapon because they finally shuffled off. She bent over again, long enough to produce twinges in both her neck *and* her spine.

Shephard, as it was turning out, tended to be chatty. 'So why is your ME under scrutiny from the county?'

Don shrugged.

Theresa said, 'Isn't everyone?'

'Think they'll find anything?'

'No,' both scientists answered in unison.

'Nice to see people with faith in their boss.'

'It's not that,' Theresa said. 'It's just that the medical examiner's office isn't a likely center for corruption.'

Don translated: 'There's not a lot of money in dead people.'

Theresa spoke while following the black and white ridges under the loupes. 'On the rare occasions that a coroner or medical examiner have been prosecuted for wrongdoing, it's usually because they were overcharging for private or out-of-county autopsies. That's one of the few avenues to bring in extra cash around here. But I've never noticed us having a significant number of non-county autopsies.'

'Me, neither,' Don said. 'Or jobs, the county loves to trade in jobs. But we don't have that big of a staff, so it's kind of hard to hide a full-scale giveaway in a place like this. I don't know anyone here who's related to this or that bigwig. Anyone who is has managed to keep it really quiet.'

'And that would never work,' Theresa said. 'You can't keep a secret in this place to save your life.'

Perhaps an unfortunate choice of words, since apparently someone had a secret, and lives were exactly what keeping it had cost.

She straightened both prints and started over, going over every area on each one, just to make sure.

After a while she stood up and dropped the pointers on her desk.

Once she had disarmed, Shephard asked, 'Well? Is it him?'

Theresa shook her head. 'Whoever was lying on that gurney when I came in this morning, it wasn't Justin Warner.'

TEN

T hat, as they say, changed things.

'Are you sure?' Shephard asked for the third time. Don knew better – Theresa never said anything about a fingerprint if she was not sure.

'The print from the gurney is from the hypothenar region,' she said, illustrating with her own hands. 'The section of the palm toward what we think of as the outside of the hand, under the pinkie.' (Examiners may not write it, but that doesn't mean they don't *say* it.) 'The other two sections are the thenar, the side by the thumb, and the interdigital, which is across the top, above the lifeline and below the fingers. The ridges in these areas have pretty distinct flows and patterns, making it easy to distinguish one from the other. So, I'm satisfied that I have the right region, hypothenar. Justin has a somewhat unusual hypothenar, with a whorl in it.' She held up his fingerprint card and pointed to wear the ridges swirled to form a circular pattern in the middle of his palm.

'Maybe it's his other palm,' Shephard suggested.

She thought of pointing out to him that she still had her spiky pointers within reach, but didn't. She never assumed her own infallibility, especially with such a positive identification as fingerprints, and said, 'He has one in both palms. People usually do, with hypothenar patterns. If they have a vestige in one, they'll have a vestige in the other—'

'So you're sure.'

For the fourth time. 'I'm sure that the man who put this palm print on this fingerprint card did not put that print on the gurney, yes.'

He rubbed the bridge of his nose.

They were sitting at the Trace Evidence Department table again, the big, high one in the center of the lab which got used for everything from opening the mail to monthly meetings to bedding examinations (it could be difficult to get a good look

at a king-sized comforter on a three-by-six examination table).
Even Neenah had grown bored with them and had gone back
to typing reports, when not fielding phone calls from elsewhere
in the building to rehash Darryl's grisly end and the relative
odds of Justin's guilt in same. So far the betting went ten to
two, and not in his favor.

Don handed her a fresh cup of coffee – apparently the only
sustenance they were going to get that day, the way things were
going – and asked if the print could have been left by another
deskman, someone who washed down the gurney earlier.

'Sure,' she said. 'You would think they'd grab the bars on
the sides for washing and stacking, but it could have been
there already, though it seems kind of unlikely that someone
could climb on and off the gurney without smearing it, and
it's in the correct position for someone sitting up on top of it,
but of course anything is possible.'

'Could it be Johnson's?' Shephard asked.

'Darryl's? Again, anything's possible, but if it is then it's
probably not relevant. There was no blood by the print, and
his hands were covered in it after the murder. If he left it there
it would have been before the attack and wouldn't really tell
us anything. He could have washed the gurney last.'

Shephard stared at her while he mulled this over. He had
been working his math of two minus one equaling one, and
now somehow he had two minus one equaling two. It obviously did not make him happy.

Tired of calling him by his last name, she asked him what
the L on his name badge stood for.

'Louis,' he said.

'Oh.'

'Maybe this third guy used the gurney to move Justin's
body,' Don said, sitting next to Theresa.

'Or unconscious form,' Theresa said. She had already lost
two co-workers and maybe another. She wasn't going to give
up on Justin, even mentally, until she had to. 'It would explain
why he was still here an hour or so after killing Darryl.'

'Why take him and leave Johnson?' Shephard asked.

Don said, 'Maybe he meant to take them both. He had put
Justin in his car—'

'Or Justin's car,' Theresa said. 'Since it's missing.'

'Then he comes back for Darryl, but is interrupted.'

'By me,' Theresa said, and for the first time it really hit her that she had walked right past a violent killer without the slightest inkling, utterly at ease in the place she thought of as a second home. It would never have occurred to her to be wary inside the medical examiner's office. She felt safer there than anywhere, even home, because at the office there was always someone else around, and that someone was usually both friendly and relatively large. Yet this morning she had been ten feet from someone with blood on their hands. 'Why didn't he kill me, too?'

This time she couldn't keep her voice from shaking, and Don got up and hugged her shoulders. Restrained by the presence of Shephard and Neenah she didn't hug him back but wrapped her arms around one firm biceps and let her head rest in the fragrant crook of his neck for the briefest moment before, reluctantly, disengaging.

'I mean,' she went on, coughing to get her vocal chords under control, 'he had just killed one man and possibly two.'

Shephard had been studying her, perhaps wondering if Theresa could have been spared because she might be somehow involved, or if all medical examiner's personnel were so huggy. 'Maybe he was sated, maybe he wasn't a stone-cold exterminator, maybe Johnson's murder wasn't planned – or it would have gone much smoother. He planned to remove both bodies, clean up the place, and let their disappearance confuse everyone. Or it *was* Justin Warner and the print on the gurney is irrelevant. He was going to move Johnson's body and clean up, tell everyone the guy went home sick or off on a bender. Sounds like the wife wouldn't be terribly surprised if her man stayed out a couple of nights.'

That story sounded better to her. Justin would still be guilty but not a born killer, with Darryl's death simply a fight that got out of hand. A good chunk of our clientele came to the ME's office in that manner. Anger had been the cause of the first murder and would, she felt certain, be the cause of the last.

But then what about George Bain and Dr Reese?

'It would help a lot if we could find Warner.' Shephard spoke through gritted teeth. 'Then we could just ask him.'

'Nothing on the BOLO?' she asked. She assumed they'd put out a Be On The Lookout notice so that any cop in the city would call in if they saw Justin.

'No. Nothing on his car, no one at his place. Where would he go if not home? Does he have relatives, a girlfriend?'

Don and Theresa shook their heads; they wouldn't know even if he did. Theresa refilled their cups in silence and started another pot while they all pondered current events. She also pondered what Shephard was still doing there, apparently on his own time, trying to do the detective's job for them – a job he obviously missed. Shift sergeant might pay more but it was largely a management job, overseeing, coordinating, communicating with a group of patrol officers. Perhaps, like George Bain, Shephard had jumped ship too early, and now regretted it.

She muttered George Bain's name.

'What?' Don asked.

'Let's say for the sake of argument our three murders are connected.'

'Three?' Shephard asked.

'Let's assume for the sake of argument that George's death is a murder. And since we don't know where Justin figures in or whether he's a murder, a kidnapping or a suspect, leave him out completely. So we have Bain, Reese, and Darryl Johnson.'

'So what's your connection?' Shephard said. 'Other than working here?'

Don said, 'I can't see one. Different ages, races and socio-economic rank. They lived in different areas of town.'

'The only connection *is* working here,' Theresa said.

'Was there any incident that involved the three of them?' Shephard asked. 'A fire in the building, did they all get stuck in the elevator at one time, did they wrestle a distraught family member to the ground, were they brought up on charges for some reason?'

'No, no, no, and we don't have "charges" in the medical examiner's office.' She thought that was funny, but Shephard didn't smile. 'No scandals involving them that I know of, I don't think all three would *fit* in the elevator, and no physical crises in the building.'

Don said, 'Unless you count evacuating due to the presence of an explosive, but that involved everyone, not just them.'

Shephard raised one eyebrow, but Theresa didn't feel like getting into her checkered past just then. Instead he asked, 'What about a case? Maybe there's a family member out there who feels they're not getting the whole story, that mom came in here with fourteen thousand dollars worth of diamonds around her neck that didn't make it into the coffin. Or that their loved one was actually Elvis in disguise. Or shot by cops and you're covering it up.'

'Yes, we're agents of the state,' Theresa said. 'We've heard that before. But there haven't been any controversies lately. A funeral home lost a pair of shoes that the family is still complaining about. A homeless guy got drunk, crawled into a car and froze to death and his parents insist that he was murdered. Other than that—'

'We've got that poor mom who comes down every time we have an unidentified body, insisting that it's her missing son,' Don offered.

'Yeah. Other than that, we don't really attract a lot of controversy,' Theresa explained to Shephard.

'If we're looking for one case that all three had something to do with—' he began.

'Hundreds,' Don said.

'Thousands,' Theresa said.

'Maybe into the five digits,' Don said. 'All three men had been here for a long time – at least ten years, maybe fifteen.'

'Say we focus on just the past year – or rather the twelve months before Bain retired. Is there a way we can get a list?' Shephard asked.

A pause.

'Neenah?' Theresa asked.

'No,' the secretary said. 'Uh-uh.'

'Use Reese as a limiter,' Don suggested, to no one in particular. 'That's the easiest way. He will be front and center of the report for any case he autopsied. The other two guys probably won't even be listed.'

'Find a case where George transported the body. And Darryl would be on the intake screen if he filled out the sheet.' Theresa meant the legal-size form filled out when the victim arrived, listing their vitals, name, address, apparent method of death and all clothing and property with or on them. The deskman had to sign and date this inventory, but it would remain hand-written. Nothing went into the computerized database except the name and address and the deskman's initials, since no one felt a need to digitalize every T-shirt and sock. 'He would also list the property, if the victim came in with property, meaning valuables. Many don't, especially if they're coming from a hospital – the family has already collected it.'

Don continued to calculate a ballpark figure. 'It might not be that bad. We average three thousand cases per year.'

Shephard looked puzzled. 'I would think it was more than that.'

'Only about fifteen percent of deaths come here,' Theresa explained. 'Most occur under a doctor's care and don't require additional examination. Of those fifteen percent we only autopsy a little more than a third, plus the ones we do for other counties. Say twelve hundred. Reese was one of six pathologists . . .'

'So he probably does about two hundred autopsies a year?' Shephard finished, showing off his own math skills. Theresa felt like she should get out a package of self-stick gold stars.

'Neenah?' Don said.

'Uuhh-uh. You don't want to do that.'

'Just search the past year. Show the sergeant here what we're up against.'

'Don't act like it's my fault,' Shephard said.

'Fine,' she said, and typed a few commands on her keyboard. The computer thought. And thought. And thought some more.

'Told you so,' she said.

Finally – after the computer froze once and had to be rebooted (the county's IT budget wasn't exactly generous) – she swiveled her monitor slightly to the right so they could see the scrolling list of case numbers.

'Now search those results for Darryl's initials on the intake screen.'

'Sure,' our secretary said. 'How exactly do I do that?'

Don moved his lanky form next to her to help find a way through the menu options.

'It might be easier to simply take the list of cases and go through the ledger downstairs by hand,' Theresa told Shephard. 'Every case – every deceased person – that comes in is entered on a numbered page, and the deskman's initials will be next to the entry.'

'You still write things by hand?'

'There's a lot to be said for it. It can't be hacked. It can't be corrupted or destroyed by an electromagnetic pulse.'

'What if the building burns down?'

'I didn't say it was perfect. But there are advantages. When I started in this field we were still stapling the bags shut and writing the evidence number on them with a Sharpie marker, using this slightly complicated numbering system that the first Trace Evidence supervisor devised. But, unlike the stickers – labels – that we use now, Sharpie marker couldn't fall off. You could pick up a piece of evidence twenty years later and, in about four minutes, find out what it was, where it came from, who signed it in, what was analyzed on it and what the results were, and who it had been released to. Not so bad.'

He raised that eyebrow at her again.

'I'm not proposing we go back to movable type and quill pens. I love Google as much as the next guy; more, even. But it work—'

Theresa broke off. Shephard said something, she could see his mouth moving, but the words were lost in the haze of her revelation.

She moved over to her desk, rummaged around its surface, and found the piece of paper upon which she'd scribbled down the numbers from the note in Justin Warner's locker: *1432, 1433, 1555, 1830.*

She could be wrong, of course, but – she could be right.

Shephard had followed her, apparently intrigued by this sudden trance. Don did too, after a moment, leaving Neenah's computer churning through its paces.

'What?' Shephard asked her.

She held up the paper so Don could read it, saying, 'They could be evidence numbers. Old evidence numbers.'

He squinted at the sheet. 'But there's no year.'

They stared at each other.

'*What*?' Shephard asked again.

ELEVEN

Sergeant Shephard watched them with arms crossed as Don and Theresa pulled the old ledgers out of their supply closet. Each book – one for each year – measured about eighteen inches long by a foot wide and was covered in red with the year embossed in gold, very similar to the deskmen's ledgers she had just described to Shephard. She wondered if you could still buy them, if anyone still manufactured them, or if they'd gone the way of pagers and Walkmans in a world where kids weren't even taught cursive writing any more. (A policy she remained on the fence about, should anyone care to ask.)

As they bustled, excited as archaeology students outside KV63, she tried to explain her idea to Shepard. 'I just said we used to inventory everything we received using a system our first director devised. Every piece of evidence, or sample, or clothing, or whatever, was written down and assigned a number. The number started with two digits for the year, then a letter or letters – E for evidence, A for autopsy sample like blood or gastric contents, C for victim's clothing, etc. – and then the number of the item. We started at one on January first and they simply went numerically until the next year. We kept a tally sheet so you could see what was the last number used when you went to enter something, to avoid duplicates.'

'Sounds complicated,' Shephard said.

'A little more cumbersome than having the computer simply generate the number for you, yes, but, again, it worked. You could pick up something from ten or twenty or thirty years previously, pull out the ledger for that year—' she hefted the book in her hands to demonstrate – 'and simply follow the numbers up to the correct entry.'

'And you think those digits are evidence numbers?'

'Or sample numbers, or something. About seven years ago we went to a computerized inventory—'

'Only seven?'

'It took a while to find the right system. The Powers That Be hemmed and hawed over each proposal – can't really blame them, they had to decide between two computer systems once before and wound up choosing what could be called the Betamax over the VHS. Once burned, and all that. Plus, scraping up the funding is always a challenge in our county, especially in a down economy.'

'So—' he prompted.

'So we went to the RMS system – Report Management System. All nice and digital, relatively paperless. Bar codes and scanners instead of staples and Sharpie markers. But, of course, we no longer needed the old system with the year and the letter categories. All samples and items are numbered in order regardless of type.' She scanned the pages of the 2005 ledger as she spoke, sprawling the book open across Don's desk. He stood next to her with 2004, their shoulders bumping.

'And these numbers from Warner's locker couldn't work in the new system?'

'They could if they're old, and if he left out the zero as the first digit – when we came online we started with 00001 and went from there. So *zero*1462, *zero*1463 etcetera could be RMS numbers, but I just checked and in RMS those numbers correspond to three different cases; three of the items are blood and toxicology samples from a traffic accident and a heart attack, and the fourth is a pair of shoes from a suicide by hanging. I didn't see any similarities or connection between the three cases at all. And Reese didn't autopsy any of them.'

'But this list of numbers might have nothing to do with the murders.'

That stopped her for a moment. 'That's true, but I don't have any better ideas at the moment. Do you?'

'And there's no year. Or letter.'

'Because Justin already knew the year and the type. He didn't need to write it down. Or,' she admitted, 'because these aren't evidence numbers and have nothing to do with anything.'

'So you're going to go through every single book?'

She didn't answer that, since obviously they were. 'Starting with the last year before we went to RMS. As you can see, it doesn't take that long. The system did have its advantages.'

Beside her, Don made a *hmmm* sound.

'What?' she asked.

'What?' Shephard asked.

Don held his finger down on the pale-green, lined sheet. 'The first two numbers could be evidence from this case, a ligature and vaginal swabs. The third, fifteen-fifty-five, is here too . . . her fingernail scrapings.'

Theresa checked her slip of paper, because she couldn't remember a number for more than half a nanosecond. 'And the last? Eighteen-thirty?'

He slid his finger down as she read over his shoulder, the paper crammed with tiny writing, their notations as to the results and disposition of a number of items from the same case. His finger stopped under a crammed-in notation, in Theresa's handwriting, of a set of tapings – hairs and fibers collected from the surface of the victim's shirt.

Theresa's gaze traveled to the beginning of the entry, to the name next to the five-digit case number, and it sucked the breath out of her lungs.

'What?' Shephard demanded.

'It's Diana,' she said.

She had known Diana Allman would be trouble the first time she saw her, on Diana's second or third day at the ME's office. She had to be; it would not be possible for those kinds of looks to get through the world without attracting way too much attention, both the good kind and the bad.

Diana had been hired for the secretarial pool, or rather the more professional-sounding administrative assistant pool (which everyone still *called* the secretarial pool), to spend her days typing the doctors' scribbled notes and transcribing their dictations at a small desk among other women doing the same thing. Her reception at first ranged from neutral to downright chilly, but she soon thawed her fellow secretaries. She listened to their tales of husbands and children and cats. She brought in home-made brownies. She did her job well, her typing speed the envy of anyone who heard her fingers flying over the keys as if possessed. And she never let on that her social life included clubbing and celebrity events to which she found herself invited, or that her photo occasionally appeared in the society columns (as much as Cleveland has society columns; the city prides itself on being down-to-earth); she never let on that her nightlife might be vastly more interesting than everyone else's. She told Theresa because Theresa didn't care; Theresa wouldn't have been interested in clubbing even if she'd had the energy ten years ago. Especially ten years ago, when she had still been married and her daughter was young.

But the looks, Diana couldn't do much about. Flawless, caramel-colored skin, high cheekbones, ridiculously slender thighs and healthy but perfectly proportional breasts – she couldn't hide all that, and didn't try.

They would eat lunch together in the med school cafeteria, across the tiny courtyard from the ME's office. Theresa was only ten years older than Diana but they were critical years, full of marriage and child raising, so she probably felt the gap more than Diana did. The younger woman took Theresa back to her college days, full of laughter and outrageous conversations, keeping her up on current events and attitudes with hilariously apropos summaries. Other lunches were typical workplace gripe sessions – Theresa knew better than to trust anyone (other than Don) with her true opinions of the place, but she had learned, carefully and over time, that Diana could be trusted with a secret. Diana had a number of her own, and most of them revolved around her husband, James. Not Jim, not Jimmy. James.

They had been married only a year. James wasn't a bad guy, Diana said – always a matter for concern when someone began a description of their spouse by damning with faint praise – he just didn't have a particular trade or profession, and he fell too easily into the typical pitfalls of coming from a not-great area of town. Didn't know his mother. Father good-hearted but drank too much. Barely graduated high school. Worked as a car mechanic or assembly-line grunt here or there but always wound up on the wrong end of a conflict with the boss. Champagne tastes, beer budget. Craved respect without any interest in putting in the effort to earn it.

But he could be so great, too, Diana told her in more cheerful moods. He would bring her donuts from Presti's and remember her go-to choices at their favorite restaurants and sing to her in the kitchen and basically do all the sweet things that a young man in love does, sometimes, and not for very many years. But he did them. And he didn't beat her, or sleep with her sister, or even flirt with her friends, not much. James' only real flaw was his inability to hold a job and his inability to adjust his finances accordingly. And the drug use.

Still, Theresa didn't give their future great odds. Diana didn't need much but she did want stability, and though she might be sweet, she wasn't stupid. Eventually, she would do the old Dear Abby test: *are you better off with him or without him?* and Theresa doubted the answer would come up in James' favor.

She thought Diana had reached that point one day when Theresa found her on the loading dock, face turned up to the snowflakes as they fell gently from a dull gray sky. The deskman – it was Darryl, as Theresa recalled – stamped out his butt and went inside, leaving them to their girl talk. Neither woman smoked, but they still utilized the dock whenever they felt the need to get outside, step away from the phones or their supervisors and breathe some fresh air. Plus that day there had been an autopsy going on in the special room set aside for decomposed bodies. Everyone in the building felt in need of fresh air.

Diana stared at the clock on the med school, a frown wrinkling her brow. 'He pawned my Prada bag.'

'I didn't know you had one. Of course, I wouldn't know a Prada bag if Ms Prada gave it to me.'

'You mean mister. It was real, too, not a knock-off. Tim – I dated him before James – gave it to me. His sister-in-law got a discount or something, but it was real.' She stamped her feet, probably burning off nervous energy since it wasn't that cold, even with the snow. 'He's been going on about needing a new tire on that thing he drives, and I *just don't have it*. Not if I want to pay the rent and the utilities in full. He's always, oh, just pay partial this month and we'll make it up next month

– but we *won't* make it up! There won't be anything to make it up with! Why does he not *get* that very simple math?'

She practically shouted the last few words, a real outburst for a woman who had learned to keep her head down – the dangers of beauty, how to fly below the radar of vitriolic envy. Theresa opened her mouth to say something comforting, but Diana had already gone on.

'Then I come home yesterday, and it's gone. And he's got a new tire. He won't admit it, that's the really irritating part. He says he fixed a guy's car on the next street, that's where he got the money. And my bag? He's got no idea where it is, it just disappeared right off my closet shelf into the Twilight Zone.'

Then Theresa did say something comforting, something purely eloquent like *that sucks* or *that's a real bummer*, and thought to herself that this may be the beginning of the end, and maybe that was a good thing.

But nothing happened immediately, and they went back to talking about movies and food and rumors of office affairs. The next month James pawned an old gold bracelet of Diana's and she got angry, angry enough to rush to the ladies' room in the middle of lunch and return pale and sweaty, but after another day she decided that the bracelet had no real sentimental value to her, and so that incident passed as well. Diana only wanted security – her own childhood had not been the most stable. She must have kept hoping she would find it in James, a plan doomed to disappointment. She never actually said the word *divorce*, while her conversation circled ever closer to it.

Theresa never saw Diana outside of work, only because of simple convenience; she lived on the opposite side of town from the younger woman and took public transportation to get there. Once the workday ended, Theresa had to rush home to make dinner and do laundry and pay bills, and the last thing she felt like doing was making the commute in the evening as well, just to hang out with someone much younger than herself and talk over all the things they had already talked over at the lab. It was a work friendship only, sincere but limited. She truly liked Diana, and felt it important to have someone there besides Don whom she could trust with her thoughts, but if either of them had moved on to another job they would not have stayed in touch.

Then, on a Tuesday in the fall, Theresa came to work and Leo, her boss at the time, had said that he and some homicide detectives needed to talk to her.

Now she said, to Don and Shephard, 'We're going to need to get into the vault again.'

Don shook his head. 'Janice isn't going to like it.'

TWELVE

D iana's file was an inch thick, which didn't seem like much for the murder of one of their own but still outweighed the surrounding files by at least seventy percent. After all, beyond the autopsy and accompanying toxicology, histology and trace reports there was not much that could be done. The police officers would conduct the rest of the investigation, interviewing witnesses, apprehending the suspect, checking alibis. A good portion of the file consisted of clipped newspaper stories. Theresa read silently and the two men with her did the same, rotating the scraps of print among them.

On that Monday afternoon a neighbor heard a heated argument coming from Diana's house. The weather was still nice enough for windows to be open, and she had heard a man and woman shouting at each other – not for the first time, so the neighbor, Wanda Simmons, simply *tsk-tsk*ed to herself and went on making dinner. She had glanced up from her kitchen window after hearing a door slam and seen James stalking across the lawn, crossing from his own grass on to hers, and she thought to herself that at least it would be quieter on the street. Then her son came home from work, they ate her meatloaf, and she took out the garbage. It was her son's job, but he was on the phone and she wanted to be sure they didn't forget. While dragging the cans from the side of her detached garage, she noticed that the rear screen door of Diana's house gaped open about a foot. Behind it the inner door stood well ajar. This was not all that unusual – it *was* a warm night, and Diana wasn't the everything-buttoned-down type – but somehow she felt wrong about it. And, she admitted, she was also nosy and wanted a chance to ask Diana what the fight had been about; Diana had been much more chatty than usual lately, perhaps due to the increasing pressures of her marriage. So Wanda Simmons abandoned her cans and walked through the unfenced rear yards, telling herself she only wanted to remind Diana that garbage day had arrived once more.

So Wanda rapped on the loose, open screen door. It didn't shut right, and unless one paid attention to the latch it would swing outward; yet another household repair that James never quite got around to fixing. She called Diana's name and slipped inside.

It seemed immediately obvious that there had been a struggle in the cramped, eat-in kitchen. The table to her left had been shoved off-center, and a chair lay on its side. A mug had fallen from the short counter on her right, scattering brown liquid across the linoleum. Wanda called her neighbor's name a second time as she moved forward, the last syllable dying off as she saw a bare foot just past the edge of the counter.

Wanda Simmons told the reporter how she'd told the police that she could never remember in exactly what order the next event occurred, but she had moved around the counter until she could see Diana's body lying equidistant between the breakfast counter, the sink and window to the back yard, and the oven range and refrigerator. She lay on her left side, but Wanda, hoping her friend had simply passed out, pushed the upright shoulder until Diana fell open, on to her back, sightless eyes staring at the ceiling, tongue swollen and protruding. Wanda jumped back and stumbled away, too horrified by the sight to touch her friend again but equally horrified to think that she should be doing CPR or artificial respiration or something before Diana died completely and left this life for good, just in case that hadn't happened yet, in case there was still some chance, but there wasn't a chance because she couldn't bring herself to go near that *being* on the floor, much less touch it . . .

Finally, her brain calmed enough to realize that Diana had, indeed, truly died and no amount of CPR would help, so she could stop beating herself up enough to find the phone – a cordless, scattered among the overdue bills and neighborhood flyers on the counter – and call 911. She gave the address and the situation easily enough, but it took another few minutes to convince the dispatcher that Diana was truly dead and Wanda had already worked through the CPR debate. They established that the victim had probably been strangled. Then the woman on the phone asked if there were anything still around Diana's neck. Afraid she would be asked to touch the body to remove it, Wanda hesitated in answering. She also couldn't make much sense of the incongruently bright object wound so tightly into the dead woman's flesh that it had partially disappeared into a furrow of its own making. Aqua blue twined with a bright purple, assaulted by occasional patches of brilliant red. It wasn't until she deciphered a tube of red plastic as a handle that Wanda recognized it for a jump rope. She reluctantly told the dispatcher and flat-out refused to touch it. Diana was dead, she insisted, and the dead had germs that she didn't want anything to do with.

The patrol cars arrived so promptly that Wanda hadn't even had time to wonder if the killer could still be in the house; when it did occur to her, the idea gave her nightmares for weeks. But the house had been easily cleared, and Wanda wasted no time in providing the police with their most likely suspect – the ne'er-do-well husband she had seen marching across the grass shortly after a screaming match with the dead woman. The same husband – the reporter added – who had a history of assault (narrowly avoided a conviction regarding a bar fight shortly after his high school graduation) and drug abuse (several small possession charges; James had a bad habit of hanging around his dealer instead of making his purchase and going). The same husband who callously pawned the sapphire ring he had taken from the hand of his beautiful wife after choking the life out of her. Conviction seemed assured, so James Allman listened to his lawyer and pled guilty. The prosecutor had started out at murder, aggravated by theft (of the sapphire ring), but perhaps concerned by the absence of any slam-dunk physical evidence he agreed to voluntary manslaughter. Extrapolating from her voluminous media interviews, Theresa wondered if the prosecutor had reservations regarding the testimony of the perhaps too-helpful Wanda. Diana had no family to enrage, and James did go to jail for ten–thirty years, so it seemed a satisfactory resolution.

The first officer on the scene was also named Allman – Casey Allman, he and James were first cousins. This was not a coincidence. He had heard the dispatch over the radio and recognized the address. He then responded without being assigned, beating the dispatched unit there.

Theresa slid the 5x7 crime scene photos out of their envelope. Probably because of the quick resolution of the case, not many had been printed and all were of the kitchen. Though she knew what to expect, Theresa still took a sharp breath in to see her friend, dead, the rope biting into her neck so deep that it seemed ready to separate the head from the body. Theresa made herself look, but to her relief saw nothing to linger on. Diana had been wearing a blue T-shirt and white shorts, a white scrunchy in her hair, and nothing on her feet. Scratches on her neck illustrated how she had clutched at the thing around her neck, trying to breathe, trying to live.

Theresa flicked through the Trace Evidence Department report Don had written up. No DNA under the fingernails, except the victim's. Clutching one's own throat was instinctual, but why hadn't Diana tried to wound or scratch her assailant? Her fingernails were certainly long enough. They'd been the envy of the secretarial pool.

Close-ups of the hands showed the broken nails, the slight crimson edges where she had drawn her own blood. No jewelry except for her wedding ring, no bracelets, and one gold Hello Kitty watch.

Theresa glanced over Don's shoulder as he flipped through the autopsy report, and sure enough, Dr Reese had noted how the jump rope had been knotted from behind. Diana hadn't gouged her assailant because she couldn't reach him. Theresa went back to the crime scene photos. Shephard continued to read through the newspaper articles.

Diana's kitchen, fairly tidy except for a pile of junk mail, had only a few loose items on the counter and three more empty coffee mugs by the sink. Close-ups revealed dregs at the bottom, and the rims had been swabbed for DNA, according to the evidence inventory. The swabs had never been tested – no need, given the plea.

Behind the coffee cups sat the container of Dunkin Donuts decaf coffee, an unlabeled canister, a wicked-looking steak knife, a jar of vitamins (B complex) and a two-liter bottle of generic ginger ale (diet, of course). A box of Zesta saltines was next to a box of animal crackers, somewhat incongruous in the home of two adults, at least one of whom watched her carb intake religiously.

On the breakfast counter sat a *Cosmopolitan* magazine, a box of Pop-Tarts, a labeled prescription medicine bottle, and a pen, next to a blank white envelope. Another shot showed a close up of the bottle, a prescription made out to Diana Allman for metformin, which confused Theresa because Diana had not been diabetic. At least, not that she knew of . . . though of course Diana could have been and it simply never came up in conversation.

And these were the items surrounding Diana Allman at the end of her life.

Theresa found herself staring at the back cover of the Manila file.

'Ten years is a long time,' Shephard said. 'Were you working here then?'

'Yeah. Still married then, with a daughter in middle school. Don here had just started.'

'I was still on the road,' Shephard said, meaning he had been a patrol officer with an assigned area. 'So what does this murdered secretary have to do with Reese and Johnson and the missing Justin Warner?'

Don held the autopsy report. 'Reese did the autopsy. Just as they did today, they emptied the building—'

'I remember that,' Theresa said.

He patted her shoulder. 'Leo told you to stay home – in one of his rare shows of compassion – knowing that you two used to hang together. I collected the fingernail scrapings, stored the ligature and taped the clothing.'

'Ligature?' Shephard asked.

'The jump rope she'd been strangled with. Where's the clothing list?'

Theresa pulled it out, the white copy of a three-part form. 'Here.'

'Who was the deskman?'

'Darryl Johnson.'

Shephard inhaled sharply. 'Let me see that.'

Don turned it around so the cop could read it, pointing to a set of initials in one of the last boxes. 'The personal property – earrings, wedding band, watch – were dropped in the Property Department drop box.'

Theresa pointed to a set of initials in the corner of the form. 'George Bain transported the body. Well, he and his partner, Cindy Messina.'

'We should call Cindy,' Don said.

'She doesn't even live here any more, remember? She went back to North Carolina and full-time ministering. She has a small church in Greensboro.'

'That's right. Still, might not hurt.'

Shephard exhaled. 'So that's all our victims. But no mention of Justin Warner, right? Did Warner know Diana?'

'She died ten years before he started working here,' Don pointed out.

'They could have known each other outside of here. They were about the same age.'

'But why would Justin suddenly get curious about Diana's death? It had been solved. It's not as if anyone here—'

He broke off as Theresa grasped his arm.

She thrust one of the newspaper articles announcing the plea deal at him, pointing to a picture of the defendant. It was an inch-square, grainy, badly lit black and white photo, but still—

'No way,' Don said.

'What?' Shephard demanded of them both.

'Justin Warner,' Theresa said, 'might be James Allman. Diana's husband. The one who went to jail for her murder.'

THIRTEEN

'I don't know,' Don said. 'It doesn't look exactly like him. Something about the mouth—'

'I'm not positive either,' Theresa admitted. 'If it is him then he's at least fifty pounds lighter.'

'How can you not know what the woman's husband looks like?' Shephard demanded.

'This is a morgue,' Theresa said. 'Family members don't tend to visit or hang out here. And the case pled out – none of us ever had to testify, so no, we never met the man. I do remember seeing a grainy picture in the paper, but that was ten years ago. And I could still be completely wrong.'

Don said, 'But if you minus the beard—'

'And shave the hair.'

'And add a smile.'

Shephard ignored them, occupied with a phone call to the prison to find out just where James Allman now resided.

'It's possible.'

'Just possible,' Don said.

Shephard hung up, jabbing the buttons of his phone with agitation. 'He's out.'

'What?'

'*What?*' Theresa said.

'He got parole. His sentence had been ten to thirty and the judge gave him twenty-seven. But you only have to serve the minimum of your sentence to be eligible, not the two-thirds of the actual sentence like it used to be. Plus he got eight months off for good behavior. So he's out. He's been out for about five and a half months.'

'Plenty enough time to be working here for three,' Don said.

'They're going to call me back with his parole officer and current address. Do you two want to tell me how you can have a felon on parole, who happened to kill one of your employees, working for the highest-ranking law enforcement official in the county?' His voice rose a decibel with each word.

'I have no idea,' Theresa said. Nor was it her fault, but this wasn't the time to insist upon that.

'We don't know that he *is* James Allman.' Don, as always, the voice of reason. 'He may simply look like him. He may be a relative. James Allman might have sent him here. Seriously, it's not our department, but the county *does* do background checks, fingerprints—'

'Prints,' Theresa said, thinking about the print on the gurney and how it did *not* match those in Justin Warner's personnel record. Was that because Justin Warner was not their killer, or because the prints on Justin Warner's fingerprint card had not come from the man she knew as Justin Warner? 'If he could fake the prints, he could do it.'

'How?' Shephard demanded.

'Our employees have to go get fingerprinted at the city, but then the card is given to them to add to their application packet. He could have himself printed, then roll someone else on a blank card and fill in all the proper stamps and ORI number, forge the tech's signature—'

'Where would he get a blank fingerprint card?'

'Maybe he palmed one on the way out of jail, I don't know. It's not that hard – they're just blank cards, not necessarily under lock and key. He could get some friends to pretend to be references, use their phone numbers and tell them what to say when the county calls. Then all he would need is a clean drug test, because those results are sent directly.'

'Allman would have failed that,' Shephard said. 'He had a history of drug offenses.'

'He had ten years to clean up. I never saw any signs of drug activity in Justin, and that's something we keep a very close eye on here, naturally. He wouldn't be able to use and fool everyone in this building at the same time. But either way, if Justin is James Allman or someone sent by Allman – why would he come here? Why would he kill the people involved in his wife's case?'

'Revenge,' Shephard said. 'For getting him sent to jail.'

'He pled! There was never a trial, never any testimony. How

would he even know who had performed his wife's autopsy, and why would he care?'

'His attorney would have had copies of all the forms,' Don said. 'He might have seen them through him.'

Theresa felt a chill. 'Where's his attorney? If he's taking out people who helped him into a jail cell, he's probably been telling himself that his attorney talked him into the plea.'

Shephard flicked open his cellphone again. Allman's attorney had given several statements to the press, her name clearly printed. He only had to call the public defender's office and hope she hadn't moved on; most young lawyers at either the PD or the prosecutor's office jumped ship for more prestigious and better paying positions once they had a few years of experience under their belt.

She had, landing as senior counsel to a small firm of personal injury lawyers. Small enough that she answered the phone herself and assured Shephard that she had not been beaten or killed or even contacted by James Allman. In fact, she hadn't heard from him in years and did not know that he had been released on parole. If he had wanted to find her it wouldn't prove difficult – she had married but retained her own name for professional reasons, and the PD routinely gave her contact information to former clients and other attorneys who might want to reach her about past cases.

Shephard gave her a vague update on the situation, but enough to impress upon her the importance of caution in the next few days to weeks. Just because Allman hadn't contacted her yet didn't guarantee she wasn't on his list. He might be getting around to it. The presence of a husband in her home might be the only reason she had been spared – so far.

'Though he seems to be focused on the medical examiner's office, for some reason,' Shephard said to no one in particular after he hung up. 'Strange.'

'Very strange,' Theresa said. For all the people she had helped put in jail, she never seriously worried that one might come back at her. After a criminal had been arrested by the cops, testified against by witnesses, friends and sometimes family, prosecuted by lawyers, judged by a jury and sentenced by a judge, they were not likely to have any ire left for a lab tech or pathologist. Theresa had certainly never worried about it and truthfully didn't feel she had reason to worry now. Her name appeared only once in the medical examiner's report – where it stated that the tapings from the clothing had been submitted to her for fiber analysis. She had never done it – by the time she could face looking at them, the husband had been caught and a plea seemed certain. 'You're in the file more than I am,' Theresa said to Don. 'You're in the actual autopsy report.'

'Just the fingernail scrapings.'

Which normally would have been her job, but on that day he had told her, gently but firmly, that he would take care of all the trace evidence tasks relating to Diana and she should go home. And she had. She had not seen her friend's body, not that day, not at the funeral. The strangulation had made an open casket too difficult, and it would have been a further crime to see a woman as beautiful as Diana looking less than stellar at her final appearance. 'And you got DNA off the jump rope.'

Don switched his attention to the trace evidence report. 'But we never received James Allman's buccal swab to compare it to. He entered his plea, and that was that. I also never tested the swabs of the coffee cups. No point in wasting reagents on a closed case.'

She picked up the toxicology report. 'I wonder if his attorney would have seen a copy of Dr Cooper's report.'

'Doubt it. He doesn't finish those for weeks after the death. Sounds like James had already pled and been sentenced by then. Anything in it?'

'N, N-dimethylimidodicarbonimidic diamide hydrochloride. Doxylamine succinate. Oh, and three, four-pyridinedimethanol, five-hydroxy-six-methyl-hydrochloride.'

'You're not helping,' Shephard complained. 'Summarize it.'

'Nothing illegal, nothing mood-altering, nothing that would have contributed to her death.'

'See how easy that was?'

Don said, 'Basically, we reported nothing from this office that either sunk or exonerated James Allman.'

Theresa said, 'So why is he killing men who work at the medical examiner's office?'

'Don't get comfortable with the "men" part. He could expand his parameters to any name in that file at any moment. Face it – we need to go into defensive mode. From now on it's the buddy system. You don't leave my sight until he's caught.'

'And you don't leave mine.' She tamped down her smile but couldn't erase it completely. 'We can make popcorn and build a fort out of the sofa cushions.'

'I'm serious, Theresa.'

'So am I. Believe me, I'm serious.' But also delighted.

'I'm fairly serious myself,' Shephard intoned from across the table. Then he made some more phone calls – to the arresting officers, then to the prosecutor, who he told to warn the judge. *Allman was out and might be looking for revenge.*

Or something.

Theresa steeled herself again and slid the autopsy photos out of their assigned envelope. She knew what she would see, but still the sight of her friend's naked body lying flat on a cold steel table took her breath away. The slender arms, full breasts and dark hair all seemed as graceful as they had in life, but the swollen, mottled face did not belong to the Diana she had known.

She passed to the next photo. Close-ups of the limbs, the slender but unremarkable feet and legs, arms, the nails of her right hand, chipped.

'Reese did the autopsy,' Theresa said aloud. 'But who acted as diener? It probably would have been another pathologist.'

Don flipped to the front of the autopsy report. 'It's not filled in.'

Theresa flipped to the next photo. 'What about Reese's notes?'

'Yeah – here. It's . . . crap, can you read that?'

She glanced over. The ink scrawl next to the printed title *Diener* appeared, like so much of Dr Reese's handwriting, to be illegible. 'No idea,' she said. 'But I can make a guess.'

'Really? How?'

She held up a photo of Diana's left hand, showing the damaged nails and a slight smear of blood under one of them.

The limp hand had been held open by someone who wore blue latex gloves and, beyond all these sets of fingers, a silver John Cena belt buckle.

'Causer,' Don said.

FOURTEEN

Only a few autopsies had been completed by late afternoon. The rest – including the cooling body of pathologist Reese – waited in the walk-in refrigerator, anonymous in their zipped-up bags. The office had toughed it through Darryl Johnson's autopsy, but Dr Reese's murder added up to too many shocks in too short a time, so despite the Police Department agitating for a report, the procedure had simply been shelved. At last it had been decided that the medical examiner himself would come in early the next day and complete the autopsy before the rest of the staff arrived. This would avoid any more taxpayer-funded hours off for county personnel. Dr Banachek, voted Least Likely to Complain, would function as diener. Everyone knew what a report would say, anyway: death due to cerebral trauma. Homicide.

And so Theresa found Mitchell Causer alone in the autopsy suite, mopping the floor. The dieners were responsible for clean-up, as well as making the Y-incision and snipping the ribs with garden shears. They could not leave until every bit of blood had been washed away and the stainless steel gleamed. If this occurred as early as one in the afternoon, they still got paid eight hours – if it occurred at four thirty, not so much, but still it was a perk of the job as well as the most effective incentive for workplace efficiency ever.

For everyone except Causer. He either disliked the drudgery too much to force speediness or he had no home to go to, because while everyone else had cleared out he had swabbed only half the floor and had a sink full of trays, forceps and knives to clean. The tiny specimen room still had a stack of jars to be labeled and dispersed through the building. Causer pushed the mop up and back, missing the corners and humming tunelessly to himself. He had thin black hair, swept back with gelled flair, thin clothes, a thin frame and nicotine-stained fingers. No official wrestling belt buckle today, but a silver number embossed with a gold skull. The pot belly had faded over the years, but he still seemed to own more belt buckles than he owned shirts.

'Ms MacLean,' he said the moment her foot hit the threshold. He leaned, quite literally, on the mop and swept her from head to toe in one unblinking gaze, pausing slightly at chest level. 'What can I do for you? And please feel free to say what you can do for me.'

'Do you remember Diana Allman?' She didn't waste time with pleasantries or small talk or to ask how he fared in the wake of two co-worker deaths in the space of one morning. He would not pretend to care about any of that, which, in a way, made this easier. She didn't feel up to any sentimental reminiscing about Diana, Darryl, Dr Reese or anyone else right now. Emotions were bubbling too close to the surface for comfort.

'How could I forget?' he said. 'A figure sharp enough to pop a balloon and lips that I bet could— Yeah, I remember.'

'Did you act as diener for her autopsy?'

'Me? No.'

That threw her off her stride for a moment. 'Are you sure? There's a picture of you from the autopsy, holding her hand for the camera.'

'Oh, I was *there*.' He resumed mopping, thought better of it, and rested the handle against the tiled wall to give her his full, reptilian attention. 'But I wasn't diener.'

'Dr Reese did the autopsy—'

'Yes.'

'Then who acted as—'

'Stone.'

She goggled, which amused the man. 'Oh, yes. He might be the lord and master now, but ten years ago he was just another rookie pathologist straight from passing his boards, turning green from sectioning the bowel and sneaking a smoke in the specimen room to keep himself from puking. Kind of surprising that he's risen so far so fast, eh? Makes you wonder if he's got a picture of the mayor with a goat or something like that.'

Theresa thought back to the autopsy report. The scrawled name *could* have spelled 'Stone'. 'If you weren't diener, then why were you there?'

'Miss a chance to see Diana D-cups naked? Not on your life.'

After so many years working around the dead and violent and depraved, there were very few statements that could shock Theresa MacLean, but this very nearly did. And despite how long she had known Mitchell Causer, she still had to fight the urge to throttle him on the spot. 'She was *dead*.'

'And still a D cup. Impressive girl.'

Theresa bit back what she wanted to say. 'What do you remember about that day? *Besides* the D-cups?'

Of course, Causer could not answer a simple question. That would have been out of character. 'Why do you want to know?'

She couldn't think of a lie and thought the truth might stimulate him to search his memory more stringently than a vague inquiry anyway. 'We think the murders of Darryl and Dr Reese might be somehow connected to Diana's murder.'

'Her husband killed her,' Causer said immediately.

'I know. We can't figure it out either. So, what do you remember?'

'Got a cigarette?'

'No.'

She watched him try to think of some other appropriate bribe . . . They weren't in a bar, so she couldn't buy him a drink. They weren't in a restaurant, so she couldn't pick up his tab. He glanced her over as if considering what would happen if he requested a sexual favor; his conclusion must have involved bloodshed because he apparently thought better of it and leaned against the steel table, the mop forgotten. 'Well, let's see. They found her at night, but of course the county wouldn't pay overtime so she stayed in the cooler with the rest until the next morning. They let everyone come in and then sent them home. Like they did today – they wait until you're already up and then they call and tell you to go back to bed. Kind of pointless, but that's the county.'

'But you did go back to bed,' Theresa couldn't resist pointing out. 'This time, you didn't come in when you didn't have to.'

'Like I want to see Darryl Johnson naked?' Causer gave a derisive snort that could be heard on the third floor. 'So yeah, I sidled in here that morning anyway. I was married at the time and would have gone to the sewer plant if it got me out the house. And there she was, naked as a jaybird. Not even those diamond studs she used to wear in her ears. Her face didn't look so good – Diana's. Mottled, swelled up.'

Theresa swallowed, hard.

'But the rest of her looked okay – yeah, not just her breasts. No bruises or cuts, if that's what you're wondering. Nobody raped her, the doc said. No injuries to her goody bag, nothing gooey hanging around, you know. I thought that was strange – what was the point of throttling her until she went limp if you weren't going to—?'

For once, he exercised the extremely small amount of discretion of which he were capable, and stopped there.

'But you were photographing the—'

'I'm helpful that way.' And he probably wanted to be able to say that he had put a hand on Diana Allman's flesh. Even if that flesh had been cold and unmoving. 'Anyway, once Stone cracked the ribs I sort of lost interest. But I remember that her lungs were clear – didn't smoke. Nothing much in the stomach, what looked like pretzels or crackers or something. Probably how she kept that figure.'

'What did you guys talk about?'

'Other than—'

'Other than the breasts, yes.'

He frowned, apparently thinking hard. 'Don't remember. Nothing comes to mind. Reese was tut-tutting and glaring at me because I dared to breathe in his presence without letters after my name. Oh, and his college had named a reading room after him or something like that – he must have given them a boatload of money – and he had to write a speech for the ceremony that night. He probably didn't even notice the D-cups if you ask me, the old pansy. Then Stone bitched about having to be diener 'cause he had some issue at home that needed tending to – read, missus giving him hell. You think Harris whines, you should have heard Stone back then.'

'Did they discuss any theories on her murder?'

He gave a surprised look. 'We knew who killed her – her husband. Not much to discuss, other than wonder which of the myriad ways a woman has of making her guy feel particularly murderous had finally done it.'

Theresa kept her face blank. 'But James hadn't been arrested yet. What made you so sure?'

'I dunno. I just remember talking about the husband.'

'What did he look like?'

'Who, the husband? I don't know. I never met him.'

'Mmm. Anything else?'

He frowned again, started to say something, then stopped. 'No.'

'Are you sure?'

'Yep.'

'You looked like you thought of something.'

He fidgeted, which gave Theresa pause. Something that made Causer feel awkward would likely make most human beings faint dead away.

'Her uterus,' he started. This time she couldn't stop her face from grimacing in wary anticipation, and he hastily went on: 'It looked swollen to me.'

Theresa, not a pathologist, took a moment to catch up. 'You mean she was pregnant?'

'I don't know, do I? I just thought it looked a little . . . fullish. But the doc said no, so I guess I was wrong. Rare, but still possible.'

Theresa thought over the crime scene photos. Maybe Diana simply liked ginger ale, but it could also serve as a good stomach-settler for the queasiness of morning sickness. Ditto for saltines. And B complex vitamins were also known as folic acid, recommended for a healthy pregnancy. But there had been no mention in the autopsy report, and no reasonably competent pathologist would miss a pregnancy. Certainly not the particular and thorough Dr Reese.

And Diana would have told her, Theresa. She certainly would have told her *that*. 'Anything else?'

'No . . . no disrespect to your pal, but not really worth getting up early on a day off.'

'So sorry to disappoint.'

'Oh, I wasn't *disappointed* – the D-cups were real. I lost a ten-dollar bet with Johnson, but it was worth it to know. Like I said, impressive girl.'

Theresa couldn't wait to get away from him.

FIFTEEN

Shephard found Theresa with her eyes to the ocular lens of a stereomicroscope, poring over the ten-year-old acetate sheets with pieces of tape stuck to them. A sharpie marker labeled each sheet: *Shirt-front. Shirt-back. Pants-front.* 'What is that?' he asked.

'The tapings from Diana's clothing. I never looked at them.'

He slumped into a task chair, scooted it up to the counter. He looked as tired as she felt . . . and probably looked, she thought with discomfort. When *had* she last combed her hair?

'And what can they tell you?' he asked with a sigh, as if he didn't really care about the answer, only that someone else do the talking for a while.

So she started from the beginning. 'We press adhesive tape to the surface of the clothing or bedding or upholstery, and it picks up loose hairs and fibers and other trace evidence, like paint flakes. With luck, the hair will belong to the suspect and the fibers to the clothes he wore.'

'Really.' He seemed a bit perplexed, no doubt wondering why he didn't hear more about hairs and fibers.

So she added the qualifiers. 'I can screen the hair for similarities microscopically, but can't individualize it to the person – that would be sent for DNA. As for fibers, I can tell you it's red nylon of so many microns diameter, but even if the suspect owns a red nylon shirt, I can't tell you how many of those shirts were made, how many were sold in the area, how many are still in existence or how likely it is that a fiber from someone else's red nylon shirt might have wound up on the victim.'

'They can on TV,' he pointed out.

'How nice for them.'

This made him laugh. 'Okay, then. What can *you* tell me from these taping things?'

Now *she* sighed. 'Not much. I don't know why I'm even

looking at them, other than because they were here and easy to get to. The few hairs are long and black, so almost certainly Diana's. There's one short black one, maybe James', which means nothing since they lived in the same house. Then we have different fibers, cotton, nylon, various colors. The only interesting thing is this weird animal hair – weird only because it's neither cat nor dog.'

'People have all sorts of strange things as pets.'

'But Diana didn't have any pets. Of course, she did have a backyard and she liked to garden, so she could have come into contact with raccoons or possums or deer, for all I know.' Theresa paused. 'She was always trying to give me bulbs and seedlings, but everything I try to grow winds up a thin brown stalk. I wonder what happened to all her flowers?'

Shephard said nothing, waiting out her spell of melancholy.

'What did Yin and Yang say?' she asked him.

'Same thing we did: why would James Allman want to get revenge on the ME staff instead of the cops and the judge who arrested and sentenced him – for a crime, by the way, he pled guilty to? It's not like he went to the can protesting his innocence. The judge and prosecutor haven't heard from him. The arresting officers haven't heard from him. Yin and Yang talked to his parole officer, who thought he was working at Giant Eagle.'

'How did that get by him?'

'Because James Allman – not Justin Warner – really *was* working at Giant Eagle. Part-time, just enough to have a paycheck to prove gainful employment. Giant Eagle found James to be a pleasant and reliable employee. He had been on the late shift, restocking shelves, but recently asked to switch to mornings.'

'Because he changed to the night shift here.'

'Sounded like when he finished his stint as a deskman, he went there, worked a few hours, went home.'

Theresa pondered this, pushing around a box of Kimwipes. 'This guy worked two jobs just to keep anyone from looking more closely at James Allman.'

Shephard nodded gravely. 'Yeah. That's a lot more dedication than we usually see from the average wife-killing drug addict.'

'It's an incredible amount of dedication – and all to get revenge for his incarceration for a crime that he himself committed?'

'Guys like him aren't terribly reasonable. *Fair* doesn't enter into their thinking. Something like "it's my own bloody fault that I'm sitting in this jail cell and I've got no one to blame but myself" would never light up their brain cells. Don't expect logic.'

'It just doesn't make any sense—'

'Don't expect sense, either.'

'Then what should I expect?'

'Violence,' Shephard said. 'Expect violence. Whatever this guy is up to, he's serious about it. And Theresa – your name is on that report.'

'I know.'

Don emerged from the DNA lab room as if something had abruptly occurred to him. 'What about where he lives? Allman, I mean.'

'We *did* think of that,' Shephard said mildly. 'He's got an apartment off of Eddy Road. But he's not home. His neighbors have no idea where he might be, and no one has spotted his car. We've got a guy stationed there in case he comes home, but of course Allman had a head start. He could be hours in any direction by now.'

'I don't think so,' Theresa said.

'Why not? He probably didn't plan to murder Darryl Johnson or he would have done a better job of covering it up.'

'Maybe he intended to,' Don said, 'but Theresa interrupted him.'

She said, 'We're forgetting that he left us a message.'

'Message?'

'The one written in Darryl's blood. *Confess.*'

'And what does that mean?' Shephard asked, his patience obviously beginning fade together with the long day.

'It means the same thing that him working two jobs means. James Allman – provided Justin Warner *is* James Allman – has an agenda, and he's expended way too much effort toward it to leave town before he gets what he wants.'

'And that is?'

'I have no idea.'

Shephard rubbed an oily face with one hand, clearly displeased with their progress or lack of same. 'Okay. The situation remains the same, then – you, both of you, are potential targets, and you need to act accordingly.'

'We intend to,' Don said. 'We'll be doubling up tonight, watching each other's backs.'

Theresa nodded.

'I'm happy to hear it,' Shephard said. But he didn't look happy at all.

SIXTEEN

When Theresa had woken up to the incredibly annoying vibration of her cellphone nearly twenty-four hours previously, she certainly had not expected the very long workday to end with an intimate dinner in Don's apartment, alone with him and his pet ferret.

And she could not make up her mind how she felt about that.

On the one hand she had longed (if she were being honest) for years (if she were being *really* honest) to have Don's attention without the distractions of the lab and the work and the other county employees. She loved the kid, of that she had no doubt. But no matter how much she tried to school herself to love him like a son or even a younger brother, her mind always traveled to activities best not completed with blood relatives.

She loved his warm brown eyes and his deep, comforting voice and the gentle way he had of asking questions that needed to be asked. Don didn't do small talk. When he asked how you were he really wanted to know. An answer of, 'Fine,' would not be accepted if you were clearly in distress, when most men would be finding an excuse to sidle out of the room. Out of everyone else in the world, her mother and Don Delgado would always be in her corner. She loved him, and seeing him in a snug T-shirt instead of a lab coat was just about doing her in entirely.

However, she also wore a T-shirt, and it didn't seem to be doing anything to him. The relaxed serenity she found so appealing at work did not abate at suddenly putting up a co-worker in his home. He lived much closer to the lab than she did, and since they couldn't shake the feeling that some-thing more could happen at any moment, they had eliminated her home in the suburbs from consideration. Theresa's daughter Rachael was safely ensconced at college, and her mother had gone out of town to visit a sick relative, so if Justin – she still thought of him as Justin – showed up at her home he would find no one around to attack. Even the dog had been collected by a neighbor, and no one could find the cats when they didn't want to be found.

So she had gathered up whatever extra clothes and toiletries she kept in her desk drawer for long-day or really-sweaty-crime-scene emergencies and went home with him. Just not in the way she'd been imagining.

Now they sat at a bistro table in his tiny eat-in kitchen, knees nearly touching under the tiled surface. Apparently, Don considered Chinese to be comfort food – which would not have been her choice; not only had she eaten enough fried rice to last a lifetime during her marriage, but the sodium content would plump up the extra five pounds she perpetually tried to lose. But since she had invaded his space she felt he should get his way on this, and truthfully she would eat live squid if that would make him happy.

'Sorry about the mess,' he said over an order of General Tso's.

'This isn't messy at all.' Compared to the hundreds of homes she had seen in the course of her work, a few cereal boxes out of place and loose socks visible on his bedroom floor still left him eligible for a *Good Housekeeping* spread. 'I like your colors. The pillows on the couch really tie it in with the burnt sienna walls.'

'I can't take credit for that. A former tenant picked out the paint, and the pillows were a gift from my ex-girlfriend.'

'Oh.' Carefully casual, she asked: 'Are you dating anyone now? You haven't mentioned—'

'No. Not since the shoe psycho.'

Theresa laughed. 'I remember her.'

He held out one perfectly-formed arm. 'I still have the scar from that stiletto.'

She caught his wrist and pressed her lips to the smooth skin of his inner arm, without giving herself time to be horrified at her boldness. 'There. Better.'

'Definitely,' he said. But then he added, with the air of asking whether she'd bought a new set of tires: 'Are you seeing anyone?'

Her last love interest had a homicide in his past and, when in danger from it, had led that danger straight into her home. Whereas Don had opened his own home just to keep her safe. 'No.'

Don paused over a piece of broccoli. 'You were friends with Diana.'

'Yes.'

'What did she say about her husband? Can you remember anything that might explain what he's doing now?'

'No. I've been thinking of little else for the past five hours, and I can't. She complained about his spending habits, his taste in movies and his avoidance of any and all household chores. Just routine marriage stuff. I have a hard time reconciling the guy she spoke of with someone who would work two jobs, fake his fingerprint records, dot every I and cross every T while working with dead bodies just to – just to kill people.'

'None of it makes sense,' Don agreed.

'All her misgivings about him – it seemed like typical spouse-type griping. All his crimes – some drugs, some theft – were completely non-violent. I never thought he'd kill her.'

'She probably didn't, either. It's not your fault. You couldn't have known or even suspected.'

'I even thought it was getting better. The last few months – she seemed happier, somehow. Humming tunes all the time, smiling more. She had that glow that women have when—'

'When what?'

When they're around a man they find fascinating, Theresa thought. Aware of every vibrating molecule in the atmosphere and thrilled by each one. *Like I am with you.* 'When they're happy.'

'So they'd been getting along all right. Well, you know how that can turn on a dime.'

'True. She didn't say anything specific . . . and the last thing I wanted to talk about right at that point in time would have been marriage. I probably didn't seem too open to discussion on the topic.'

He put one hand over hers. 'You can't blame yourself.'

She started to curl her fingers around his, but he patted the back of her hand and said, 'What else did she say about him? What was his job? Hobbies? Who were his friends?'

Theresa swallowed and poked at a piece of chicken. 'He worked in machine shops or auto repair places, but seemed to be out of work a lot. It wasn't always his fault – one of the car repair shops got busted for chopping stolen cars, and he barely avoided going to jail with the owner. I think he'd been out of work for a while when the murder happened.'

'Another stressor.'

'Yeah. If he had any hobbies other then drinking and occasionally snorting, she didn't mention them. She didn't care for his friends, street bums who – according to Diana – were always trying to drag him back down into the gutter.' Theresa stirred her tea. 'He did have a cousin who was a cop. Diana said once that he was the only friend she didn't mind James hanging around with. She hoped he'd be a good influence, the cousin. Do *you* remember Diana? You had just started working at the lab.'

She remembered his first day, him sweet and a little shy and yet completely competent from the very beginning. She flushed, more from the vision than from the warmth of the tea.

'Only four or five months when she died, but yes, I remember her. You couldn't be male and not notice Diana.'

Biting down on her jealous bone, Theresa went on: 'Did she ever talk to you? You would have been about the same age.'

Don paused, chewing, thinking. 'Just to say hi to.' Then he stood and dumped his plate into the garbage can – a typical bachelor, he had learned the convenience of paper dinnerware – and closed up the fried rice carton before handing her one of the two fortune cookies. 'Here. See what's going to happen to you.'

She broke open the cellophane wrapper and extracted the slip of paper. 'The surest sign of intelligence is a willingness to learn.'

He opened his. 'You will have an unexpected visitor.'

She thought about their current location. Don's tidy

apartment building in Cleveland Heights had a well-lit lot and keyed entries, but beyond that it wasn't any place she would want to see Rachael living in, meaning it was no fortress. The stairwells were unlocked. No interior security cameras. A deadbolt but no chain or bar on the slender wooden door. Having now visited Don's apartment, she wanted him to move. She also wished she had a gun. Maybe two.

She stood, slowly. 'I don't like the sound of that.'

Don smiled at her. 'Silly girl – it's you. An unexpected visitor.'

'I wouldn't be so sure. We're the only two names left in the autopsy report. The bodysnatcher who transported, the deskman who received the body, the doctor who did the autopsy. The toxicologist who did her bodily fluids isn't in there because their reports are always separate. Even we couldn't read Stone's name as the diener, so he should be safe. Histology doesn't get listed since the final call on the tissue samples is made by the pathologist. That just leaves trace evidence – you and the fingernail scrapings, and me and the fibers. You're listed, aren't you?'

'What?'

'In the phone book? It doesn't matter anyway, he's been working there for three months, he could have picked up your address any one of a dozen different ways.'

'Theresa. Don't worry. We'll be fine. There's two of us and one of him.'

She bit her lip. 'I found their bodies, Don.'

'*Hey.*' He put his arms around her, and she found her face nestled against his collarbone, hard and strong underneath the soft cotton fabric that smelled faintly of aftershave and soy sauce. She dared to let herself go and allowed her arms to encircle his midsection, breathing deep. Let me have this moment, she thought. *Just let me have this one moment and I won't ask for anything more.*

'It will be all right,' he said.

'If he wants to get to you he'll have to go through me,' she said with embarrassing fervor, sounding like a bad movie and unable to remember when she'd ever meant anything more.

He stopped hugging her and put both hands on her shoulders,

pushing her back just enough so they could face each other. 'Don't assume he's going to stick to male victims. You're next in the report. But at least if he goes to your house he'll find it empty. And there's always a chance he's a state or two away by now. We'll be fine.' He moved both hands to her face. 'We're going to be fine.'

She felt swayed, of course, by his words, but even without them she wouldn't have cared if James Allman had knocked on the door in the next two seconds, with an arsenal of weapons in his back pocket. Kiss me, she wished hard enough to have said aloud. *Kissmekissmekissme—*

'Besides, I've got a deadbolt on the door and I doubt he could shinny up two stories of drainpipe,' he said cheerily, and released her. 'Now let's find you some blankets.'

An hour later Theresa lay cocooned on the sofa, watching lights from the passing cars play across the ceiling. Don's apartment faced Euclid Avenue, and the traffic remained steady, even when people should be in bed. Well, people her age. Especially people her age who had only gotten about two hours of sleep the night before and then had had a number of shocks throughout the day. People her age who knew there was a violent felon roaming around town with, apparently, a list of names which included hers. And yet her eyes stayed open and the neurons in her brain kept firing, not over the reliability of the deadbolt or the reasons Justin Warner/James Allman might have for his recent activities, but pondering instead her current romantic situation. Or rather, stunning lack of same.

The ferret – named Garlic, and Theresa hadn't asked why – scratched at the glass of his large terrarium. Every time she so much as breathed deeply, the animal darted back and forth in the cage, no doubt wondering why someone had invaded his living room. Either ferrets were nocturnal, or she was not the only mammal losing sleep that night.

If Don felt more for her than simple friendship, he probably would never have a better opportunity to let her know. If he had wanted to kiss her, he could have. Unless he was restricted by concern that he would be taking advantage of her vulnerability in the wake of an overwrought day, that perhaps she didn't feel the same, that their age difference would prove too great to bridge – or that an order of General Tso's chicken would have detrimental effects on the breath – he could have.

And hadn't.

So this idea that had been milling about in the back of her mind for a robust number of years had finally been dragged to the forefront – only to be shot down and then stabbed for good measure.

Tears pricked at the corners of her eyes.

Stop it. It had been a stupid schoolgirl crush in the first place, no matter how real it felt, no matter how her heart ached, no matter how her neurons seemed to fire more rapidly the moment he walked into the room. *He doesn't love you.* He doesn't need you. He needs a sweet kindergarten teacher, with a good sense of humor and breasts like rocks and twenty-five-year-old skin so tight it snaps, so he can settle down and start raising a family of his own, not a divorcée on the wrong side of forty with a child already halfway through college.

But he *hadn't* found a kindergarten teacher, so . . . maybe . . .

She awoke with a start, and her head shifted on the gift-from-ex pillows. Don had not offered to give her his bed – apparently, even he had a Limit of Awkward, and she wouldn't have let him do it anyway – but the sofa proved fairly comfortable provided she didn't try to turn over. That and exhaustion must have taken over; it seemed that she had only just closed her eyes, but the noise from the street had lessened to only the occasional rumble and the room seemed darker, as if a few storefronts had closed down for the night. She did not know what had woken her, and she thought with one wild stab of hope that Don had decided to press his home-field advantage after all, and after lying awake thinking of her had emerged to—

But no one hovered over her still form. No one obstructed her view of the ceiling. She saw nothing to make her think anyone else on the planet stirred except for her.

Then she heard a sound, the hushed whooshing *shuck* of a door being closed and the knob releasing its bolt, very, very quietly, back into the jamb. This would not have been so worrisome had it come from Don's room – a bathroom break, perhaps, or maybe he really had rethought their relationship . . . but the sound had clearly come from the short hallway leading to the outer door.

Garlic the ferret sat up, rustling his wood shavings.

Someone had just entered the apartment.

SEVENTEEN

I t will be a girlfriend, Theresa thought furiously to herself, one of several he has, one who decided to be super-cute and show up in the wee hours wearing nothing but a trench coat and high heels, to announce in a husky voice how she couldn't sleep—

Or perhaps Don himself had gone out and now returned. Maybe he had made his own booty call, reassuring his current squeeze that Theresa was simply a co-worker, an older lady he needed to look out for. Perhaps he'd taken up a smoking habit . . . No, she would have smelled that.

While her mind flipped through the myriad and mostly harmless possibilities, her body rolled off the cushions – which gave only the slightest creak – and into the space on the floor between the sofa and coffee table. Her right hand snuck under the sofa frame to locate the steak knife she had liberated from the wooden block on Don's counter after he'd gone to bed. Thus prepared, she peered from behind the upholstery, her chin touching the floor, her body as still as death.

For a moment she saw nothing but the tan walls and the framed picture of the Grand Canyon and thought that her imagination had been playing tricks on her, but then a lighter piece of shadow moved apart from the gloom of the hallway. It did not belong, she felt certain, to Don's slender form. It seemed to be a giant, an amorphous being of hulking menace.

It – he – stood at the edge of the dark, gazing into the living room, slowly scanning the area from left to right. She did not move, praying he wouldn't come closer – how could he not see her? Perhaps the coffee table blocked enough of the ambient light from the window to cast her nest into a shadow deep enough to hide her. Perhaps he simply didn't expect anyone else to be in the apartment. Or the rustling ferret distracted him. She held her breath until her lungs felt like bursting. Then he moved.

Don had shut his bedroom door – further dashing any tender hope of hers – and the man-thing put his hand on the knob.

Theresa debated what to do. This was not some late-night lover, unless Don liked them hefty enough to start for the Browns, and she could think of no other reasonable explanation. She had a knife, and this man or thing or whatever was going after Don. It had killed George Bain and Darryl Johnson and Hubert Reese. Don came next on its list.

Theresa wished she had readied a flashlight along with the steak knife. Then she could blind him.

It turned the knob. The door swung silently open.

She had two options: a blitz attack, slide that blade into his midsection before he even realized she was there, or – based on the very slim possibility that there might after all be an innocent explanation for this midnight visitor and adding in her lack of experience in stabbing people – she could shout, startling the intruder and warning Don.

She made the choice without conscious thought.

In one movement she leapt to her feet and shouted, 'Stop!'

It – he – straightened and turned from the door so sharply that she could have sworn she had scared the shit out of him, to the point where it would have been comical had he not immediately launched himself at her. He flew through the air and struck her mid-section as if he really did play for the football team, smashing her to the ground and slamming her right shoulder against the edge of the coffee table, her head against the base of an armchair, and her tailbone against the thinly carpeted hardwood. It all hurt like everlasting hell. Not to mention that his weight on her chest prevented her from breathing.

She did not, however, lose her grip on the knife.

But neither could she get much of an arc going to use it with her arm stuck under the coffee table and her entire upper body pinned to the ground.

But she tried. She snaked the knife out and drove it into what should have been the intercostal space between the sixth and seventh rib – not, perhaps, with all the might she had, more like an experimental tap to see, first, if she could do it at all, and second, if it might be enough to spur him to a more reasonable exchange.

She could, and it didn't.

He hit her. He drew back one arm and slugged her in the face, snapping her head to one side and making her vision turn to nothing but white, shooting stars. She tried to suck in some oxygen and couldn't. The knife hand sagged.

The ferret dashed from one end of his cage to the other, making some sort of concerned, snuffling sound. The room flashed into sudden illumination. Someone had hit the lights.

Vaguely, she heard a thump in the distance, and then Don loomed behind the intruder, shouting something she couldn't quite make out. The weight on her torso lifted, abandoned her, and she sucked in air as if she hadn't tasted it in weeks. This cleared some of the stars, but by no means all.

It – he – rose, knocking the coffee table completely over, and moved toward Don. Slender, peaceable Don.

Theresa rolled over, still gasping in oxygen, and pushed herself up with her aching arms. The man advanced on Don, who had his arms up and fists ready.

She still had the knife.

'Stop!' she shouted again, or at least tried – her starved lungs couldn't produce much more than a squeak. The man ignored it.

He raised his right fist as he moved. Theresa had no idea what his fighting abilities might include and did not intend to find out the hard way.

She took three steps forward and sank the knife into the man's upper back.

Though *sank*, as it turned out, put it a bit too strongly. The blade went in about a half-inch before it seemed to hit a shoulder blade, and stopped. Or perhaps that represented the limits of her strength. In any event, all it did was piss him off.

He turned, his arm stretched the length of Theresa's, and grabbed her shoulder. With one jerk he pulled her from where she stood and twirled her around him so she now dangled between himself and Don. With his other hand he encircled her fist, which held the knife, and pushed the blade up against her own throat.

Damn, he was fast.

And strong. His fingers and arm might as well have been

cast from solid iron; she could no more shove the knife away from herself than she could move through his body to back away from it.

'Stop moving,' he hissed.

The hell she would. She kicked at the inside of his knee, a single thrust outward as she had learned in a short-lived, long-ago karate class. It would have broken his leg, if she could have gotten more momentum and his iliotibial band hadn't been made of steel. Annoyed, he pulled the knife closer to her throat until she felt a stinging, paper-cut kind of pain slice through her skin.

'Theresa!' Don cried. The ferret snuffled.

She stopped moving.

'James,' she rasped. 'What are you doing?'

'Finding justice,' he said.

EIGHTEEN

She couldn't see him, could only feel the muscles in his chest and legs as he crushed her against himself, and her gaze instead fixed on Don. Nearly close enough to touch, and yet on the other side of an unbridgeable gap formed by the knife at her throat. She could see the struggle in his face – afraid to move yet terrified not to. She had never seen him show fear before – death-defying situations rarely arose in the forensics lab – and it paralysed her.

The knife stayed at her throat, but James moved his other hand long enough to pull something that clanked from one of his pockets and toss it at Don.

Then he grasped the wrist of Theresa's knife hand hard enough to numb it and, before she could figure out what he was doing, pulled the knife out of it. She barely had time to draw a deep breath before the blade returned to her throat. She pulled at that forearm with both of her hands, the attempt as useless as every other one of her actions to date.

'Put your hands out.' It sounded more like a growl than actual speech.

No one moved.

'You, Theresa. Put your hands out straight.'

It took a moment, but she made herself let go of the arm that held a knife to her skin. Slowly, trying to avoid any rebound motion. It stayed in the same place, not breaking the surface but resting on it, tense enough to make swallowing feel foolish.

She stretched out her arms.

'Put them on her.'

'No,' Don said. It seemed to be a gut reaction. 'Let her go. I'll do whatever you want but—'

'Put them on!'

'What do you want? Just let her go. I—'

The blade shifted slightly. 'Put them on or I'll cut her open right here and now!'

She watched Don swallow, considering his options and failing to find an acceptable one. Even in her abject terror, her heart melted a little to see his distress. He may not *love* her, but he surely loved her.

He opened the metal circles, not the bare-bones cop variety but with, incongruously, hot pink padding along the edges. He locked one around her left wrist, then did the same with her right. And even though she didn't argue, knew this had to happen, she couldn't help but feel a little shock of something like betrayal when the second one clinked into place. They weren't even particularly loose.

She lowered her hands, refusing to embarrass herself any further by tugging at James' arm. 'All right,' Don said. 'Now what? What do you want? Why did you kill—?'

The chest plastered to Theresa's back expanded and contracted, its voice rumbling in her ear. 'I want my wife's ring back.'

Don blinked.

Theresa felt herself do the same.

'What?'

'What?'

'Someone at the ME's stole Diana's sapphire ring. The cops thought it was me, that it made the case airtight. But I didn't steal it, and I didn't kill her. She was alive when I left that house and she still had that ring on her finger. Someone else did both those things. *You*—' clearly he meant Don – 'were at the office when her body came in. Suddenly at the autopsy, there's no ring. Explain that.'

'But you pawned—' Theresa began.

'I pawned a ring, yes. But it wasn't *that* ring.'

They were silent for a moment. Then Theresa said, 'James, you need to start from the beginning. Let's sit down, and you can tell us what happened.'

The blade tightened across her larynx. 'Oh, I'll explain. Then we'll see what your baby boy here says.'

He freed one hand only to plunge it into her hair, pulling it hard enough to make some of the stars return.

'Don't!' Don shouted again.

'Shut up.' James moved backward, stepping between the

sofa and overturned coffee table, up to the end of the sofa. Then he moved his grip downward, dragging her hair by default, until she took an uncomfortable seat on the sofa cushions, with him standing behind its arm. The blade stayed at her throat, and with a small movement he could thrust it downward and into her chest if he wanted. If her theory about a cut on his right hand had been correct, then obviously the wound didn't bother him much.

'You, lover-boy – sit there. Now.'

Don did as told, thrusting himself into the armchair, mashing the cute matching throw pillows his ex-girlfriend had picked out.

James' voice emanated from above her, his grip on her hair not lessening in the slightest.

'I'll make this quick. I went to my home. Diana and me, we – we had a fight, okay. I went and got my shoes from the bedroom and figured, sure, if she wants to be like that . . . so I took a look in her jewelry box, helped myself to a ring. Which *I* bought her, got it? I left. Later, the nosy neighbor came over, found my Di—'

A pause. She heard a breath shudder through his body, felt his hand tremble; then he went on. But she could see only Don; he didn't appear to be breathing, sitting with each hand on a knee and a look of both paralysed fear and complete confusion. Even the ferret stayed quiet.

'Found my Di dead. She called the cops. The cops get there. Diana has two rings on, her wedding band and this silver thing with blue and white stones that she'd been wearing lately, said she bought it at Tower City, just a cheap thing. It didn't look cheap, though. The body goes to the ME's. A deskman – I think it was Darryl Johnson, but I can't tell because the copy my attorney showed me had been cut off at the bottom – fills out the clothing list but under jewelry just writes "earrings, watch, ring". Or maybe he writes "rings". I thought it was Darryl's handwriting, so I asked him, showed him the copy my lawyer gave me. *He* said he can't tell if he even wrote it, much less what it says. Like I was gonna believe that.'

'You killed him,' Theresa said.

A pause. It seemed that his grasp on her hair lessened just a millimeter – or perhaps the muscles were simply getting tired.

'I didn't mean to,' he said.

NINETEEN

'You beat him to death,' Don said. 'You flooded the deskmen's office with his blood.'

The grip tightened again. 'He wouldn't tell me the truth! He kept saying he didn't remember, but I know he was lying. He had that sly way of looking at you, like he was laughing at you, taking you for a fool the whole time he'd be pretending to like you—'

'He looked at everyone that way,' Theresa said. They needed to calm him. They needed to soothe him. Nothing else would get them out of this. 'He wasn't very nice.'

'Kept saying he didn't remember anything about that day. Said he didn't even remember Diana. You ever *met* a man who didn't remember Diana? He hit on her every day she worked there. She told me.'

'She told me, too,' Theresa said.

Behind her, James drew a ragged breath. 'Anyway, even when he was dying, he wouldn't tell me anything about the ring.'

'So he was probably telling the truth,' Don extrapolated.

Another sigh. 'Maybe.'

'And George Bain?'

James jumped back into his narrative. 'He had the whole trip to the office, just him and Diana in that ambulance. He could have made a pit stop to take a closer look at her.'

'George didn't work alone,' Don pointed out. 'The body-snatchers work in pairs.'

But James had done his homework and would not be distracted. 'That Cindy woman moved away. And she was a minister – ministers don't steal, at least not most of them. But Bain didn't strike me as any sort of upstanding character, so I went an' asked him about it.'

'You started with him,' Theresa supplied.

'He wasn't working there any more. He didn't know who

I was, didn't know that a Justin Warner now worked at the ME's. But I barely started asking him—'

'Aggressively?' Theresa asked, as gently as she could.

'He tried to throw me out! All I did was ask about what happened that day, and he got all offended and tried to kick me out. I said that wasn't going to fly, and then he gets so uptight he has a heart attack and dies, right there in front of me. So I look through his papers – why do old dudes always have so much paper? – and his jewelry box, but he didn't have any women's jewelry. And if he sold it, there's no sign of it.'

A short silence ensued, but Theresa kept to the plan of letting him talk it out. 'So you went on to Dr Reese.'

''Cause then I started thinking about the bags, right?' She felt his leg on the edge of the sofa behind her, as if he had hitched one hip on to it. He must have gotten even less sleep than she had, and this time his grip really did loosen, not enough to free her but enough that her scalp kept aching. The blade stopped pressing into her skin but remained resting against it, so she did not move. 'The cops at the scene bagged the hands. Ring was there. We – deskmen – aren't allowed to take those things off. Only you guys, you trace evidence guys. So Darryl and the other deskmen and George Bain, they were the wrong guys . . . maybe . . . because that ring would have been inside the bag where they couldn't get to it. But you were. The autopsy report said you removed the bags.'

Don said, 'I did, but – I didn't take Diana's ring. I don't steal from our co— our victims. I certainly wouldn't have stolen from *Diana*.'

Theresa flashed back to another memory, this one unbidden and unwanted of Don when he first began work at the ME's. He'd been desperately broke, with crushing student loans and his first apartment to pay for. His mother had recently died, far too young. He'd been counting every penny and particularly upset that the county never provided for overtime in any way, shape or form.

She shook her head, physically, which only reminded her of the knife at her throat. Ridiculous. Don would never have done such a thing no matter how young or desperate he might have been. And he certainly wouldn't have done it in a case he knew would be so thoroughly scrutinized.

'So what happened to it?' James demanded.

She watched Don's face contort and crumble into a frantic fear. 'I don't remember.'

James' voice rose. 'You don't remember what you did with it?'

'I didn't take it – I just can't remember anything about her hands or what rings were on them—'

'This lady's blood is going to be soaking your couch in another second if you don't—'

'I didn't take it!'

The knife pricked her skin again.

Theresa spoke, straining for her firmest, most first-grade-teacher-like voice. 'Start from the beginning.'

'What?' Don asked.

'Go back to that day,' she said, enunciating each word. 'Leo told you to take care of the trace evidence duties – the fingernail scrapings, the clothing – so I wouldn't have to come in. Right?'

'Yeah.'

'Careful. Don't lead the witness,' James warned her, sounding almost amused. He let go of her hair, finally, but moved that hand to her shoulder where he gripped it hard enough to interrupt the carotid where it emerged from behind the collarbone. The knife did not move.

But Theresa persisted. 'Where was she?'

'In the amphitheater.'

'And were the hands bagged?'

'Yes. I mean – I don't remember, but they must have been because it's in the report.'

'Okay.' Theresa sucked in a careful breath. 'So you cut the bags off.'

'I must have.'

'And what condition were her hands in?'

He gave her that desperate look again, as if trying to convince her instead of James Allman. 'I don't remember. I'm sure I did it, I collected the fingernail scrapings, but I don't actually remember doing it. I know I can't tell you what kind of jewelry she had on.'

'How could you not—' James began, angrily.

Theresa said, 'Because we look at one or two sets of hands a day, every day, all week long, and have done for the past ten years.' She remembered some details from cases that old – the color of someone's shirt, a pair of shoes, a tattoo – but there were umpteen million other details which she would never recall.

'But this was *Diana*,' James pointed out, reasonably.

'All I remember is her—'

What? Theresa wondered. Boobs?

'Face,' Don finished, his gaze slumping to the floor. 'Her face looked so – awful.'

The hand on her shoulder tightened. She'd pass out from lack of blood to the brain at this rate.

'And how upset Theresa would be,' Don added, looking at her again. 'I knew you two were pretty close. Leo insisted on calling you with the news, and I knew he'd do a crappy job of it.'

'He did,' Theresa admitted. 'Human compassion never having been his strong suit.'

James stayed on point. 'So you got no idea whether this ring with blue stones was still on Diana's hand?'

Don shook his head. 'None.'

Theresa cleared her throat. 'So you collected the fingernail scrapings. What did you do then?'

'I wheeled her into the hallway, outside the autopsy room.'

'And then?'

He gave a small shrug. 'Then I went back into the amphitheater and taped her clothing. I stored the clothing in the trap room and took the samples up to the lab—'

'But *Diana*,' James interrupted. 'What happened to Diana?'

'I – I didn't have anything else to do on – with – her after that.'

'So you just *left* her there? In the *hallway*?'

Don visibly struggled to find a comforting phrase. 'That's how we always do it. The building had been emptied, anyway . . . and when I left the amphitheater with the samples, they had started doing the autopsy.'

'Who was in the autopsy suite?' Theresa asked.

'Two, three guys – I don't know. I didn't look, I just went past . . . I didn't want to see her like that.'

That must have seemed appropriately sad to James because she felt a deep breath ease out of him. But in the next moment he said, 'That is not very helpful. Not at all.'

'There's nothing else I can tell you!' Don said, a catch in his voice. 'Just let Theresa leave. I'll stay here with you. Just let her go.'

'Wrong plan.' James stood and pulled Theresa to her feet as well, plucking her upward like a child and keeping her body wedged between his chest and the knife. 'I got a better idea. You stay here, and she comes with me.'

Don shot to his feet. 'No.'

'Here's the situation. You say you're innocent, fine, you didn't steal my baby's ring. That means I need to move on to my other suspects. I need to know who was in that autopsy room. I need to know if Darryl was the deskman on duty or what, who worked the Property room then, who was diener. I need her file.'

'Her—'

'I couldn't get that sweet little piece Elena to get it for me. So you can go back to the office and get it.'

'They won't let me—'

'They will if you tell them I'm going to slice this girl's throat if you don't.'

'James, seriously—'

'*Seriously*?' His voice cut through her like a winter wind off the lake. 'Something about this make you think I'm not serious?'

'How am I going to get into the vault without someone noticing—?'

'Don't kid me. You guys are in there all the time, looking up something from one of your little reports. You can do it. And I don't care if they notice you, but if they stop you, she dies. You tell the cops and they try to stop *me*, she dies. You understand that, right?'

'Okay,' Don said, holding up his hands. 'Okay, say I get this file. Then what? How am I going to get it to you?'

'You let me worry about that. Just get your ass to the office and get them to open the door. And I know you're thinking that you're going to be on the phone to the cops as soon as I'm in the hallway, right? But like I said, they take me down, she goes with me. If I so much as see a black-and-white in my rear-view mirror, I slice her throat open. Do you understand that?'

Don gazed at her, their conclusion obvious: they were in a room with a man who had already killed four people. So yes, they understood.

'I've got nothing left to lose,' James warned, and dragged her backward to the apartment door.

TWENTY

It always amazed her how many other people were awake and about in the middle of the night. She drove up Quincy, hands still cuffed together, passing other cars and more than a few pedestrians. They traveled in a beat-up Chrysler sedan of unknown origin, not the Cavalier registered to Justin Warner; a bundle of exposed wires made her think he had stolen it. James seemed to be fairly savvy about avoiding any BOLOs. He had refused to take her car and had given her a very brief but humiliating frisk before shoving her into the vehicle to make sure she did not have a cellphone on her person. She was dressed in nothing but a sports bra and a T shirt and thin pajama bottoms borrowed from Don – suspiciously small, which made her think they might be left over from a previous love – she hadn't wanted to wear them at all but the alternative would have been even more embarrassing – which left her with no pockets, so she carried nothing, no cellphone, no car keys, no ChapStick, no mascara. She hadn't been able to either brush her teeth or wash her face and felt distinctly unhappy over both. And when the sun came up she might want a pair of sunglasses since James' plan seemed to be to drive aimlessly until either Don got the file or they ran out of gas, whichever came first.

James told her to turn a corner. She did, as smoothly as possible with her hands cuffed together. The padding did help; they only hurt when she forgot about them and tried to do something like scratch her nose.

She had cut him, twice, but he had barely noticed and didn't seem to be bothered now; the stabs were as mosquito bites on a bull.

'So, Justin,' she said. 'I mean James.'

'Theresa,' he intoned. He held the knife in plain sight, across his thigh but pointed at her. It frustrated her to be forced into the role of victim, and she consoled herself that cooperation did not equal capitulation. She would only get herself hurt by arguing with him; if she went along, she would learn more about his past crimes and could testify to his statements in court. Most importantly, every minute he spent with her kept him away from Don – and Stone, and Causer, and anyone else he might decide to put in his sights. He did not seem to include her on his list of suspects, but that might be only because he hadn't noticed her name in the autopsy report – once he got Diana's file that might change. But so far he had bludgeoned his victims, not stabbed them, and there could yet be the slightest chance that he would hesitate to hit a woman. The slightest chance. Diana had never accused him of physical abuse, but then there could have been many things that Diana had not told her. And Diana had died, almost certainly by his hand. Theresa needed to stop thinking because it wasn't making her feel any more hopeful.

So she spoke: 'You got a job at the Medical Examiner's specifically to track down this ring.'

'Yes.'

'You said the cops at the scene saw it . . . If you don't mind my asking, why don't you think they took it?'

He glanced out the passenger window at an all-night diner, checking out the clientele. 'Because he's blood.'

'Oh. Yes. Well, that's one thing we have in common.'

'What is?'

'I also have a cousin who's a cop.' At his quizzical look she added, 'Diana told me.'

'Great,' he sighed. 'So you got some blood at the PD who's going to be taking me out through a scope.'

She debated whether to let him believe that, but it seemed to worry him and she needed him as calm as possible. 'No. He's out of town at the moment.'

'Turn here.'

'So your cousin happened to be the first responder—'

'They dispatched another unit, but he recognized the address. So he responded.'

'—and he noticed her jewelry.'

'He'd seen it before. A family barbecue, the girls were oohing over it. Diana said she got it at Claire's for cheap. I could see my cuz didn't believe her. When I thought about it, I didn't believe her either. But I wasn't thinkin' about a lot of things in those days.'

She considered this. 'So you think this cheap ring that maybe wasn't cheap is going to – do what? Help your case somehow?'

'I got convicted because of that ring, because the judge said it was "so callous" how I – this is his words, now – took it from my dead wife's hand and pawned it for drugs. But that isn't true. Someone at the ME's helped themselves to that ring, figuring Diana wouldn't need it no more and I wouldn't be in a position to argue about it. If I can prove that, then it changes the whole *tone* of the case against me.'

'James – I'm not trying to irritate you, but . . . you were convicted because you confessed.'

'I didn't *confess*! I never confessed – because I didn't do it. *I did not kill Diana.*'

Treading carefully, but also quite confused, Theresa persisted: 'But you pled guilty.'

He stared out the window for a while, at the tenements, a convenience store, a battered stop sign. 'Yeah.'

'Even though you say you aren't.'

Trying to keep him from becoming agitated was not going so well. He snapped out: 'What chance did I have? I was the no-good, drug-addict husband who stole his wife's jewelry to buy crack. I was smokin' so much back then that I couldn't even *say* what happened that afternoon, not and make any kind of sense. My lawyer said if I went to trial I could get the death penalty, so there it was – I could plead or I could die. I see now that I made the wrong choice, but like I said – then, my brain was fuzzy.'

So fuzzy that he might have killed his wife and then spent the next ten years convincing himself that he didn't. And now he felt willing to murder more people just so he could keep believing that.

'Turn here,' he said.

'It's a little tough to steer in these things.'

'Quit complaining,' he said with a slight smile. 'I got you padded ones, didn't I?'

'Sure. I like the pink, too.'

'They came in with a victim. The family said to toss 'em, but I thought they might come in handy.'

'If you don't mind my asking—'

'I'm sure I will,' he said, settling back against the passenger door so he could keep her fully in sight. 'I heard all about you, Ms MacLean. Diana said you never let anything pass. But go ahead. We got time.'

'How did you get into Don's apartment?'

'Key.' At her surprised look, he added: 'From the super-intendent's office.'

'Did you—? Is he all right, the super?'

'I dunno. You think he lives in that dump? No, he's got this crappy little office way down in the basement where no one will hear if you take a crowbar to the door. And there's keys to everybody's place, all nicely labeled. Terrific security. Why were you flopping at Don's, anyway? I'd say he was a little young for you, but then you was sleeping on the couch, so—'

'We were sticking together. Safety in numbers, and all that.'

'Oh. Sure.'

It occurred to her that it had worked. Don was still alive, not choking on his own blood – the idea made her bowels quiver – which might not have been the case if she had gone to her own home tonight. She felt a small tickle of satisfaction at that. Granted, she had wound up at the mercy of a multiple killer, but so far he did not seem inclined to harm her. She did not figure into his list of suspects. At least, not until he got the rest of Diana's file. And the longer they spent together, the more reluctant he might become.

Then she remembered that he had worked with Darryl Johnson for six weeks before killing him. Apparently, famili-arity did not breed safety. So keep talking. 'How did you get your fingerprints through the background check?'

'I went and had myself printed at the Police Department, just like they said to. Then I took blank cards and rolled someone else's on them. A kid from my old block, touched in the head. He's in adult assistance programs and all that. I figured if the cops caught up to him, even they would be able to figure out that he hadn't been out committing no crimes and that they couldn't blame him if I talked him into using his fingerprints. So he'd be okay. 'Cause the Feds don't care if your prints don't match you, they only care that they don't match a criminal history. They didn't, so they came back clear.'

'And the drug test?'

He seemed to bristle, slightly. 'I haven't used in ten years. Nothing. No-thing. My blood is as pure as a baby's.'

There is no rehab quite like prison, Theresa thought. His system had been cleansed and his body buffed. James' only occupation for ten years had been to work out his muscles, and she could attest to that. Overcoming him with any sort of force ranked as a ridiculous fantasy. He had five inches and a hundred pounds and four thousand hours of free-weight work on her. 'I never met you when – when you were married. But I saw a picture of you in the paper. You look different. I can't really say different how . . . It's not just the weight—'

'Three years and two months in, a guy started a little dispute with me about the lunch tables.'

Theresa didn't ask for details, figuring it didn't take much to start 'a dispute' in prison.

'He had his posse, I had mine. So he waited until one of my best had the flu and another one got a special detail, and then brought it on in the hall. Those meal trays are plastic but they're just as hard as metal, and sharp when they break. He was tryin' to slice up my face with the edge of one of them when the guards pulled him off.'

She actually moved to squeeze his hand, before the jerk of the cuffs reminded her where they were.

'So I'm bleedin' in the infirmary, and this white kid comes in and tells me he's a doctor – or a resident, whatever they call them student doctors – and he's specializing in plastic surgery and wants to get some practice by putting me back together. I told him to knock himself out. He took his time about it, kept coming back to check on stitches. Even brought in a portable laser once for the scars – experimenting on me, but I didn't care. I didn't care about much of anything right then. And he did a hell of a job. Made me beautiful.'

He smiled, teeth gleaming in the dim interior. Theresa could not decide how she should respond to this, so she kept her eyes on the road.

'I didn't recognize myself for six months. Then finally, I did, once all the swelling went down and the scars faded. But I looked different.' He paused. 'That was when I got the idea.'

'To become Justin.'

'And go right to where you all worked. I already knew a lot about the place, from listening to Diana. I studied up on medicolegal investigator work, worked on my spelling and typing – all you really need to be a deskman is basic computer skills, upper body strength, and a strong stomach.'

Theresa nodded, and they drove in silence for a while.

Then she said, 'You never quite explained Dr Reese. We got distracted talking about the bags on the hands.'

'What about him?'

'Why did you attack him?'

'He was next on my list.' For a man with four murders under his belt, he managed to avoid saying much about them.

'Why did you look in the filing cabinets?'

'For a pawn receipt, in case they pawned the ring. Or a receipt for buying it in the first place.'

'You thought they'd keep evidence of either a theft or a purchase made for a mistress?'

'You spend that much money on something,' he intoned somberly, 'you don't throw the receipt away. It was worth a try.'

'Did you eat a Pop-Tart when you were done?'

He gave her an odd look, but perhaps he was more puzzled by the need for the question than the question itself, because he said, 'I was hungry.'

Theresa didn't want to ask any more.

'I was pretty sure Darryl was the deskman for Diana's case – I can't be positive, but I'm pretty sure, even though he wouldn't admit it.'

'His initials are on the autopsy report,' Theresa said.

'Oh. I didn't catch that. But that's what I thought – Darryl Johnson and George Bain would have the best opportunity to steal the ring. But after that would be the pathologist. He's all alone in the autopsy room, and no one questions anything a doctor does.'

Reese hadn't been alone, but Theresa wasn't about to shove Stone and Causer into James' sights.

'And there were some other things I wanted to ask Reese about. When it got . . . out of control with Darryl, and I couldn't clean it up in time because you were coming back, I figured I'd better move on to Reese immediately. The cops would be looking for me. They *are* looking for me, right?'

'They're looking for Justin Warner.'

'Yeah. That's why I can't go to my apartment or use my car.'

'Why did you hang around in the deskmen's office for so long? The blood had mostly dried when I passed you coming in.'

'Figured out it was me on the gurney, huh? Would have scared the shit out of you if I suddenly sat up!'

'Yes,' she said, 'it would have. But why were you still there?'

'It took him a while to die. Like an hour, it seemed. The clock in that office ticks loud enough to hear when it's quiet, did you know that? Every time I thought he was dead he'd make another sound or seem like he was breathing.' James' voice trembled, and he suddenly seemed quite a bit less than cold blooded. 'I didn't know what to do. Whether I should call a doctor, or just hold my hand over his nose. If he lived, he would have been able to say I did it. But with him dead everyone would figure I did it anyway – or Justin did. Maybe I could disappear . . . Then I'd think, no way. Then I'd hope he'd wake up so he could tell me the truth. I'd tell him that I'd call an ambulance for him if he'd tell me the truth. But he didn't wake up, didn't die, and the clock kept ticking. So finally I took a shower and changed clothes and was just going to leave when I heard you unlock the back door.'

She fought to remove that image from her mind and hastily moved on. 'So Dr Reese—'

'Pretended he barely remembered Diana and didn't remember her autopsy. He certainly didn't remember her jewelry. He got all puffed up, that way he did. Like he couldn't believe I had the nerve to speak to him.'

'He was probably scared.'

'Oh, yeah,' James said simply. 'I'm sure he was that.'

'Maybe he really didn't remember. And maybe he didn't

take Diana's ring. Now, you think the guilty party is still out there – so you do realize that that means you've killed three innocent men?'

She spoke as gently as she could, but made her words clear. If she could make James face the extent of what he'd done, perhaps he would let himself feel enough remorse to give up—

'That's not on me.' He fairly hissed the words, his body a coiled force on the other side of the front seat. 'That's on them. I asked simple questions. All they had to do was answer them.'

'They *did* answer them. You just didn't like the answers.'

'No. All I wanted to know was if they took Diana's ring. Yes or no. Instead they gave me all sorts of crap, pretending they didn't remember, asking who I was, how did I know about that – just kept *asking* questions. Not answering them.'

Theresa tried to rub one hand across her face, but the cuffs stopped her again. The car wavered on the road. 'And you'll probably kill me, once you get the file.'

'I don't care about the file,' James said. 'That's just an excuse for you and me to spend some quality time together.'

Her stomach, which had been flopping around in her torso for the past forty-five minutes, plunged to her knees. 'What?'

'You heard me.' He leaned forward slightly, his voice an ominous rumble in her ear. 'Now I get to ask *you* some questions. And I had better like your answers.'

She stammered, and hated herself for it. 'What are you talking about?'

'You and Diana were close. All that girl talk.'

She wanted to say that they weren't *that* close, and that men often assumed that women shared many more details than they actually did. But that would feel disloyal, distancing herself from her friend just to save her own skin, so she nodded.

'So I need you to tell me who it was.'

'Who—?'

'Got her pregnant.'

TWENTY-ONE

They stood at a small bluff overlooking the coastline, about eighteen miles east of downtown near the mouth of the Chagrin River. A lifelong west-sider, Theresa had never been there before. The sun began to fill the sky with a dull rosy glow far to her right, and the waves crashed with angry force into the large rocks below. A seagull landed on the edge not far from her and watched carefully to see if she might be willing to share some food. The breeze off the lake stayed robust enough to make her shiver as it cut through Don's old T-shirt. But the momentary discomfort seemed well worth it in order to breathe fresh air. And to get out of that damn car.

'This is where I proposed to her.'

Beside her, knife ever at the ready, James gazed out over the water. 'I packed a picnic lunch with two real glass flutes and a bottle of champagne. She worked at a bank then, doing secretarial work in the Loan Department – boss was a real bitch – and they were closed Mondays. So she had the day off. We sat right here.'

A wooden bench faced the water, and he sunk slowly on to it. He held the knife loosely in both hands as if it were a hat or his car keys. He stared at the waves, but she would bet he didn't really see them. The seagull edged closer.

Now that she had better light and time she got a closer look at him. He appeared to be the same Justin Warner she'd said hello to for three months – high cheekbones, thick eyelashes, just enough acne scars remaining to keep him from prettiness. But now the eyes she had thought were curious and thoughtful seemed still, cold. Dead.

The clothes he'd changed into, clean Dickies work pants and a navy hoodie, carried only one visible spot of blood – on the thick burgundy T-shirt, hovering over the sixth and seventh rib.

'Are you feeling all right?' she asked. 'I *did* stab you.'

He gave her a wry and not reassuring smile. 'Pinpricks. My blood clots really fast, always has. You can't hurt me.' And indeed the stain seemed dry, though he couldn't resist a quick rub with the appropriate hand, and a small wince.

No one's indestructible, she thought, but didn't argue. He had gone on, anyway.

'I told her she'd make me the luckiest man who ever existed if she would be my wife. That part was true. Then I told her that I would be a millionaire before my thirtieth birthday – I forget why I thought that, I guess I had some plan to open a sporting goods store with a guy I met in juvie – and I'd make her life perfect. We'd have four kids and send them to private school. We'd go in on a boat with my cousin and sail up to the islands on the weekends. I'd give her everything she could ever want. That part wasn't true,' he said. 'I guess.'

Guess not, Theresa thought. *Unless being strangled in her own kitchen had been on her bucket list.*

Still, it had been a much more romantic and thoughtful proposal than she herself had gotten. At least James had been, at that moment, sincere. The question remained: had he been equally sincere when he decided that killing her would be preferable to losing her?

'She started to cry when I showed her the ring. It wasn't a diamond – I wanted to be different, of course – but a sapphire with two diamonds on either side. Her birthstone.'

Mine, too, Theresa thought.

'It was stolen. A friend of mine liked to specialize in jewelry stores, and I told him to keep his eye out for something special. Gave it to me for ten percent. No one ever caught up to him, though.'

He looked up at her. 'That's the ring I was pawning when someone killed my Diana. A sapphire with diamonds. But she had stopped wearing it, left it on her dresser. The ring she had on her hand that day, that the neighbors saw, that my cousin saw, it was also a sapphire with diamonds. But not the same ring.'

Theresa opened her mouth to say something, couldn't think of anything that would help, and shut it again. She tried to remember Diana's hands, typing, gesturing, stirring her Diet Coke with a straw.

'I know I screwed up. I wasn't giving her the attention that she needed. I spent too much time with my buddies and my crack. But I loved her. I never stopped loving her.' His eyes filled with water, and his voice trembled. It seemed impossible not to feel sorry for a man in such pain, though at the back of her mind Theresa wondered if love could ever overcome the handicap of beginning a marriage with a stolen ring. 'You have to believe me.'

'Okay.' She didn't know what else to say. Besides, believing that he loved her did not at all imply believing that he might be innocent of her murder.

'I didn't kill her. But I *got* her killed. I drove her away. I pushed her to another man. He knocked her up, then killed her to keep her from having his baby.'

'That's the part I'm not quite getting,' Theresa admitted. 'Diana was *pregnant*?'

'That's what we argued about. On account of it wasn't mine, since we . . . Anyway, we argued.'

Another man's baby. If anything would send a husband into a jealous rage, that would be it. How many women had died that way?

'She said how I need to leave her life, me being a loser who would never make good . . . Maybe she was right about that . . . Point is, now you need to tell me who that man is.'

'I don't know.'

He gazed up at her from his seat on the bench, his pose deceptively casual. 'That's the wrong answer, Theresa.'

'She didn't tell me she was pregnant! She certainly didn't tell me she was having an affair. I – thought it was you.'

Confusion made him pause. 'Me?'

'Making her happy. Because she *did* seem more light-hearted that last month or two, more—' *Excited*, Theresa thought, but didn't think it prudent to say. 'But she never said anything to indicate a boyfriend. And she couldn't have been pregnant.'

Though, in a way, it made sense. Pregnancy would explain the glowing skin, the saltines and folic acid on her kitchen counter;

it would explain why Diana excused herself from lunch one day and came back from the ladies' room pale and sweating. Not because she'd been angry, only nauseous.

And yet—

'I read the autopsy report, James. There's no mention of pregnancy.'

This didn't seem to concern him much. 'She couldn't have been more than a month along.'

'That wouldn't matter. They – they dissect the uterus, James. The doctor would have seen it.'

His face clouded, either at the image of his wife being cut up like a high school biology project or at this blow to his theory of the murder. 'But—'

'No,' she insisted, as gently as she could. 'That's not something Dr Reese – especially Dr Reese, he took great pride in dotting every I and crossing every T – would miss. Pathologists check every female for— There are obvious signs inside the uterus, no matter how early the pregnancy is. They couldn't have made a mistake about that.'

His frown deepened as he listened to her. 'But why would she lie to me about that? Especially when she knew how angry I'd get?'

How angry *did* you get? Theresa wondered. 'Maybe she was mistaken. Maybe she *thought* she was pregnant. She might have simply missed a period and assumed the worst. She wouldn't be the first woman in history who'd made that mistake.'

He appeared to give that careful thought – always a good thing, in her opinion. Anything that kept him from getting agitated bought her time and improved her chance of survival.

Finally, he shook his head. 'I don't know. It doesn't really change anything, whether she was or wasn't. She *thought* she was, which means she had been getting it on with somebody and that somebody might not have wanted to be a daddy. You cold?'

'What?'

'You got goosebumps.'

I'm standing on the shore in nothing but a T-shirt. In April!

'Um . . . a little.'

He smiled, but with a curve of the lips that did nothing to warm her. 'Then let's go.'

'Where are we going?'

'To the scene of the crime.'

TWENTY-TWO

The sun still hovered just above the horizon, and tall trees along the backs of the houses cast the neighborhood in to a deep gloom. The small ranch home at the end of the street seemed almost swallowed up by the darkness.

'It's empty,' James said, in the seat beside her. They had parked in the driveway, most of the other houses blocked from sight by the ranch.

'Since the murder?' Theresa asked.

'No, just since last month. Owners moved out, realtor can't find a buyer yet. She has to disclose the history, I guess. Some people are superstitious. Stupid – Diana would never haunt that house, she loved it. But then maybe that makes her more likely to stick around, I don't know.'

'Uh-huh.' Theresa didn't know the rules for haunting. She did wonder what the rules were for driving around town while restrained and under duress. But every moment she spent with James kept her co-workers safe, and he did not seem eager to harm her – despite the fact that he clearly believed her insistence that she knew nothing about Diana's affair was a lie. He had simply shelved the topic for now. Perhaps he thought Diana's ghost would give Theresa permission to spill her secrets. 'Do you have a key?'

He gave her a look designed to make her feel foolish for asking. 'Of course not.' Then he got out of the car, not caring that the slamming door reverberated through the quiet area, and waited for her to join him. He did not threaten or prod, and she did not plan to run, scream, or fight. No option would end in a good way, and besides, she had begun to feel curious about Diana's last day on earth.

That soporific feeling evanesced when James broke out one of the glass panels in the back door with a brick from the flower bed. The broken pieces tinkled on to the linoleum inside, and again he didn't seem concerned about the noise. Theresa supposed with several murders hanging over your head, a B&E charge wouldn't give much pause.

He had the door open in no time. 'Go in.'

She moved slowly over the threshold, walking into the pitch-dark interior of a home where this man had murdered the last woman with whom he had been there alone.

Or had he?

It seemed vaguely familiar, from the crime scene photos, though all the accouterments of a home were absent. No table or chairs, no canisters lining up on the counter.

No body on the floor.

He watched her, his very large, very dark shadow blocking the exit. She wondered if he were even breathing.

On the other side of the counter the room opened into the living area. The uncurtained picture window let in a small amount of ambient light and showed the peaceful picture of the neighboring homes. But even they seemed ghostly, ominous, and certainly uncaring. She had been left on her own.

The silence grew oppressive. 'Tell me what happened.'

It took him a moment to begin. 'I came home to get some cash. It was in the afternoon – I don't know, four? Diana was washing dishes, I remember that. Right at that sink, there. She – she was so beautiful . . .'

'Came home from where?'

'The bus stop. My car wasn't running.'

'But where had you been?'

Even in the dim light she could see him squint at her. 'Why you asking that?'

'Why did you bring me here?'

'Because I want you to see I didn't kill Diana.'

His thought process finally clicked for her. 'And investigate who did?'

'Yes!'

'Okay. Then that's what I'm doing – getting as complete a picture of Diana's life as I can. Where did you come *from*?'

His shoulders slumped an inch, looking decidedly sulky, and he rubbed his side again. 'I'd been with my crew.'

'Crew? What crew?'

'Look . . . I did a lot of stuff back then—'

'Oh. You were doing drugs?'

'That don't matter!'

'Fine. So you had been taking drugs during that day, and you came home to get more money so you could do some more. That about sum it up?'

'Why you going on about that?'

'I told you – if you want me to investigate, then I need to create a picture of that day. What time did you arrive home? You said four?'

'I guess four. Maybe five, I don't know. It was still plenty light out, I remember that. It was still summer, and the days were longer.'

'And what did Diana say when you came in?'

He shrugged, his form becoming easier to see as the sky lightened outside. 'She glared at me. She knew where I'd been. We argued about the money—'

'Wait – before that, did she say anything else? What she'd done that day, if she planned on going out, having company over—'

'I don't remember. I think I picked up her purse and she got mad.'

'Did you take something out of it?'

'I think so, maybe a couple of bucks. That was all she had,' he admitted without a note of regret in his voice. But, to be fair, he seemed to be concentrating mightily on recalling as many details as he could. Without much success.

'What was she wearing?'

'Wearing?'

'Yes, James. What clothes did she have on?'

'I dunno. A shirt – pink, maybe? Jeans?'

In the crime scene photos Diana had been wearing a blue T-shirt with white shorts. 'Okay. Then what?'

'I went into the bedroom.'

'Can you show me?'

Again, no reason other than delay. He seemed more grieving than agitated, for the time being, and not yet provoked into any sort of homicidal rage. Surely, the police were looking for them, perhaps the car's real owner had just called in the theft, perhaps the nosy neighbor still lived next door and would notice action in the supposedly empty house? Shephard knew his killer had to be James Allman. Wouldn't he have assigned a patrol to keep an eye on his former home? Or would they reason that, for a man who had been out of jail almost six months, this would hardly be the time for a stroll down memory lane?

She felt a momentary nostalgia for Shephard. If only he were there, with his cop's training and his cop's weapon. He would make sure nothing happened to her.

This time James led the way, and she followed. Without a cop's training or a cop's weapon.

The bedroom, about ten by ten, had fresh light-colored carpeting and nothing else. James crossed it to the far wall and gestured lightly with one hand. 'Our dresser was here. Her jewelry box sat at this end. I took the sapphire ring and, I think, a plain gold bracelet. It was real thin.'

'Did it occur to you that that was her engagement ring?'

'Huh?'

She repeated the question. It was as if he'd been transported back to that day completely and didn't see why any sort of sentimental attachment should have an adverse effect on his drug habit. 'I think so. I knew what it was. I think I thought that if she wasn't going to wear it, was going to wear that other one, I might as well sell it.'

The utterly self-serving justification of an addict. 'What else did you do?'

He moved to the other wall, where a long set of doors were slightly ajar. 'I think I went through the closet. I might have been checking her pockets, or old purses. Sometimes I did that. Sometimes I checked my own.'

'Where was your jump rope?'

'My what?'

'Your jump rope.'

He blinked at her as if she had suddenly asked about the international price ratio. 'I don't know.'

'Where did you keep it?'

A shrug. 'We had some weights and stuff in the other room, with the computer and the bookshelf. It was probably in there.'

'Okay. Then what did you do?'

'I guess I went back into the kitchen.' He moved past her to the hallway.

She asked if he had entered the spare bedroom. He didn't remember, didn't think so, and didn't pause on the way back to the kitchen.

'I told her I was leaving – I mean, leaving the house,' he added to Theresa. 'Not like I was leaving *her*. But she must have saw the jewelry in my hand and got mad. She said I wasn't going to leave the house with her engagement ring.'

Theresa stood by the room opening, very still. 'And then what?'

'I said I *was* leaving . . . I *think* I said I was. And then I guess she yelled some more.'

He thought, he guessed, he couldn't remember. Theresa wondered if that entire afternoon or day or week or year had been one drug-hazed blur. 'Try and tell me *specifically* what she said. And what you said.'

'Just shit. Yellin', and – wait, and then she stopped and said that I might as well get rid of her engagement ring. I remember this because she said it real cold and snappy, like making every word super-clear. I might as well get rid of it because this marriage was over.'

'I see,' Theresa breathed.

'But she said that all the time,' James warned her, with the carelessness of someone who had made a lousy spouse. 'So I just turned to go. But then she said, "I know it's over because I'm in love with someone else. Not you." Real clear.'

Theresa had to prompt him . . . softly, as if poking a sleeping bear with a stick. 'And then what, James?'

'I said something like no, you're not, and she said she was. That she was pregnant with his baby. That she was going to have the four kids with him instead, the private school, the clothes and the shoes, some shit like that. I think I stood here – right here, by the door, for the longest time. I thought I should hit her, but it seemed like too much work just then, you know what I mean?'

'Sure,' Theresa said, when he waited for a response.

'I'm pretty sure I said well, if you're knocked up, then it's a good time for me to say adios and sayonara. And I left.'

'That was it?'

'I walked out the door. I mean, I could have said some other stuff, but then I walked out and across the lawn and went to the bus stop. I – that was probably the bills and change I took from her purse, what I used to get on the bus. Then I went to the pawn shop.' He shrugged, as if it felt lighter, somehow, to have relived that day and gotten through it.

'And you didn't come back?'

'I couldn't. The cops picked me up somewhere, I think it was on Prospect, about two the next morning. I don't know how they found me.'

She considered this. 'And you had pawned the ring?'

'Yeah. I went to that place a lot, it's over on Eighty-Second.'

'And . . . that day when you left, the kitchen table was here?'

The change in topics visibly perplexed him. The sun had risen all the way, and she could see him plainly. The house no longer seemed so inimical, simply empty and a bit forlorn.

'Yeah.'

'And chairs?'

'Yeah.'

'And Diana's body was found . . .' She purposely didn't finish, but neither did he. Finally, she asked, 'Did you see the crime scene photographs?'

'No. My attorney didn't want to show them to me.'

'That was probably best. She was here.' She waved her hand over the linoleum boxed in by the counters. 'Right about here.'

James stayed by the door, but straightened. 'You've seen the photos?'

'Yes.'

'Did you see the ring?' He moved over to her so suddenly that she backed up in alarm. 'Did you see it?'

'No! No, you – her hands were at her sides, with the palms up. I can see she's wearing rings but not what they look like.'

'But how many?'

'I – I don't remember,' she admitted, though she had looked at the photos only, what, sixteen hours previously? But she hadn't paid attention. She hadn't thought it was important. 'I'm sorry.'

His shoulders slumped again, but he didn't back off.

Frankly, that had been an error by the crime scene photographer, Theresa thought. Getting a close-up picture of both the front and the back of the victim's hands was Crime Scene 101. No one from the medical examiner's office had come out, though, which was another bow to the personal feelings of the staff; the police officers had processed the scene instead.

A musical tinkle of children's laughter interrupted their tableau. James glanced out the dining area windows and she followed suit, to see the woman next door ushering two impossibly small girls out of her side door. They wore matching pigtails and pastel-colored sweaters, and were heading for a slash of school-bus yellow at the edge of her field of view.

James grasped her arm. 'Come on.'

She didn't argue, assuming he meant to leave before witnesses spotted them in the supposedly empty house. They could get to the car and still stay out of sight of the woman's side door. But instead of turning toward the driveway, he began to drag her in the opposite direction, across the dewy grass between the two houses, where she would be sure to see them. He paused only to remove his hoodie and drape it across the cuffs, spreading it out to hide the pink pads around her wrists.

'What are you doing? James!'

She felt a sharp point at her back, just to the right of her spine. 'Stop squirming and play along, unless you want this blade in your lung.'

'But what are you—'

At the end of her driveway, the woman waved goodbye as the bus released its air brakes and started to move. As soon as she turned she spotted them, of course.

'Hi,' James said, in what he must have believed was a friendly tone, but Theresa could hear the strain. 'We were just looking at the house next door.'

After the slightest pause, the woman – long dark hair, about thirty, dressed in pink pajama bottoms and a tank top without a bra, arms crossed over her chest to avoid flashing her daughters' classmates, bare feet, a tattoo covering one shoulder and the hint of a limp from an old injury – continued her path toward them. Yes, it might be bizarrely early in the morning for house-hunters, and their different ages and races made James and Theresa seem an odd couple, but still, the house *was* for sale, and one always wanted to check out potential neighbors. If one liked their looks they would be told the house and neighborhood were solid and healthy. If one didn't, they would be told about the kennel on the next block, how the power went out frequently, and that there had been a 'boil water' notice three times in the past year. Oh, and someone had been murdered there.

'Have you lived here long?' James asked.

'Yeah, about four years.' She, wisely, stopped a good ten feet away. Friendly but not stupid.

'Did you know the woman that lived in this house before you?'

'You mean *my* house?'

'Yeah.'

The beginnings of suspicion crossed her face. 'Why would you be asking about *my* house?'

Theresa said nothing. She had no idea where James wanted to go with this, and she did have a knife at her back. Unless he decided to harm this woman—

'I used to live around here and I remember her. Wanda was her name – right?'

The woman relaxed. 'Yes.'

'Are you her daughter?'

'Me? No, we just bought the house.' Her gaze fell on James' hand as it gripped Theresa's arm. A slight frown creased the area between her eyebrows. Perhaps she had also noticed Theresa's bare feet, but then it wasn't the kind of neighborhood that required formal attire.

'Oh, I see. Do you know where she went, where she lives now?'

'No-oo.'

In his agitation he pressed the knife into Theresa just enough to make her wince. 'You sure?'

'What's going on?' the woman asked. She glanced at Theresa's arms as if the hot pink cuffs might be sticking out. 'Who are you?'

'We'd just like to know where Wanda went,' Theresa made

herself say, trying her best to sound natural. 'We were friends when we used to live here.'

She looked as if she didn't buy that for an instant, but knew she wanted these people off her lawn, and since they weren't asking about *her* family . . . 'She moved to Arizona, the real estate agent said. Her son got a job out there or something.'

'Oh. Thanks,' Theresa said, hoping like hell that would satisfy James.

'Are you *sure*?' he asked again. The knife blade didn't waver.

'That's what they told me. I think, I don't remember much,' the woman said. 'I never even met her.'

Still he didn't move.

'Honey,' Theresa said, in the most soothing tone she could muster. 'That's all she can tell us. We should go.'

'Don't you want to know about the house you're looking at?' the woman asked, her skepticism now clear. She again peered at the sweatshirt draped over Theresa's wrists.

'That's all right, the real estate agent told us all about it,' Theresa assured her.

But she had decided, reasonably enough, that she didn't like their looks. Not at all. 'A woman was murdered there. Her husband strangled her.'

'We heard,' Theresa said. 'We should go. Ja— dear. Come on.'

'Right in the kitchen,' the woman added.

James' hand tightened on her arm until the lack of circulation made it ache. But the sharp point disappeared from her back. He must have secreted it in a pocket or waistband, because when they turned away from the woman, she didn't screech or immediately run to call 911. When Theresa glanced back she still stood there, watching them go.

TWENTY-THREE

Again, Theresa drove, James in the passenger seat with the knife in his hands. The medical examiner's office would be opening now, and Don would have had a few hours to explain the situation to Shephard and for them to decide on a plan. She had no doubt that Don would have called Shephard immediately, despite the warnings James had issued. This was not television. Forensic scientists did not try to deal with four-time killers on their own. It did not reflect any feelings, or lack of same, that Don had for her, of that she felt sure. And she found it oddly comforting to think that Shephard might be out here, looking for her. Or at least monitoring patrol officers who were. Yin and Yang might have the homicide investigation, but surely the sergeant on duty would be coordinating her particular investigation since she had been abducted, not murdered.

Not yet, anyway.

'Why did you want to know where Wanda was?' she asked.

'She would be able to describe the ring – Diana's ring. She said she saw it just before Diana . . . was killed.'

'James, *I* can describe the ring – I mean, in general,' she added when he turned toward her with apparent excitement. 'I remember it had a large square blue stone and small white diamonds all around it . . . they looked like diamonds, anyway, or cubic zirconia.'

'That's it. See, the ring I pawned had a round sapphire and a single diamond on either side. Tell the truth, they look like diamonds to you? Around that square stone?'

'Yes, but I just glanced at it.'

'A woman your age knows fake from the real thing,' he stated flatly. 'Tell me. Was that ring real?'

'I'm not much into expensive jewelry. Never been able to afford it.'

'*Would you just answer me?*' The knife moved toward her side, and once again the car seemed entirely too small.

'Yes! I think so. It looked real to me. But I could be wrong – seriously, *I don't know*. I'm not joking about never having been able to afford it.'

'Did you ask how Diana afforded it?'

'No. I didn't ask anything about it, just said it was pretty. She told me the same thing she told you – that she bought it at the mall. Maybe that was just the truth, James.'

'It's still gone, ain't it?'

'So maybe it doesn't matter whether it was real or not, only that a thief thought so.'

He appeared to think about that.

'What about the one you pawned?' she asked, trying to get him on to a new topic. The time they'd spent together had not warmed him to her, or vice versa. If anything he seemed more sullen, more impatient than ever. The stress and the exhaustion and, if she were lucky, the remorse were catching up. 'What happened to it? Did your attorney try to get it back?'

'Yeah, but the asshole at the pawn shop sold it as soon as he saw my picture in the paper. He figured I wouldn't be coming back for it so he didn't have to worry about the thirty-day rule. The newspaper article didn't say anything about the ring so he didn't think it would be important. By the time my attorney got around to question him – too late.'

'But didn't the pawn shop have a picture or description of it?'

'Just the standard form. It said "sapphire ring with diamonds". That's it.'

'Did your attorney try to trace the new owner?'

'Some guy who paid cash. The store don't ask for names or addresses, so she had no way to trace him.'

'That's stunningly bad luck.'

'Tell me about it. That ring is the whole reason the judge pushed a plea bargain on me. He said if it went to trial he'd give me the maximum sentence.'

She stopped at a red light at Union Avenue. 'James – why *did* you plead?'

A long pause. 'Some of that stuff, it takes a while to get out of your system.'

That didn't sound exactly like an answer, but she waited.

'I couldn't believe she was gone. I couldn't believe people thought I did it. And prison sounded better than dying while somebody stuck a needle into my arm. My head was this hurricane of thoughts, and I couldn't keep any of them straight, for maybe a year. Then all of a sudden I woke up one morning and wondered where my wife got a ring that looked like it cost four months of her salary.'

That still didn't sound like an answer. Theresa had begun to believe that the reason James couldn't recall many of the details of that day might be because he didn't really know. His brain had been out of focus, and now he couldn't sharpen the images. Like a gas station surveillance video, he couldn't increase resolution. Look closer, try to blow up the images, and it pixelates into one big blur.

He might not have killed his wife. But he might have.

She no longer knew which seemed more likely.

'Then she had told me about this being pregnant thing. So after lyin' around in a cell for months and months, I finally put it together. This other guy, he gave her the ring. She's having an affair, and it's somebody who can afford private school for their kids. See?'

'Yes,' Theresa said. 'I'm following.'

'And you work in a building full of doctor types, who have money.'

'I see. So you think her boyfriend worked at the medical examiner's.'

'Even if the ring is fake and he's handing her a line about how much money he's got, even then – Di doesn't have a lot of spare time. So where did she meet this dude? And when do they have time to—? So I figure, it's got to be a guy at work. After a few more months of lyin' around, I start to put in more time in the exercise yard. And I start to picture them, picture this guy who maybe doesn't want a baby, or maybe has a few of his own at home already with a wife and can't afford for his piece on the side to start making noise, screwing up everything for him. He's got to deal with this, right?'

'I see,' Theresa said, and she did. But he finished anyway.

'And that's who killed her. Someone you work with.'

'So that's your end game, here? The real killer. But then why are you spending so much time on this missing ring?'

He leaned over and poked a finger into her right temple, twice. 'Don't pretend like you're not following this! Who would have a reason to take her ring, other than the guy who gave it to her? Once she was dead he had to figure they'd be digging into every aspect of her life. He couldn't have known the cops would railroad me into a prison cell before her body got cold! No, he had to cover his tracks. He forgot to take it when he killed her, so he had to get it back afterward. At the ME's office.'

'So if you find the thief—'

'Then I find the killer.'

They parked in Calvary Cemetery, under the railroad bridge that bisected the property. The graves, trees and wet grass were deserted except for a plodding maintenance worker they had passed on the way in.

The tunnel was not wide, and the sun broke through the clouds long enough to brighten even its shadow. Theresa started to roll down the window.

'What are you doing?'

'I need some air.' She lowered the glass a little more than halfway, breathing in with a gasp that told her how claustrophobic the vehicle had become.

With the window open she could hear birds chirping and the rumble of a train in the distance. Nothing else. Calvary was the largest Catholic cemetery in the city and one of the largest in the state – 105 acres – with graves dating to 1893. Frank Lausche, mayor of the city during the second world war and elected governor of the state for two non-consecutive periods, had been buried there. A large stone memorial along a treeline somewhere on the grounds commemorated Frank Yankovic, the Polka King. And some day Theresa hoped to have the time and safety – this was not the greatest of neighborhoods – to search for her paternal grandparents.

Provided she didn't join them shortly. 'Okay. So you're guessing that the thief is also the killer. I agree that's likely, but it's not proven. Whoever took the ring might have simply seized an opportunity, especially if the stones were real. Tell me again why you're sure it couldn't be one of the cops at the scene.'

'Because I'm related to him.'

'Oh, yeah. The cousin who's a cop.' Theresa didn't dare cast aspersions on this still-unnamed relative. 'But surely he left the scene at some point, securing the house, waving in EMS? Another officer or emergency responder could have taken it.'

'He bagged the hands himself, my cousin.'

'Oh.'

The tracks above them began to rattle. 'And no one could have gotten the bags off without breaking the evidence tape, right?'

Something occurred to her, one of those insights that seem so absurdly simple that you can't believe you didn't think of it before. 'No. But – if one wanted to – they could be replaced with new ones. All you'd need is two fresh paper bags, some evidence tape, and a sharpie. And a moment of privacy.'

'And then they'd, what, forge my cousin's initials on the seal?'

'Sure.' She had never heard of such a thing being done, but it would be easy. The bags were simple paper bags, the size made for a child's lunch, bound around the wrists with the easily breakable red evidence tape. The investigator would jot their initials and the date across the crushed and crimped paper and tape, conditions which hardly made for good penmanship. No one at the ME's such as, say, Don, would recognize the handwriting of one of the many officers on the force; the signer himself would be hard-pressed to swear to a scribble on crumpled brown paper. The bags would be stored in evidence and, almost certainly, never looked at again.

The train passed over their heads, a rush of power and noise that surely must cave in upon them, that couldn't possibly be held up by a small span of hundred-year-old stones – except that, of course, it was.

The hardest part of this scheme would be finding a moment of privacy. There is a lot of activity during a homicide investigation. EMS comes and often hangs around, happy to be out of the station. The press shows up, neighbors get nosy. Cops arrive, then their sergeants and lieutenants and other cops who are in the area and are tired of checking storefronts and supervising kids getting out of school. Family members. A crime scene is not a quiet or undisturbed area.

But the ME's would be, she thought. Especially when ninety-nine percent of the staff have been sent home for the day.

'Let's play a game,' he said suddenly, once the deafening noise fell off.

'I don't know that I'm up for games.'

'Let's pretend that you believe me. That I didn't kill my wife – okay? You believe me?'

This had a worrisome feel to it. But she did wonder about the folic acid, the saltines, the way Diana had seemed to hum with a new energy during the last month or two of her life, when conversely her conversation had dipped to nearly mute. Plus James had a knife and an extra hundred pounds in a confined space, so she said, 'Yes.'

'How would you prove it? What can be done, now, ten years later, to prove it wasn't me?'

She thought. 'We could do DNA on Diana's fingernail scrapings. There probably won't be anything there except her own cells, but it's worth a try.'

'Okay. That's good.'

'We could try DNA analysis on the jump rope – of course, you used it regularly and the killer only used it once, so your cells might wash out his.'

'What else?'

'You didn't have any pets, did you?'

'What?'

'Pets. I found some animal hairs on Diana's clothing. Not a cat or a dog, I don't know what it is.'

He almost smiled at this. 'No. No pets.'

'It could also have been trim on her own clothing, something in her closet that rubbed off on everything else.'

After a pause he asked, 'Is that it? That's all you got?'

Admitting it was didn't sound like a good idea, so she said nothing.

'You see why I need this ring? And a confession? That's the only way anyone is ever going to believe me.'

'So you're just going to go around beating people to death until someone tells you what you want to hear?'

'Until one of them tells me the *truth*! And I ain't beat you yet, have I?'

'Because you know I couldn't have . . . couldn't be—'

'Couldn't have knocked up my wife, yes. That's it exactly. That makes you the only one there I can trust.'

She didn't point out how odd it seemed to talk about trust as he held a knife on her. But his mind then turned to another matter.

'What about the baby?' he asked. 'Why can't we do DNA on the baby – even if it's just a couple of cells big, you can still get the guy's profile, right?'

She needed to step carefully but clearly. 'James – there *was* no baby. Diana wasn't pregnant.'

He didn't seem as willing to accept that as he had before, and he shook his head. 'She wouldn't make that mistake. She'd been pregnant once, about four months after we were first married. She – we lost it. It was right after that, you know, that I went back to the crack.'

So he had a good *reason* to be a drug addict. Searching for a distraction, she asked, 'If you only wanted to ask me about a possible boyfriend, why didn't you just ask me at Don's apartment? Why am I here?'

''Cause I thought he might be the guy, the baby daddy. And I didn't expect to find you there, wasn't thinkin' that fast. But once you were, I figured you could come in handy.'

Great.

His phone rang, the shrill tone searing her nerves with an electric shock. He answered, said *yeah*, *what*, and *yeah* in quick succession, then put it on speaker and held the phone between them.

'Theresa?' Don's tinny voice came from the flat rectangle.

'I'm here.'

'Are you all right?'

That seemed too complicated a question to answer, and the strain in his voice brought tears to her eyes for reasons she could not define, so she simply said yes and left it at that.

'I'm in the vault. I have the file.'

James said, 'And? Who's in it?'

They could hear him rustling the papers. 'You already know Bain was the bodysnatcher, along with minister Cindy. Darryl did the intake. Dr Reese was assigned to do the cut – autopsy.'

'Stop telling me what I already know. Are you alone there?'

Just the barest of hesitations. 'Yes.'

'You didn't tell the cops about me?'

'No.'

'You can't lie worth shit, bro,' James said with a humorless laugh. 'That's all right. I knew you'd go running to them the minute my feet hit the pavement.'

Theresa heard a wind-like noise as if Don had breathed out in relief, and then the DNA analyst, cleverly, tried to distract. 'Stone acted as diener.'

'The ME?'

'Yes. And Causer was there too.'

'Mitchell Causer?'

'Yes.'

Painting a target on their backs, but Shephard would have them surrounded by cops. James would never get close to them. He had to know that. And yet, his reasoning process had some holes.

'And me,' Don added. 'You know that I did the fingernail scrapings. Julie Barnes worked Property then, she logged in the personal effects the following day, Tuesday. She listed a wedding band, watch and earrings.'

James said, 'So Darryl either stole it, or it was already gone.'

'You're right. Either way it never got to Property.' No harm in casting aspersions on to Darryl – he could no longer be hurt.

Theresa asked if he had the toxicology report. She had only just glanced at it before.

'Yeah, it's here. Clean. No surprise there. Only drugs found in the house were vitamin B, vitamin C, and a prescription metformin. No alcohol.'

'Diana didn't drink,' James pointed out.

They heard the rustling again. Shephard, no doubt getting restless. Theresa wouldn't have been surprised if half the command staff of the police department, the medical examiner and two or three pathologists were currently crammed into the records vault, hovering over Don's cellphone.

'Okay, that's the file, James. I did what you asked. Let Theresa go.'

'Here?' James peered through the dirty windshield at the empty park. 'I think she'd be safer with me. Lot more than ghosts to fear in this neighborhood.'

'Uh – someplace else, then. Just let her go,' Don said, in what sounded very close to anguish. Theresa's heart did that tiny fluttering again, as if she had a defect in all four chambers at once.

'I got a better idea. I was trying to eliminate suspects one by one—'

Literally, Theresa nearly snorted.

'—so let's just cut to the chase.'

'What does that mean?'

'I want you to exhume my wife's body.'

TWENTY-FOUR

In the background, she heard Shephard forget himself and exclaim, '*What*?'

'She had a baby inside her,' James said simply. 'I want to know whose it is. Because that will be the guy who killed her.'

'But she wasn't pregnant,' Don said.

'James, that's not going to work,' Theresa said.

'She *was*,' he insisted, both to the phone and to Theresa. 'If she said she was, she was. How close was your doctor looking, anyway? She had been strangled, not – nothing to do with her inner parts. He would want to get it done and over, someone he knew like that.'

'Not Reese,' Theresa said. The man had invented the word *meticulous*. 'And besides, James, there's nothing that can be done now.'

'Yes there is. You can still get DNA from a fetus. I know you can. I had a cell mate for a while, that's how he wound up in the can.'

'But—' Don said.

Theresa said, 'The fetus isn't there. The – look, you know what happens at an autopsy, right?'

'Yeesss . . . ah. I never actually *watched* one. Not the whole thing.'

She turned toward him and spoke quickly but carefully, aware of the audience on the other end of the cell tower link. 'The chest cavity is opened and the organs are removed. The doctor examines each organ, sections them – that means he slices them open – and cuts off tiny bits of the tissue if he wants to take a closer look.'

'I *know* that.'

'Those bits go into a quart of formalin, and histological samples will be made later if the doctor thinks he needs a closer look. But the organs go into the red biohazard bag.'

'And that goes back in the body,' James said.

'Yes, it does. This large garba— *biohazard* bag, full of the organs, heart, lungs, stomach, intestines, etcetera, is placed in the now-empty chest cavity, which is sewn back up. Then the body goes to the funeral home.'

'Yeah. Anderson-Day, that's where Diana went.'

'At the funeral home they need to embalm the body, drain whatever blood is left and send embalming fluid through the veins and arteries.' The interior of the car had grown airless again; she rolled the window the rest of the way down and unlatched her safety belt. Her bottom had gotten tired of the driver's seat, and her legs were quivering in miniature spasms. 'James, they take that biohazard bag out. There is no way to embalm each individual organ for placement back inside the chest cavity, and of course if they just put the whole bag back as it is, those organs will rot, and of course they can't have that because the whole purpose of embalming is to prepare the body to be viewed by loved ones.'

His eyes narrowed to slits. 'So what happens to them?'

She forced herself to speak. 'The funeral homes have incinerators for small amounts like that.'

'They burned her?'

'Just the—'

He seemed to swell right in front of her, sucking in air until his shoulders blocked out the passenger side window. 'Insides? They burned up her insides?'

'James, there's nothing else they can do. There's no way to preserve—'

'So you're telling me that my Diana in the ground, there's nothing inside her? She's just an empty shell?'

He won't kill me, she told herself. He's been angry all day, this is just one more thing and it isn't my fault— 'Yes. I'm sorry, James. I'm trying to explain that exhuming her body won't do you any good.'

To her surprise he turned and opened his door, phone still in hand, and stepped out.

Good. Let him walk off a little nervous energy and they—

To her *great* surprise he reached in, grabbed her by the shirt front and dragged her across the passenger side and out of the car. Too shocked to scream, she bumped one knee on the gear shift and sank to the other one before she could get her legs underneath her. The asphalt felt cool and gritty under her bare feet.

He shook her with one hand, hard enough to make her head snap. 'How could you do that? She was your friend!'

'Stop it! James, stop it. That's how all autopsies are done. There's no way to preserve everything. There's nothing I or anyone else could have done about it. Besides, she *wasn't pregnant*!' she added, her hands futilely trying to pull his from her shirt, straining against both the cuffs and his wrist.

This did nothing to calm him. 'Stop saying that! You're just trying to help your office cover it up! I thought you were on my side. I thought you were on *Diana's* side.'

'I am! But I can't change reality.'

A voice squawked from somewhere; James still clutched the phone in his free hand, and she could hear Don's frantic tones calling her name. James looked at it. Then he looked at her. A crow shouted from the top of a maple. Otherwise, they were alone in the world. No mourners came to visit, and the lone maintenance worker was off somewhere with his rake.

James stopped shaking her, but didn't let go of the shirt.

He brought the phone to his cheek. 'Change of plans. Forget the exhumation. I just want to know two things: who stole my wife's ring, and who she had been cheating with. That's not too much to ask, since they're probably the same person.'

On the other end Don said something, but James cut him off. His gaze never wavered from hers.

'I've got this woman here, and I'm stashing her until you answer those two questions. And the first time you tell me you can't, I pull her back out and slice her throat open. No second chances. Then you can burn her organs too and bury the empty shell. Got that?'

A flurry of words she couldn't make out.

'I said, *do you got that?*'

But he didn't pay much attention to whatever it was Don said, because he moved her around to the back of the car, set the phone on the trunk, unlocked the trunk, then replaced the keys in his pocket and picked up the phone.

'James,' she said, 'no.'

'You've told me everything you know, you say. So we don't need to converse no more.'

'No!' She did what she should have done in the first place – screamed, kicked at his balls with bare feet, clawed at his arms and face. But he held her far enough away to protect his eyes and shifted his massive thighs to shield his privates. Her voice echoed off the roof of the tunnel, and yet another approaching train threatened to drown it out entirely. She had no more effect on James than a small child, and as if she were one he picked her up and tossed her in the trunk hard enough to knock the breath out of her body. She raised her arms as she sucked in air, but he slammed the lid before she could mount any real defense – not that would have done any good against his weight and force. As the lid clicked shut she heard Don's panicked voice over the cellphone in James' hand. She couldn't make out words, only her name as he shouted it over and over.

She did all the useless things people do in movies. She pounded on the inside of the lid with her cuffed hands and screamed until she got dizzy. She kicked at the corners where the taillights should be, which only hurt her feet. Of course, none of that helped.

Nor did it have any effect on James. When she finally paused in her shrieking she heard the door open, feeling the vibration of the movement more than the actual sound, and then the vehicle rocked. The door shut. An instant later, he started the engine.

This was not going to be fun.

TWENTY-FIVE

J ames pulled out from under the tunnel and drove smoothly away through the rolling hills. Smoothly in that he didn't peel out, and he then turned the corner on to what must be the outside street in a reasonable manner. But she definitely felt the uneven curb, and the road needed to be paved after one too many freeze-and-thaw Cleveland winters . . . One of the disadvantages to being kidnapped and locked in a trunk in the less ritzy area of town.

She made herself stop screaming – with an effort – and tried to think. First, assess your surroundings. At least the trunk was not full of old gym clothes and cockroaches – she didn't think so, anyway. It smelled of grease, and the carpet felt less than clean, and the bolt that held down the spare tire had stabbed her in the back upon her entrance, nearly missing her spine, but at least no insect life presented itself. The weatherproofing around the seal had held up over the years, for not the slightest crack of light appeared between the frame and the lid. She lay in utter darkness.

She felt around, sliding slightly as James took another corner. For a stolen car it had a very clean trunk, and she wondered if he had stolen it from a used-car lot. Larger ones had so many vehicles that staff couldn't always keep track and had a bad habit of leaving the keys in them. Unless they had a solid fence and good lighting, a car might not be missed until a salesman went looking for it. And this trunk held nothing but the spare tire on its bolt and a whiff of Febreeze New Car Scent. No car care kit or emergency flasher or, what would have been really handy for both extricating herself from the trunk *and* beaning James once she did, a tire iron.

She wriggled around until her back lay against the outer wall, and she kicked at the seat back with both feet. Heavy boots would have made this much more effective. Stilettos would have made it more effective. As it was, the impact jarred her frame and made both feet scream in protest, while having no effect at all on the seat.

James shouted something, but whether he might be speaking into the phone or shouting at her to stop it, she couldn't guess.

Next she moved closer to the seat back and ran her hands over it, paying special attention to the upper corners. Shouldn't there be a release in case the owner wanted to lay the seat down in order to fit something extra-large into the trunk?

Apparently, that had not been an option in this model. She didn't even know what kind of car she was in – there had been a Chevy emblem on the steering wheel, but beyond that . . . Being dragged from Don's apartment in the middle of the night and focusing on James and his tendency to murder had left her little time to be her usual observant self.

There should be a trunk-release cable with a little plastic handle somewhere around there. She felt around, covering every inch of the area with her hands. When did they start requiring those in vehicles – 2002? Could this car be that old, or had James clipped the thing off before going to Don's? Had he thought that far ahead?

James went over a slight bump, and the movement knocked her head against the trunk lid. On top of that, several exposed bolts protruded from the lid – trunks were not meant to be passenger areas – and one cut into her scalp. She had also begun to sweat; a cool spring day didn't feel so cool inside an enclosed metal space, and she would have given anything for just one breath of fresh air. The walls around her seemed to be getting closer with every rotation of the wheels, cinching inward until—

'James!' she shouted. 'What are you doing? How do you think this is going to help?'

He said something back. She couldn't make out the words, but from the cadence she would guess he had said, 'I can't hear you.' And probably meant that literally.

Her fury at herself edged out her fury at him. How could she have been so stupid? How many tales of abduction, murder and other woes had she heard in the line of her work? She should never have gotten into the car with him. How many times had she promised herself, and told Rachael the same thing: in the case of an attempted abduction, don't go! If he says he'll shoot you, tell him to go ahead. Better it be in a parking lot where help might pass by before you bleed out than lost on an isolated country road. If he says he won't hurt you, don't believe him. And if he says he'll hurt you if you don't, he had planned to anyway. Once you get in the car the needle on your life expectancy meter falls from debatable to less than slim.

But this was different! she could say if she wanted to defend her own actions. James wasn't a rapist or a serial killer in the usual sense. Harming her had never been his goal. She had cooperated because, first, it got him away from Don, who seemed a more likely victim, and second, because she thought her friendship with Diana might put her in a position to bring the situation to a close without further bloodshed. She had thought she could handle it. She had thought she could handle him.

That had been her most foolish mistake.

Okay. Stop with the recriminations and think. How does one get out of a car trunk?

She had read once that an intrepid Girl Scout had pulled out the taillight and then stuck her arm through the hole and waved until someone noticed and reported the vehicle to the police. She wriggled carefully and ran her hands over the outer corners, though she knew what she would find from her first pass. The frame covered the taillight area completely. They were not accessible from inside the trunk. She pulled back the molded upholstery just to make sure, but the metal felt smooth and unbroken. The taillight wouldn't help. Maybe if she had the actual Girl Scout.

She heard a tinkling sound and stopped moving to listen. The car slowed – perhaps for a light, because she could hear other vehicles around them – and then James' muffled tones penetrated the seat back. Someone must have called him, meaning he must have hung up at some point. It was probably Don calling back to keep him talking, communicating and, she hoped, negotiating.

The car curved to the side and sped up. They were getting on the freeway, most likely I-77. He was driving much faster than he would dare on city streets.

There were so many things that could happen next, all of them bad.

Upset, manic, distracted, James could get into a car accident, in which a large truck or even a tractor-trailer plowed into the back of him, and Theresa would have to be scraped up in small pieces for the funeral. Rachael would—

Don't think about Rachael.

James could be planning to drive out to hilly Geauga County and dump the car in a copse of trees. Theresa would not be found until she had long since died of dehydration, her body crawling with maggots and lying in its own—

Best not think about that, either.

He might, for whatever reason, think that the vehicle would best be hidden in the lake and drive it off the end of a pier, escaping through the window she'd opened while the trunk filled up with water with nowhere for her to go.

Or James could get an answer he didn't like – a nearly inevitable outcome, since how could Don and Shephard and Stone and the rest of the group at the ME's possibly figure out who might have been Diana's lover/killer this many years later? The guilty man certainly wouldn't be willing to admit it, and, if James had been right about the pregnancy, they had incinerated the only evidence. Unless the histological samples held a surprise . . .

He seemed to be shouting into the phone now, though she still couldn't make out any words. Definitely an answer he didn't like.

Probably, the *best* scenario would be if James bailed out and left her parked in a populated lot, where a hapless shopper might hear her pounding before she collapsed from a lack of water and oxygen.

Maybe the car's owner had reported it stolen, and the cops were looking for it – either because it was a stolen car or because Shephard had put the two things together and suspected it to be James' current mode of conveyance. In which case the cops on the street would be keeping an eye out for a multiple murderer, not a car thief. That changed things. Cops would be extra determined not to let him get away. They might not know she was in the car – perhaps a dispatch cut out before they got that info, or they wouldn't see her inside the car and would think he had let her out somewhere else. James could lift the knife and, seeing a flash of metal, they think it's a gun. Or maybe they set up a roadblock and he tries to ram the officers and their vehicles. There were so many scenarios that could end in a compacted crush or a hail of bullets, cutting through the relatively thin metal compartment where she lay—

She pulled on the thin carpeting beneath her, stiff but not tacked down. A piece of plywood covered only the spare tire, not the entire expanse of trunk floor, so she could move it aside with a minimum of scrapes and splinters to get at the grimy lower crevice. Unfortunately, the lower crevice was peppered with exposed bolts and contained a jack that removed her kneecap from the rest of her leg. At least, it felt like that.

As she rubbed her knee he turned another corner. Her head would have slid into the fender frame if the exposed bolt holding the spare and jack down hadn't caught her handcuffs, arresting her movement.

Suddenly, she had an idea.

A large wing nut held those items down, and in the pitch darkness her fingers found it. At first it seemed frozen by who knew how many years of inactivity, but she twisted it with a desperation more of anger than fear. At last it started to turn.

James stomped on the brakes for some reason, and the resultant bouncing thrust the back of her neck into the trunk lid. If she got out of this without permanent paralysis, she'd have done well.

The nut took an annoyingly long time to rotate off – guaranteed to further frustrate any unlucky motorist who needed to change a flat tire – and she pulled the jack off the top of the spare. It didn't seem very big, but then it would have to be able to lift a car, right?

Her hands ran over the basic diamond shape of the item. It had to have a handle, which would double as a tire iron with a crowbar end for removing hubcaps.

But she couldn't find it. In a car this old it might have been missing for years, and the jack would be useless without any way to crank it open.

In the pitch dark, and trying not to let her face bounce down on to the protruding center bolt, she felt all over the crevice. Nothing, save for decades old grease spots and insect carcasses.

The car came to a stop and didn't start again. In fact, James killed the engine. Theresa stopped moving for a moment to listen. She heard (and felt) the car door slam as he got out. No other car engines, no traffic noises. No voices. Maybe they were in some isolated area where he intended to leave her to die. But on gravel, to judge from the faint crunching as James stepped away from the car, so it couldn't be *that* remote.

She didn't shout or pound. Her dignity had limits, and it wasn't as if he could have forgotten her presence. He either intended to let her out, or he didn't, and pounding wouldn't make a difference. Besides, if she stayed quiet he might get curious or concerned enough to check on her welfare.

But she continued her search for the tire iron, her hands roaming without sound.

Then she heard another car engine approach, and stop. A door slammed. James – at least she thought it was James, she couldn't be sure – said something.

Suddenly, a loud *bang* split the air, and a bullet tore through the trunk.

It happened so fast that she didn't have time to scream. She wouldn't even have been sure what had occurred, but the resulting hole in the frame let in a tiny point of light that alerted her to reality. Her body reacted with animal instinct, forming the tightest ball it could even as she felt a shower of metal shavings sprinkle across the hands over her face.

She didn't move.

After a second she heard another shot.

Theresa held her breath. If whoever had the gun out there knew she was in the trunk he could pepper it with bullets until she bled out. But if he didn't know, she wasn't about to alert him.

Unless it was James doing the shooting, but she couldn't quite see the logic in that. He might have met up with a friend who sold him a gun, but then why would James shoot his seller? Hell of a way to get out of a bill.

If James had encountered a patrol car and resisted arrest, she would be hearing police radios and a flurry of activity. As it was she heard nothing except a faint crunching. This must have been the person walking away, because then she heard the thud as the car door slammed and, a second later, the engine started up. The other car drove away, churning up the stones underneath its tires.

Still she waited. She made herself count to sixty to give the shooter a full minute to leave, as if that might create some magic buffer zone that would keep her safe, a grace period which guaranteed he would never return.

'James?' she called.

No answer.

She rolled over and tried to peer out the small hole left by the bullet. It had actually passed through two walls of metal, and so she could only see through by moving her head to the exact trajectory. This required shoving her scalp into the tight corner of the trunk where the layers and spaces of the metal frame grabbed her hair and ripped some of it out, but finally she could glimpse a sliver of the outside world.

Gravel, trees, and a clothed leg. It lay flat against the ground and wore the same pants James had been wearing.

She shouted again. No movement. No sounds at all, which did not bode well for the idea of rescue. She really needed some passer-by to notice the body and call the cops, but from the dead silence outside the vehicle she knew she couldn't count on it.

Back to the project at hand. James could be lying outside the vehicle bleeding to death, but she could do nothing about that right now. If either of them were to have a chance of survival she needed to *get out of that car.*

The bullet had actually helped the situation; between even that minuscule amount of light and no light at all there gaped a large and substantial difference. And now that the car wasn't moving she could wriggle around without constant knocks to her head and neck. Almost.

She lifted the spare tire off its post, feeling around at the very bottom of the recess, trying not to think about the greasy, unknown things her fingers encountered. She found a booklet that seemed thick enough to be the owner's manual, a leaky quart of extra oil, and, at last, the tire iron. Or jack handle, or whatever its proper name might be.

At first she tried dispensing with the jack entirely and wedged the flat end of the handle into the weatherstripping between the trunk and the lid, trying to prize them apart. *Give me a lever and I can move the world.* Perhaps he had thought so, but Archimedes had never tried to open a car trunk from the inside because Theresa got exactly nowhere. She only created some rectangular divots in the edge of the car frame. She would have to use the jack, but she had no idea if it would even work. She feared it might just pop through the metal of the lid without releasing the latch.

Again, the tiny bit of light came in handy. She positioned the jack in the center of the trunk rear, right next to the latch, and held it in place with one foot, since the cuffs kept her hands too restricted to both hold the jack and pump the handle. Insert iron, begin to crank. This would have been so much easier outside in the open where her knuckles wouldn't scrape against the trunk lid with every pump.

The thing rose with agonizing slowness, no matter how frantically she worked the handle up and down. After what seemed like a half-hour the saddle finally touched the inside of the lid. Theresa continued to pump.

The top of the jack began to press against the lid interior. Then it created a dent in the lid interior, or at least it looked that way in the limited ambient light.

She kept pumping.

The car began to make a sort of groaning noise, which started as a small thrum but grew to a throaty purr. The jack handle showed a touch of resistance.

She kept pumping. A new sound presented itself, and after a moment she realized that it came from her, her lips forming the words *please work please work please work* over and over.

The latch fought until the bitter end, but still the car's groan increased until, with a short screech of metallic agony, it slipped off its rod and the lid popped open. It didn't fly back with a *ta-da* air, but it seemed dramatic enough to Theresa. She pushed it up and leapt out, leaving her friend the jack without so much as a thank-you. Only then did she take a deep breath, look around, and recall that they had landed in a gravel lot and that she wore nothing on her feet.

She and the car sat behind a large, plain building, possibly a warehouse from its lack of windows, doors or other accessories. A lightly wooded and deeply littered area ran to the other side. No other cars presented themselves. She had no idea where she might be.

James stretched, face up, about ten feet from the car. The gravel bit into her feet as she ran to him.

A hole in his T-shirt blossomed blood, spreading through the fabric and leaking on to the dirty white rocks below. But she would guess it had been the one in his forehead that ended his life before he could even cry out. Much more than a pinprick.

It seemed strange to crouch there next to the dead body of a man with whom she had spent the morning in close quarters. He had kidnapped her, cut her and locked her in a trunk, so she couldn't quite grieve his loss. He had killed three men, men she knew, brutally. But Theresa thought he had loved his wife, even if he hadn't known how to be a good husband to her. And now it seemed that perhaps he hadn't killed her, either – otherwise why would someone lure him to an isolated spot only to drill him through the brain?

So she spared a moment to express her regret to James for the way things had turned out.

Then she looked through his pockets for his cellphone.

TWENTY-SIX

'You're *where*?' Shephard asked.

'At a place called Brynwood Manufacturing, off Woodland and East 79th. The guy here says we're right by the tracks.' She sat on an old steel desk talking on a phone so dilapidated that she didn't want to put it to her face and so instead held it a quarter of an inch from her skin. She was surrounded by at least five men, who eyed her as if she were a hamburger accidentally dropped into the lion cage. That she had shown up in, essentially, pajamas as well as handcuffed with a pair of hot-pink bracelets had no doubt prompted all sorts of theories as to her history, each one more salacious than the last. Yes, they were having a mental ball filling in the gaps.

The interior of the factory, by contrast, had been painted a brilliant white, and there were at least one or two windows, forming an odd backdrop for the workers in stained, rumpled clothing. 'Get here. *Quickly*. James' body is sitting out there by itself. Whoever killed him also took his cellphone, so I had to walk until I found an open door.'

'Units are on their way, and I'm getting in my car now.'

'Bring Don.'

'Of course,' he said, without inflection. 'What do they manufacture?'

'Toys, believe it or not. Tricycles, and something that looks like a Big Wheel.'

Two of the men had already lost interest and wandered out for a smoke, since no work seemed likely to occur in the next half hour or so, or maybe for the rest of the day. The other three stood and listened to her every word, including the foreman who had directed her to the phone after she'd shown up at the door with feet hurting and eyes still blinking at the overcast but bright sky.

'We call it a Big Spinner,' one of the guys told her, his

focus on her chest. Which wasn't even particularly big, and what, had these guys been in isolation for the past ten years, chained to their work station attaching plastic pedals to large plastic wheels?

'Why "believe it or not"?' Shephard asked.

Because, she thought, you would not look at these men and think that they and innocent children could possibly exist in the same world. But she didn't say so. They were her rescuers of a sort, and she would appreciate them accordingly. 'Just get here. I'll be with the body.'

She hung up.

'We might be able to find you a pair of shoes,' the foreman said.

'Thanks – I appreciate it, but my feet are pretty tough.'

'Want some more water?'

'No, I'm good.'

'Do you want us to do something about those cuffs?'

She looked at them as if she'd forgotten their presence, because she very nearly had. They restricted her movement and therefore made her less able to fend off any unwanted advances. On the other hand, waiting for these gentlemen to rustle up a bolt cutter meant she would have to remain in their custody for the duration. 'No, thanks. The cops will be here any minute, and they'll have a key. I need to get back to the body.'

'You might as well wait in here.' The third guy had eyes like a rodent, round and dark. 'We sometimes have a pretty good time.'

'Sure,' said another, his gaze roaming over her in frenetic cycles, as if he couldn't take it in quickly enough. 'We don't often get visitors.'

She wanted to ask if they had been bussed in from the local penal colony, but they might answer in the affirmative. Instead she fixed the Big Spinner spokesman with a look that summed up how she felt, and spoke slowly and clearly. 'I have had a *really* bad day.'

The rodent-like eyes stopped roaming, and the other guy straightened up.

'*Really* bad.'

It took only another minute or two for the gallery to break rank and wander away, and she hopped off the desk and pushed past them to the door. The foreman insisted on coming with her; if there had been a murder on his boss' property he needed to stay abreast of the developments. Happily for her he wasn't chatty; other than sneaking glances at her bottom, he kept all thoughts to himself.

The large building had, at least, a small sidewalk in front of it, so that she hit gravel for only two sides of the horseshoe shape she had to make to get back to where James' body lay next to the car. No one else appeared in the long, wide alley behind the plant.

'Any cameras back here?' she asked the foreman.

'Used to be. They broke.'

'Great.'

'We don't have much of a problem with crime,' he added as a defense, and she supposed that would be true; Big Spinners most likely did not form a major segment of the black market.

She crouched next to the body. From that angle she could see the faint indentations where the other vehicle had stopped. James had stood in the middle, meeting him halfway. He'd brought only a knife to a gun fight, yes, but still it seemed to her that the shooter had been someone James trusted . . . or at the very least, not someone he expected to shoot him on sight. Though she had been occupied with the jack at the time, she recalled little, if any, conversation. The killer had driven up, gotten out, shot James, and left.

If he had known Theresa was in the trunk he didn't care – neither about her safety after a round went through it, nor about leaving an eyewitness, since obviously she couldn't see him. But if it had been him – or her – who called James just before they stopped, then how could they be sure that James hadn't told Theresa who he planned to meet? James might have told the guy that he had put her in the trunk. Still, unless the shooter had a lot of experience riding around in trunks, he couldn't be sure she hadn't overheard the conversation.

Unless James never mentioned a name because he didn't know who he'd spoken to, only that the person claimed to have information about his wife.

Unless he had been killed over some other element of his past, and the shooter – and the murder – had nothing to do with the ME's office.

She checked his pockets again, in case she had missed anything, but James had traveled light – no surprise; he had had to cut out of the ME's office in a hurry, and he probably knew better than to go back to his apartment. The knife had been tucked into a back pocket, ready if he needed it, but never ready enough for a bullet.

She gazed at him for a moment, with no sound around her except the slight crunch of the gravel as the foreman shifted his weight behind her, and tried to observe: did she notice anything she hadn't while spending the previous seven hours with him?

Well, no. The same close-cropped hair, slim nose, a large mole on his neck. The same T-shirt under the navy hoodie, both dirty and bearing a few stains that were most likely three different types – hers, Reese's, and his own. The bullet had not exited, she guessed from the lack of any blood flowing out from beneath the body. A large scrape along one temple – probably from Darryl, she couldn't picture Dr Reese putting up much of a fight. And a gold band on the fourth finger of his left hand.

'Did you know him?' the foreman asked.

She thought. 'I'm not really sure.'

Theresa stood up and made a gentle path toward the car, studying the area for a casing. They were notoriously hard to find, though gravel should be better than grass, but she did not see it – them, there should be two. The killer had either picked them up, or used a revolver. Finally, she gave up and went to the car.

The keys were still in the ignition, and the window she had lowered was still down. She opened the door and studied the interior, now without the twin distractions of driving and being threatened with a knife.

The door pocket held a map of Greater Cleveland, a small bottle of Bath and Body Works Japanese Cherry Blossom hand lotion – she helped herself to a dollop since she seriously needed to smell better than she currently did – and several loose CDs labeled with a girlish hand. The small armrest console had a few quarters and pennies and a cigarette lighter. The glove box let her know that the vehicle belonged to a Laurel Hightower of Garfield Heights and was overdue for its E-check. The owner had had a tire repaired at Conrad's and bought something, identified by a gaggle of letters, at PetSmart. The passenger door pocket—

The foreman's face appeared in the window. 'You really did a number on that trunk.'

He had just done a number on her heart, but she didn't say so. 'Yep.'

'I think the cops are here. Siren's coming.'

The passenger door pocket carried a dead cockroach and the stubby end of a different kind of roach – naughty, Laurel – and a screwdriver. That might have been handy if she'd wanted to counter James' knife, but of course she'd have had to get to it first.

A police siren that became more ear-splitting the closer it came announced that the cavalry had arrived. They burst around the side of the building, gravel flying, and the noise became truly uncomfortable. She waited, trying to cross her arms, but the cuffs made that impossible. No reason to be peeved at them, of course, but at the moment she felt peeved at the entire world.

Don flew out of the unmarked car as soon as it stopped rolling, shouted her name once and embraced her in an awkward – given the cuffs – hug; under usual circumstances this would have thrilled her, but right now she was too well aware of her unwashed, uncombed, bruised, barely and badly clothed body that had nothing save a dab of Japanese Cherry going for it.

'I can't believe you're alive!' was among the things he exclaimed.

'There were moments I had my doubts,' she said.

Shephard stood a few feet away, watching them with an unreadable expression on his face. 'Want those off?'

She held out the cuffs. 'No, I'd actually gotten rather attached to them. No pun intended.'

'That was a pun?' He used his key. 'Are you all right?'

'Let me get back to you on that.'

He ducked his head down as he unlocked the second cuff, taking a closer look at her face. But he didn't ask again.

'Geeze, Theresa, your hands,' Don said. The wrists were chafed and reddened, a layer or two of skin scraped off here and there, but they weren't bleeding. They would turn a few different colors in the coming week.

'What can you tell me?' Shephard asked.

'He got a phone call. We stopped. He got out and someone shot him. And, almost, me.' She pointed to the hole in the car fender. 'I used the jack to get out. Expect a victim's compensation claim from a Miss Laurel Hightower.'

He nodded, solemnly. 'Where have you been all day?'

'First he had me drive to the beach—'

'The *beach*?'

'All part of a stroll down memory lane. Look, I'm starving and thirsty and really need a bathroom. Can we do this somewhere else?' Her voice wavered on the last few words, but she cut herself some slack. It really *had* been a bad day.

'Absolutely. Yin and Yang and Don here can handle the crime scene. Doesn't look like we'll get much from it, anyway.' Shephard put a hand on each of her shoulders and guided her toward his car as if she might collapse at any moment, and in truth that seemed more likely than it had four minutes before.

He shot a look at Don as they left, and it appeared, inexplicably, triumphant.

TWENTY-SEVEN

An hour later – after she had scrounged a few clean clothes from her pathologist friend Christina, and then used up every paper towel in the ladies' room trying to take the wettest sponge bath possible using nothing but a small porcelain sink – she felt nearly human. Especially after two cups of coffee and a western omelet, which Shephard had procured from the medical school cafeteria next door and presented with such pride that she hadn't had the heart to tell him she felt that green peppers and eggs were two foods which should never intersect. Now she sat in a task chair blowing on her third cup of coffee while Neenah applied first aid to her raw wrists and the other small lacerations she'd accumulated during the morning. She didn't need to call anyone; no one had had the courage to inform either Rachael or her mother of her plight, so both had gone through the day blissfully unaware of Theresa's brush with violence. And she had already decided that they would continue to do so, for the rest of their lives.

Shephard had asked her to go through the day's events again as both he and Yin – Theresa had completely blanked out on his real name – of the detective team took notes. They had that edgy air of indecision that came after a case broke. Urgency had ended, the killer put down and the prior murders more or less confessed to. Theresa had been recovered unharmed – largely unharmed, though she knew she would have trouble drifting off to sleep in the coming months without seeing a shadow creeping into her room or dreaming of a bumpy ride in an enclosed space. All should be well, with only a mountain of paperwork to tackle before memories faded.

Except for the slight problem of the extra dead body. James had killed George, Darryl, and Dr Reese, no question. But who had shot James?

'And who strangled Diana?' Theresa asked aloud.

'You honestly think he told you the truth?' Shephard asked.

'Do I think he's capable of killing his wife in a hazy, drug-fueled rage and then convincing himself he didn't? Yes, I do. But if that's true, then who killed him?'

'Allman had a criminal history even apart from the murder, and he spent a long time in jail,' Yin pointed out. 'He might have had a target on his back for completely separate reasons. He meets up with an old pal to borrow some money or a weapon, and the old pal grabs the opportunity to settle a score.'

'If that's so we might never catch up to them,' Shephard said.

'But we can't assume the obvious answer is the right one. That may be the mistake we made with Diana,' Theresa said, trying to sound firm while wincing as Neenah tied the gauze around her left wrist.

'Charitable use of "we",' Shephard said, obviously trying not to bristle.

'I thought so.'

Yin's phone rang. He listened, snapped it shut and stood up. 'Casey Allman is downstairs.'

'Who's Casey Allman?' Theresa asked.

'The cousin who's a cop,' Shephard explained, rising as well.

'Good. I'd really like to meet him.' She scrambled after both of them.

'You're still bleeding!' Neenah called, pointing to a scrape on her arm that would not stop oozing.

Theresa snatched a Kimwipe out of the dispenser box as she went out the door. They were designed to be used on a microscope lens, but worked on skin just as well.

Casey Allman looked like a cop. Tall and pale with short sandy hair, he exuded calm, authority, and many hours in the gym. His uniform fit with barely a wrinkle. He stood straight with only the slightest hunch to his shoulders to hint at some inner pain. He seemed neither cynical nor defensive, nor sad. Theresa let him and the cops into the tiny library. The conference room had been taken over by a grief counseling session 'for staff members who would like to attend due to the office's recent losses'.

Theresa shut the door behind them, neatly including herself in the meeting.

Yin noticed immediately. 'You don't have to stay for this, Theresa.'

'Oh, I do. I was with your cousin when he died,' she added to Casey, putting extra warmth into her voice. Perhaps he would believe she remained to support him instead of question him. Perhaps Yin would, too.

Shephard knew better, from the sharp look he gave her.

'What happened?' Casey Allman asked.

She let Yin summarize as she doodled with the handy pencils and supply of scrap paper kept in the library.

'I'm sorry that happened to you,' Casey told her when the detective had finished.

'I'm not too much the worse for wear. You don't have to apologize for your cousin's actions.'

'Why not? I've been doing it most of my life. James was pretty much trouble from the day he was born.' Casey Allman crossed his arms and glanced out the window. 'We grew up together, yes, but that bond has a shelf life. Truth is, I'm only here now because my mother would give me grief if I didn't show up to, I don't know, represent the family or something.'

'Tell me about him,' she said. The two cops just listened.

'Let's see – he stole my neighbor's dog when we were ten. Of course, the thing ran home as soon as it could, and I had to talk him out of a repeat. He watched an old movie once and decided we should hop a boxcar and go to California. He had this thoroughly planned out, he said. Talked me into it. It turned out his careful planning meant he put a juice box and a package of gummy worms in his pocket, and we wound up in Pittsburgh. I mean, that stuff sounds cute now and we would laugh about it, but as the years passed he did stuff that wasn't so cute any more. He sold pot at our junior high. He robbed a convenience store at gunpoint before he was old enough to drive – got away with it, but it still scared him bad enough that he stayed pretty cool for years after that. Then – well, I'm sure you've seen his record. He dragged half of my family members into every one of his dramas. I hate to say it, but the past ten years were just a little bit more peaceful with him in jail.'

Theresa nodded.

'Did you know he was out?' Yin asked.

'Yes.'

'Did you know he was working at the ME's under an assumed name?'

'What? No! He said he worked at a grocery store.'

Yin explained about the Justin Warner alias.

'You mean he'd been *planning* this?'

'Yes. That surprises you?'

'James hasn't planned a single thing since the gummy worms, so yes, that surprises me.'

'Do you remember Diana?' Theresa asked.

Casey Allman sat back in his chair, tightening his arms and looking at the slender window again as if checking his options for egress. 'Diana. Di-ana.'

'His wife—'

'We all knew Diana, bel*ieve* me.' He sighed, returned his gaze to Theresa. 'Hot as . . . well, hot. Never understood what the hell she was doing with James, and it seemed clear, after the first couple of months, that neither could she. She was nice to James' mother while she was alive, I'll say that for Diana. The rest of us she tolerated. I don't think we fit into the life to which she some day hoped to become accustomed.'

'Why not?' Theresa asked. Across from her, Shephard fidgeted with what was probably impatience. She ignored him.

Casey sighed again, but it seemed more dismissive than weary. 'She complained that James had champagne tastes on a beer budget, and he did, but so did she. She bitched that he got a tattoo instead of getting the furnace fixed, but then she bought a purse instead of a new tire when his were bald. Diana planned to tour Italy – oh, and France – and spent a lot of time talking about the Grand Canal and the Palazzo Farnese and other places that I don't think she was even pronouncing correctly.'

'Did she or James mention being pregnant?'

His eyes bulged momentarily. 'No! Was she? No one ever told us that.'

'Truthfully, we're not sure at this time.'

'Shit.' He rubbed his chin. '*Shit.*'

'She didn't say anything about it? No hints, or indications? What about your wife or the other women in the family? Might she have confided in one of them?'

'Not a chance. Diana wasn't a coffee klatch kind of girl, said all the chatting about babies and playdates and soccer practice bored her silly. As I said, she had a much different lifestyle in mind. The last time I saw her she talked about skiing – s*kiing*. I mean, seriously?'

'A lot of people ski,' Theresa pointed out. Especially in Cleveland.

'The most physically intensive activity Diana participated in was filing her nails,' Casey snapped. 'She batted her eyes at everything that walked by with a d— anything male, especially if it came with a paycheck. But if James so much as talked to another girl, then he was taking her for granted.'

'So you weren't a big fan of Diana's?'

'No.' He looked away again, down, fiddled with the ancient metal fittings around the table leg. 'Not at all.'

Except, perhaps, in the way one shouldn't feel about their cousin's wife.

'So it didn't surprise you when he killed her?' Theresa asked.

'No – honestly, it didn't.' He fell silent.

'I understand you were the first responder.'

'Yeah. I heard the address over the radio when I was only two streets away, so I took it. I was a FTO then—' Theresa knew this meant Field Training Officer – 'and I had a rookie with me. Dispatch had just said dead, they didn't say who, so my first thought was that James had overdosed.' He sighed, and this time he did seem sad, rubbing his face with a calloused hand. His nails had been bitten to the quick, black ink marked up the inside of his middle finger, and the springy hairs from some kind of pet fur cropped up here and there along one sleeve. He didn't relish, understandably, going over the murder again. Theresa's attention never wavered from his face, trying to crawl back through time and see everything through his eyes.

'And that was late afternoon?' Odd, for her to be questioning someone, but Yin and Shephard let her go. As long as the witness is talking, don't mess with the process.

'Yeah. It was a nice day, clear. We rolled up. The back door was open, and we made entry . . . found her on the floor. Cleared the house, called it in.'

'What was she wearing?'

'Wearing? Um – a blue shirt, those *Viva Las Vegas* white hot pants. No shoes. Strangled with the jump rope. I didn't know it was the jump rope then, I didn't look at it that closely.'

'Do you remember her jewelry?'

His eyebrows went up a notch. 'He told you about the ring, huh?'

'Yep.'

'I should never have told him that. He's obsessed with that damn ring.'

'What did you see, at the scene?'

He shot her the tiniest lift of his lips, as if appreciating the nicely non-leading question. 'She had on a gold band and a silver sapphire and diamond ring. Earrings. I couldn't really see if there might have been a necklace in that mess. I didn't want to get that close, and I did *not* move the body. You can ask the rookie, he's still with the department.'

'Okay,' Theresa smiled. 'What did the sapphire ring look like?'

He described stones and clusters until she held up her doodle. 'Did it look like this?'

'Yeah. That's it.'

'Okay. So you bagged the hands.'

Yin finally began to fidget as well, but Shephard seemed to have resigned himself. She figured that *he* figured that Theresa had spent a morning listening to James' self-justifications of the crime, so she had a list of statements to confirm.

'Yep. Paper bags, evidence tape. By the manual.'

'And EMS responded out?'

'They came and pronounced. Didn't move her or anything.'

'Detectives came out.'

'And the lieutenant. But I stayed until they loaded her up.'

'And that was George Bain – the body-snatcher that day?'

He shrugged. 'I don't know his name. I'd seen him before, and afterwards, but—'

'And you were in and out of the house, probably?'

'No, I stayed with her body from the time I got there until the bodysnatchers left. Figured it was the least I could do, for James.'

'Not for Diana?' she couldn't resist asking.

He frowned. 'I guess for her, too, yeah.'

'James spent the morning telling me he didn't kill Diana.'

'Don't they all?' Casey said with a shrug. 'Say that, I mean?'

'Why did you say you should never have told James about the ring?'

He puffed out a disgusted sigh. 'I would visit him in the can once in a while. Felt like I should, no one else would other than his mom before she died. Maybe a year or two after he'd gone in, he started asking for details of that day, everything I'd done, seen. Like you just did. Okay, fine. But then first he decides that he didn't do it at all, and then after another year or so he decides that this ring could prove his innocence. I kept trying to tell him, even if Diana had a ring on that disappeared somewhere down the line, it doesn't change the fact that you did pawn a ring you stole from her just before she got strangled on your kitchen floor. That ring is not a friggin' Get Out of Jail Free card, no matter what happened to it.'

Theresa nodded.

He continued, his voice growing more strident. 'But he insisted. And insisted. I think he spent every night *dreaming* of that stupid ring for the last half of his sentence. It became some magic talisman that would fix his life and make him king.'

'Did you know what he planned to do once he got out?'

He straightened in alarm. 'No! Of course not.'

'I don't mean about the murders. But did he have any plans for finding this ring?'

He appeared to think. 'No . . . he didn't say. The last year of his sentence, he dialed it down. Stopped mentioning the ring, stopped talking about the murder . . . I was only there a couple times so I didn't think about it, figured it had run its course. Obsession is a way of life inside. It gives them something to think about, and when one is used up they go on to another. If I thought about it at all, that's what I thought. James talked only about getting out, getting a job, getting his life in order, blah blah blah, the same well-meaning bullshit they practice for the parole board, and James had been practicing since he could speak . . . I mean, I see that *now*. I probably should have paid more attention.'

'You can't be responsible for your cousin's—'

'Exactly,' he said, but without a convincing amount of confidence. 'I've been dealing with his fallout since we were kids, but that's over. He was family, yes, so I visited and hugged him when he got out and said supportive things, but as far as responsible – that ended the day he killed Diana.'

TWENTY-EIGHT

'What do you think?' Shephard asked her after Yin had taken Casey Allman to identify his cousin's body.

'I think Cousin Casey the Cop liked Diana a lot more than he's willing to acknowledge, and not in a brotherly way.' They had remained in the library; it gave them a quiet place to talk, with wide and worn wooden chairs. Theresa pulled her knees to her chin, feeling as if she had completed a marathon – after the adrenalin from the continued stress of the morning finally ebbed away, it left a sort of deep chill in its wake.

'Think he did it? The cousin?'

'He could have. He admits he was in the area. Your shifts change at six, right? He could have killed Diana, gone on duty, and hung around the area waiting for the call to come in. He sends the rookie out to the car for some reason, takes the ring and bags the hands.'

'Then why tell James about the ring at all?'

'Maybe he was afraid James would eventually remember it, or eventually remember something that would implicate him. A distraction.'

'Maybe James actually did kill his wife and wasn't coherent enough to remember it.'

'Then who killed *him*?'

'Why steal this ring at all?' he asked wearily.

'Let's assume for the moment that James didn't kill her. The person who stole the ring might have done so entirely for profit. In that case they are almost certainly not the murderer, or they would have taken the ring *during* the murder. Or, the person stole the ring because he gave it to her and thought it could be traced back to him.'

'In which case he still might not be the murderer. James could have done it, but lover arrives on the scene and doesn't want his little secret getting out, either because of his wife or because he doesn't want to be a suspect. But James still did it.'

'Then why kill James? Ten years later, would a little affair still be worth killing a man in cold blood?'

'You don't know some wives.'

'Okay, we're going around in circles here.'

'Been doing that for two days,' he grumbled. 'Why stop now?'

'I think one thing we can be certain of is that whoever called James is the one who killed him. Can you get the phone records?'

'It was a burner phone.'

'Yeah, but we should have the number from the caller ID on Don's phone.'

'I've got the phone company working on it, but it's going to take a while. Days, maybe. Of course,' he added, watching her, '*Don* had the number.'

'You all had it. You were all in the room with him, right?'

He thought a moment, then nodded reluctantly. 'Yeah. Me, Yin and Yang, and half your upper staff here.'

'You seem keen to think of Don as your primary suspect.'

'And you don't. I get that. So who are our suspects?' He started to tick them off on his fingers. 'Cousin Casey the Cop. George Bain, deceased. Darryl Johnson, deceased. Dr Hubert Reese, deceased. Dr Elliott Stone, now the ME. Don, your buddy. Mitchell Causer. Who do you think is the most likely to have been the lover-slash-killer of Diana Allman?'

She thought. 'Casey Allman seems to have been in the best position to, and he still has conflicted feelings about Diana. I can't picture George as a romantic interest of Diana's.'

'Darryl Johnson?'

'That's tougher. I couldn't stand him and didn't think she could either, but . . . he wasn't bad-looking, and even horrid men can be surprisingly charming when they want to be.'

'I can be charming.'

She ignored him. 'Dr Reese, I don't see. They *did* get along, he and Diana – he usually didn't have a lot of time for people who didn't have letters after their names, but he made an exception for Diana. Men usually did. His interest seemed more fatherly than anything, but then I'm notoriously naive about these things. I'm sure about one thing, though – if Dr Reese had had an affair with Diana, James would not have been able to beat it out of him. He'd take it to his grave.'

'He may have.'

'He had a set of principles that didn't bend. So, next – Dr Stone? He'd be the most likely, I guess.'

'Seriously?'

'This conversation doesn't leave this room, right?'

He raised three fingers. 'Scouts honor.'

'He's a handsome guy, was more so ten years ago.'

'Like all of us.'

'There have been rumors over the years that he doesn't exactly consider his marriage vows to be rules so much as suggestions, and that may be why a secretary in Records went to Parks and Recs, a pathologist went to work at the Clinic, and a histologist took early retirement. And he had the money to buy a ring like that, even then.'

'So he'd have been a move up for Diana.'

'Don't listen to the cousin,' Theresa snapped. 'Diana never struck me as a gold-digger. She wanted stability, not a meal ticket.'

'Okay. Say she was in it for love – but then he won't leave his wife. She needs a way to bust him out so one day it's hey, I'm pregnant, now you *gotta* do something – they argue, but she's holding the womb card.'

'The womb card?'

'Beats a royal flush, believe me. So he kills her. Makes his getaway – he's in her own house in broad daylight, not the most discreet move in the world – and then he remembers the ring. But again, why is he so certain this ring can be linked to him? Was it custom made?'

'I couldn't tell you.'

'You can really see your ME murdering one of his employees?'

'Truthfully? No. He'd be more likely to bribe or cajole his way out of things. He's a long-time, very skilled political player – that's how he worked his way up to the top position in record time. He would have fired Diana and found a way to discredit her, or made it well worth her while to get rid of the baby and quietly find other employment. As I said, provided the office gossips are to be believed, he winds up in a similar situation every couple of years. No one else has wound up dead.'

Shephard rubbed the stubble on his chin. 'Okay. Who else?'

'Don, as you seem to enjoy pointing out. As a lover, he would be the obvious choice. They were both young and beautiful, and on top of it he was single and sympathetic. But if so then they were extraordinarily discreet. I lunched with her all the time – if she had been interested in Don she would have been pumping me for information about him, what he was like, where he went, what he did.'

'Oh yeah?'

'Yeah. Some things don't change after high school.'

Shephard laughed.

'And vice-versa. As it is, I don't ever remember one of them asking about the other.'

'Okay, fine, let's eliminate your little boyfriend. That leaves Mitchell Causer.'

'Not in any alternate universe would he have been Diana's lover. Stealing the ring, that wouldn't surprise me at all. But Diana welcoming him into her bed? Never in a million years.'

'I see you're pretty sure about that. But then we're back to: Causer could have stolen the ring and Allman killed Diana in a drug induced haze, then convinced himself he didn't.'

'And that takes us back to James' murder. Was Causer in the room when Don took the call from James?'

'Yep. We had been waiting in the ME's office, and he insinuated himself in there somehow. I didn't even see him do it. It was as if the guy walked through the wall.'

'He's good at that, getting where he's not supposed to be.'

'We're still going around in circles,' Shephard said. 'Unless the phone company can actually do something for us.'

'What about James' murder? Where were each of our suspects? What about surveillance cameras – at the entrance to the factory, a bank up the street, anything?'

'We're checking. Nothing so far. As for our suspects – I saw Causer smoking on the back dock. Your boyf— Don hovered around here clutching his phone. Your esteemed ME did an autopsy – I guess Reese's death left the place short-handed. But staff popped in and out all morning – coffee, smoke breaks, breakfast run, even me, and that factory is only ten minutes away in good traffic. We could estimate the exact time of the murder within a few minutes and cross-check with your security cameras here, but, oh yeah, you don't have any security cameras, except the single one on the back dock which any staff member would know to avoid.'

Theresa rested her chin on her knees, closing her eyes for a moment. She would need to sleep soon, long and deep, but knew it would prove difficult. At least for a while. 'I'm beginning to see what James meant. We have to find that ring. It's our only chance for some kind of answer.'

He was studying her again, with a gaze too penetrating to be comfortable. 'How are you holding up?'

'I'm fine.'

'Really?'

'Actually, I don't know.' She unfolded herself from the chair and stood up. 'But I don't have time to find out.'

TWENTY-NINE

She went back to the file. Elena fussed over her for a couple minutes and even brought her a glass of water, clucking like a woman four times her age, insisting that she didn't want to ask a word about Theresa's ordeal as it was too terrifying to think about. Theresa had no intention of opening up such raw wounds even in the face of reverse psychology, and the girl finally went away to wrap up the day's paperwork and head home.

The autopsy report, upon second reading, did not reveal anything it hadn't with the first. Diana had no injuries save the rope around her neck and the scratches to her throat. During the day Don had finally analyzed the fingernail scrapings on the off chance that they might belong to James' 'real' killer, but as expected they had come from Diana's own skin as she fought to free herself from the ligature. There were no other cuts or bruises, save one on her left knee that probably occurred as the killer forced her to the ground.

Theresa checked the reports of the organs once again. Uterus: unremarkable. No other comment. Even a very newly pregnant woman showed signs of her condition. The lining of the uterus would have thickened to form the placenta, and any pathologist who had at least squeaked by his boards would have noticed it. The supercilious Dr Hubert Reese certainly would have.

Unless, of course, he had been part of forming the baby to begin with. Then he may have wished to leave that detail out. Theresa couldn't see him in the role of Lothario, but he had been a wealthy, accomplished older man and Diana a young woman searching for something in her life without the ability to name it. How many beautiful college students fell for their doddering professors?

If that were true, then the secret had died with him. There would be no way to verify it now. Unless somewhere in that fourteen-room mansion on Fairmount Boulevard there turned up a diamond-and-sapphire ring his grieving widow didn't recognize.

She went on to the toxicology report she had only glanced through before. As noted, Diana had no illegal drugs or indication of alcohol in her system. She had died stone-cold sober, able to fully appreciate the hopelessness of her situation, feel every agonizing quiver of her starving lungs. Theresa read further. N, N-dimethylimidodicarbonimidic diamide hydrochloride had been found. Gosh, that was helpful.

'You still here?'

Janice, Queen of the Secretaries, stood in the doorway.

'I am.'

'I would think you'd be exhausted enough to want to sleep for a week straight.' The older woman came in and dropped into a chair across from Theresa – a first in Theresa's experience. But it had been a stressful two days for everyone in the building.

'I am that too. But it's making me a little crazy – James kept insisting that I should know who Diana's lover was, and I *should* have. I heard all about her marriage and her latest purchases and her favorite movies. I should have picked up some hint if she had been fooling around with someone who worked here.'

'Unless she wasn't,' Janice said. 'Unless James made up the whole story to shield himself from the truth of what he'd done.'

'That could be true. But then I keep coming back to: why is he dead? Did she ever say anything to you, or anyone else here?'

Janice shook her head.

'Did she seem flirtatious with any of the staff?'

'She seemed flirtatious with *all* of the staff. The male ones, anyway.'

'Do you remember a fancy diamond and sapphire ring?'

'Do I! She stuck her hand in front of every single one of our faces. Annoyed Patty especially, I remember, since she had just had a ten-year anniversary and her husband bought her a lawnmower.'

'Any comment on who gave it to her?'

'As I recall she said she bought it herself, that it wasn't real, just looked it. I did wonder at the need to show off an admittedly fake ring, but then making copies of reports is not always the most exciting activity in the world, so I let it go.'

'Did any of her work habits change in the last few months of her life? Quality? Quantity?'

'Diana was efficient, I'll say that for her. I didn't have to stay on her case to get her stuff done, and I don't remember any problems.'

'What about hours? Coming in late? Leaving early?'

Janice began to shake her hairsprayed curls, then stopped. 'Not leaving early. The opposite – she started to stay late. At first I didn't notice, but then . . . I'm usually the last one to leave. Everyone else bolts at the stroke of four thirty as religiously as vampires at sunrise – you know, you see them. But she would still be typing fifteen minutes later, saying she just wanted to finish something. She never put in for comp time for it so I could hardly complain, but I thought it seemed strange. If she had been angling for some kind of promotion, or trying to get herself out of a bad mark on her record then I could see . . . but neither of those situations applied.'

'So you're saying her work performance, which had been fine, actually improved at the end of her life?'

'No, I'm saying she could have been dawdling around until it was time to meet somebody. Maybe he got off work later than her. Because I wouldn't say *improved*. I didn't notice any great increase in her output, and she actually got a little persnickety.'

'Per—?'

'You know how LaShonda always burns those scented candles – anything to combat the smell in this building, Lord knows – but Diana decided that she couldn't stand Vanilla Crème another minute . . . though it's not exactly my favorite either. We had a decomp one day, and you would have thought the building was burning down – how could we be expected to work in these circumstances, etc. Same when the A/C went out.'

Theresa nodded, her gaze falling on the crime scene photos

and the bottle of metformin. 'Did she ever say anything about being diabetic?'

Janice thought. 'Not that I recall. She certainly didn't avoid LaShonda's cupcakes or Trina's Whoopie Pies. And when Christmas came – you know how the funeral homes bring us goodies? We couldn't keep her out of the chocolates. The girls would have to take some back to their desks or they might not get any at all.'

'Hmm.'

Janice cocked her head. 'Why?'

'Everything I learn about her seems contradictory. She was pregnant, she wasn't pregnant. She was having an affair, she wasn't having an affair. Sergeant Shephard called it – we're going around in circles. We've been going around in circles for two days.'

'Is he married?' Janice asked.

'Who? Shephard? I don't know, I didn't ask. Why?'

Janice shook her head. 'You know, for a scientist, you are not always very observant.'

'Tell me about it,' Theresa grumbled.

THIRTY

Theresa left Janice to lock up the vault and returned to the third floor, hoping to catch toxicologist Oliver before he went home for the day. To judge from the condition of his workbench, she shuddered to ponder what that home might look like. George Bain's organized packratness might appear as sleek minimalism compared to Oliver's abode.

Two counters and the back of one of the chromatographs formed three walls of his fortress. He had nearly created a fourth by lining up the compressed gas canisters as far into the aisle as safety regs would allow. Piles of reports, professional journals, Nalgene jars holding either samples or reagents, no less than three open boxes of disposable glass pipettes, a carton of Alconox, and small Tupperware containers with human tissue or perhaps remnants of lunches past hid every available inch of counter space. Only the gas chromatograph-mass spectrometer escaped the clutter. Not even dust had been allowed to pile on its surface.

To call Oliver a friend would constitute a gross exaggeration. To call him enormously useful would not.

As always, he showed the rest of the world his back, hunching over his keyboard with his long, mostly gray ponytail snaking along his spine. His massive frame – which was *not* all muscle, or even partly – hung over both sides of his task chair. He did not acknowledge her presence even when she knocked on one of the gas canisters.

'I need your expertise,' she said, outright flattery being the only approach to show success in past trials.

'Uh.'

'Diana's toxicology report contains some pretty mysterious terms.'

'Which ones are perplexing you? *Blood*, perhaps? Or *urine*?'

'*N*, *N*-dimethylimidodicarbonimidic diamide hydrochloride.' She had written them down on a piece of scrap paper. Oliver hated nothing so much as inexactness.

'Metformin.' He whirled around, beady eyes focusing on her face. 'I hear you spent a number of torturous hours in the presence of a serial killer.'

She didn't argue with the adjectives – that would only prolong the line of conversation. 'Yes.'

'Who was then killed, but not by you.'

'Correct.'

He watched her for a while. For a delirious moment she thought he might ask after her health or mental condition, but he seemed to think better of it. A reputation as a curmudgeon required years of work and thoughtful tending – and was not an accomplishment to be thrown away lightly. 'What other conundrums can I dispel for you?'

'Why would someone who wasn't diabetic be taking metformin?'

'Some new diet craze? I don't know. Why do people get deadly toxins injected into their faces?'

'So they can look like their granddaughters. There's something else in here, too. Doxylamine succinate.'

'Antihistamine. Nothing exciting.'

'But she didn't have a cold. I don't remember her ever mentioning an allergy. So why an antihistamine?'

'Maybe she felt one coming on. Did she tend toward hypochondria?'

'No.'

'Some hide it better than others.'

'Okay. Three, four-pyridinedimethanol, five-hydroxy-six-methyl-hydrochloride.'

He frowned. 'Give me that!'

She handed it over. Supposing – or suggesting, certainly – that he had been stumped would not help her achieve her stated objective.

He typed the terms on his keyboard, then studied the monitor – which had been fitted with a non-county-issued privacy screen, rendering it impossible to read from anywhere except where he sat, directly in front.

'Hmm,' he said. After a few moments, he said it again, until she could stand it no longer.

'*What*, Oliver?'

'Nothing terribly interesting. It just might explain the antihistamine. And the metformin.'

'Hooooow?'

'The pyridinedimethanol can be used together with the antihistamine to make a new drug called Diclegis. It's for morning sickness. Ah, your eyes widen. That means something to you? Our dear, departed Diana had been knocked up?'

'I'm getting conflicting reports on that. Is this stuff over-the-counter?'

'Nope, has to be prescribed. The FDA is very fussy about that sort of thing, ever since the whole Thalidomide debacle. That's why they panicked and took Benedictin off the market in the early eighties, leaving virtually nothing to replace it with, so ladies expecting a confinement just had to keep puking until very recently when the FDA were finally ready to admit that oops, sorry, it's not so bad after all. But manufacturers know all about how name recognition is a double-edged sword, so they changed the name to Diclegis. It's basically the same formula.'

Theresa zoned out as he discussed the current history of morning sickness medication. Diana couldn't have gotten the stuff except from a doctor, and a doctor would not have prescribed it unless they had been absolutely certain of her pregnancy. Her opinion and/or a home pregnancy kit would not suffice. She might have gotten some from a friend or some other backwater route, of course, but there would be little need for that. She had adequate medical insurance. 'You said it also explained the metformin.'

'Provided, of course, she had not actually been diabetic. Do you have any proof of that?'

'No, but let's assume it for the sake of argument.'

'Then the only other reason – to my knowledge, and I assure you my knowledge is formidable—'

'Acknowledged.'

'Thank you. The only other reason would be to combat polycystic ovary syndrome.'

He waited to see if she would recognize the term, which of course she didn't, yielding what passed for a smile of equal parts condescension and triumph.

'Women with PCOS have too-high levels of the male hormone testosterone – not something one would suspect of the comely Diana, but there you have it – which, among other things, causes irregular ovulation and menstruation. It also causes insulin resistance, which prevents the endometrial lining from getting in shape to nurture one's little bundle of joy.'

'So the metformin might have been prescribed to prevent a miscarriage. *If* Diana had this PCOS.'

'Exacta-mundo.'

She stood up, turned to go and walked into one of the gas canisters.

'Try not to blow us up on your way out,' Oliver said. 'What's on your mind? How does PCOS explain all that has occurred, in both the past and the present?'

'I'm not sure it does yet. I have to check some things out.'

She walked out of the lab, literally feeling her way along the counter, unable to see what stood in front of her, her mind so full of shifting facts and suppositions and—

'You're *welcome*,' Oliver called after her, his pissy tones bouncing between the glassware and Nalgene jars.

The basement seemed no more or less creepy than it always did, the crypts holding their secrets and the four-inch-thick doors waiting to lure in a passing victim and then encase them forever. A weak and fading light shone through the one set of windows in the entire level, a small set of clear squares that let one see a few blades of errant grass and the bumper of someone's car. She both feared and appreciated the basement; it would be impossible to ignore the childhood terrors it evoked, but at the same time she could always work there in peace and quiet. She made her way down to the end of the hallway and had just slipped her key into the lock when someone tapped her on the shoulder.

She screamed. Literally. There was no way to qualify it, she screeched like a little girl and that was that.

'Sorry!' The woman, a complete stranger, wore a black skirt

and a deep-blue blouse, black pumps and a little too much eyeshadow for her pale complexion. 'I didn't mean to startle you.'

'Who – what – where did you come from?'

'The elevator.'

Theresa honestly debated for a moment whether the woman might be a ghost. She had never encountered one in the Medical Examiner's Office, or anywhere else, but then again there would be a first time for everything and it would not be the worst thing that had happened to her that day – until she realized that the woman probably meant the *other* elevator. 'What can I do for you?'

'Theresa MacLean, right?'

'Yes.'

'I'm Claire Donovan with the county manager's office. I just have some questions for you.'

Theresa blinked. 'It's been a really long day.'

'I know! So awful, what you've been through. So I won't take much of your time. It's routine stuff, really. Is this where evidence is stored? That would be great, because I kind of need to see it.'

'A really long day,' Theresa repeated. 'Can't we do this tomorrow?'

'Unfortunately, the manager wants my report as soon as possible.' Her voice sounded sweet and soft and utterly unrelenting, as did her perky smile. I've got to learn how to do that, Theresa thought.

'Uh—'

'Tell you what, just continue with whatever it is that you're doing and we can talk while you're working. How's that? It would really help me out.'

Theresa unlocked the door and followed the labeled bags of clothing back through the years until she found Diana's. Claire Donovan paused only for a moment from the funky, dusty smell and the cavernous collection of murder and mayhem. Then she plunged back in. 'How long have you worked here? Is this door always kept locked? How do you know what is what? Do you spend a lot of time here after hours?'

To this last question Theresa answered 'no'. The county loathed overtime, so she would only be here when someone had been murdered during inconvenient hours – and they were often inconvenient hours – and the cops wanted her to go to the scene. She blew the dust off a paper grocery bag containing the clothing Diana Allman had worn upon her death.

Claire Donovan coughed. 'What about your chief medical examiner? Does he spend a lot of time here when not on duty?'

'I wouldn't have any idea. Since I'm not here myself.'

'I thought there might be talk.'

'Not to me.' Theresa headed for the door.

'Your supervisor's position has been empty for a while.'

'Yes.' *Would you like to see the storage room? The door still shows signs of the explosion.*

But County Auditor Donovan did not seem interested in salacious details. 'Any plans to hire a new one?'

'Supposedly, they're getting a recruitment effort together.'

'Who?'

'I don't know; whoever handles nationwide talent searches. HR? The county exec?'

'Wouldn't you be part of that process?'

'Haven't been asked yet.' Theresa locked the door behind them.

'And you've been acting supervisor?'

'Yes.'

'Without a bump in pay?'

'Without.' They moved through the basement, and Theresa punched the button for the elevator. 'Why?'

'Oh,' Claire Donovan said. 'Just routine.'

Routine *what*? Theresa wondered, but felt too tired to care much about it.

'Your DNA analyst, Don Delgado?'

Theresa felt a rumbling through her midsection, which meant that if she were a dog her fur would be starting to stand up. 'Yes?'

'Does he have a PhD?'

'Yes, he does.'

'But you don't.'

'No.' The doors opened, and Theresa stepped into the elevator. 'I don't.'

The auditor made some note of this on her clipboard as the car rose with its usual groan. 'I see.'

Theresa turned to her. 'What do you see, exactly?'

'That this is my floor. Take care of yourself, Theresa.' The woman stepped into the lobby, now dimmed for the off-hours. 'You should get some rest tonight. You look exhausted.'

The doors closed before Theresa's lips could form a good, sneering, 'Oh, really?'

She did what she always did in times of utter confusion. She went back to the evidence. Don had already done the fingernail scrapings, so that only left the tapings and the clothing; he had gone home at last, leaving her a note to call him if she felt like talking. She assumed Shephard had done so as well. She felt abandoned, with that sort of post-event let-down that makes one reluctant to say goodbye to people met on vacation or in a long line, despite knowing that they'll be forgotten within the half-hour, and she chided herself for it. She should go home too; they had all reached the living-dead level of exhaustion. James' reign of terror had ended, and it seemed extremely unlikely that his killer would have anyone else in his sights. And he still could have been shot by a nemesis from his past, from his neighborhood or his prison, someone who had never been within ten miles of the medical examiner's office. And if his murderer did hail from inside the ME's walls, that person would have better sense than to start up another spree and leave bodies scattered along the hallways.

The image gave her pause.

She might be working alongside a cold-blooded murderer. She might have been doing so for the past ten years. And, just as when James had been in their midst, she had no idea who, or how, or why.

She pulled out the tapings and her slides. Around her, the building quieted down into its night-time mode. Soon there would be no sound or movement on any of the three floors save for the television in the deskmen's office and their desultory conversation as they discussed what to order for their meal break. They would need those distractions tonight; it couldn't be easy to function in a space that still smelled of the bleach used to clean up their co-worker's blood.

She went back to the animal hair she had mounted and found a few more on the tapings. None had roots, which restricted her ability to identify them. They were either a tan or white color and appeared to be simple, undyed wool. But the overlapping scales of the cuticle seemed much thinner and numerous than in wool fibers. In frustration, she laid one between two pieces of plastic cut from the rings that held a six-pack together and let the little sandwich warm until softened on the electric stirrer/warmer. Then she used a clean scalpel to slice off pieces, as thin as she could make them – the poor man's microtome. Crude, but usually effective enough.

The building had truly gone silent now, and oddly enough she found it comforting rather than scary. She had been surrounded by stressed-out human beings for going on forty-eight hours now, and the peace and quiet felt like a balm across her chafed brain.

The cross-sections let her look at the inside of the fiber, which told her nothing except that it was semi-hollow. A convenient quality for a fiber, lightweight and warm, but—

Hmm.

Her mind began to travel down roads she didn't want to follow, forming images she didn't want to see.

Theresa stood up and went downstairs, feeling the darkness close enough to touch. It watched her from every angle as she slipped down the back staircase.

The two deskmen on duty started a bit when she appeared in their doorway.

'Don't sneak up on us like that, man!' one told her. 'Especially now. We didn't think anyone was here.'

She smiled. 'Sorry, didn't mean to scare you.'

'James really locked you in the trunk?'

'Yeah.'

'Bet that sucked.'

'It did. I need to look at one of the old daybooks, okay?'

They cocked their heads at her in unison, but only for a moment before waving her toward the shelves and returning to their pad thai. The deskmen's hub formed the pivot on which the rest of the building turned, and they saw not only every oddity of the dead but also most of those of the living as well. They fielded calls from relatives, agencies and the press, removed personal effects from victims ranging from sex toys of outstanding depravity to bloodstained photos of children, and kept track of office gossip with a bookie's precision. Someone browsing through the ledgers of the dead hardly merited a glance . . . in any week except this one, perhaps.

'What you looking for?' the other asked her.

'I'm not sure yet.' The tall red daybooks, similar to the ones they had used in Trace Evidence before the conversion to digital, were stacked in order on the second-highest shelf. Since only one covered an entire year, they had nearly twenty years of history sitting in the deskmen's office. When that shelf filled to overflowing the excess migrated to the vault. They would not be allowed to take up another shelf, which had all been spoken for by forms and other supplies and a thorough collection of crackers. She found the one for the year of Diana's death and pulled it out.

Each page had the date embossed at the top, its lines filled with handwritten notations regarding the victims received during the day. They were first assigned a number, handed out in numerical order on a first-come, first-served basis. Then there would be various notations of name, age, gender, home address, apparent cause of death, next of kin and to which funeral home or crematorium the body had gone after its brief stay. Some days allowed for spaces between the entries; some days required writing in the margins in ever-more cramped script.

She turned to the date of Diana's death, September 23. It had not been particularly busy. Two motor vehicle accidents, both male and single vehicle – Car Vs. Tree and Motorcycle Vs. Pothole. Theresa wondered if a biker could have a more embarrassing epitaph than *done in by frost damage*. The shooting, B/M, 22 yrs, GSW to head. Unwitnessed death at home of a W/M 55 yrs with the common notation Hx of EtOH, which meant that whatever the technical cause of death might be, the victim's penchant for hooch had finally caught up with him. And Diana, recorded in Darryl Johnson's dispassionate hand. B/F, Hom-Strangled. There the day had ended, until a homeless man who had fallen down the escalator at Tower City came in bright and early on the twenty-fourth as a W/M, unk, Acc.

Theresa turned back to the previous page. Another young man dead from an auto accident, two middle-aged men with apparent heart issues, another who had overdosed and one who had been excavating a ditch when the soil gave way and a backhoe tumbled into the space on top of him.

She even checked the day before, but the sad history there did not clear up her question.

'Did Sergeant Shephard leave?' she asked.

'Dunno. He had been looking for the ME, last I saw him. How long do you think they're going to hang around here?'

'What about the detectives? Are they still in the building?'

'Nah, they headed out all bustlin', asking us if Justin – that Allman guy, I mean – ever said anything about prison or about somebody gunnin' for him or anything like that. He never seemed too worried to me.'

'I didn't work with the guy,' the second deskman said. 'So I couldn't tell them nothing.'

The first guy went on: 'Only thing it seemed like he didn't like was the bodies. But he got used to them. Where you going?' he asked Theresa as she put the ledger back and moved to the door.

'Upstairs,' Theresa said, but didn't specify which floor. It might be best not to leave a trail.

THIRTY-ONE

Leo had managed to keep his position at the Medical Examiner's office for close to twenty years despite being malicious and cold with a wide streak of lazy. One of the more helpful qualities he maintained in order to accomplish this was a habit of socking away information for future reference like a squirrel with nuts preparing for the inevitable winter. And not just information. Sometimes the habit included other people's employment applications, the contents of other people's Rolodexes, and keys to other people's offices.

Theresa had found them after cleaning out his desk and had tossed them aside, assuming the assortment would belong to their storage areas in the basement or perhaps downtown. But weeks later, when she had time to check, the keys hadn't fit any of those locks. Another week later when she had been alone on the floor, on a whim she tried them one by one until she discovered that two fit the lab doors of their neighbors across the hall in Toxicology. This had been in violation of county rules, certainly, but more importantly in violation of the director of toxicology, who guarded their findings as if they were secret wedding locations of A-list Hollywood celebrities. The truth might give the man an instant coronary, and who knew what effect it might have on the legal disposition of past cases? Lawyers could, if they chose, make huge haystacks out of such straws. So Theresa had mentally shelved the topic, gotten busy with a rash of homicides, and completely forgotten about it.

Now she retrieved the jangling ring from a cubbyhole in Leo's old desk and wondered what other forbidden citadels they might open to her.

If she hesitated, she might falter and second-guess herself into oblivion. So she went directly to Stone's office.

The second floor sat deserted and silent as if hermetically sealed, the only illumination coming from a single set of tubes in one ceiling tile and the red and green glowing 'ready' lights on the sea of computer monitors, towers, speakers and battery back-ups along the secretaries' desks. If only Janice, Queen of the Secretaries, had stayed behind. Theresa would take on Bigfoot if Janice had her back.

The fourth key on the ring fit.

The office of the medical examiner held only the ambient light that passed through its windows: two large ones facing the street and its lamps, and two facing the secretaries' area, but it was enough for her to move to the shelf against the latter windows and find the jar marked 9/23/04. She held it up to the small amount of light from the street, double-checking the label. A supposedly cancerous uterus from a supposedly autopsied female. But there had been no females autopsied within the few days on and prior to Diana's death. Only Diana.

None of this made any sense. Yet here she held a specimen with a clearly erroneous date, in the office of the Medical Examiner, where such a thing as an error of any kind should not exist.

'Put that down,' Elliott Stone said.

She turned, nearly dropping the heavy glass jar but catching it before it could shatter on the credenza that ran beneath the shelves. Once she had it settled more securely in her hands, she stammered, 'What is this?'

He didn't appear to have a weapon, though he wore a light trench coat with big pockets. He also blocked the only door.

'It's a uterus with a burst subserosal fibroid. What about it?' His casual tone seemed annoyed but unworried. 'How did you get into my office?'

'Leo had keys. It's dated the same day as Diana's death.'

'Leo had keys to my office?'

'Apparently, Leo had keys to every office.'

'*Leo*? That compromises . . . Do you have any idea what that means?'

'Yes,' Theresa said. 'It means you killed Diana.'

THIRTY-TWO

He had always made the most sense from the beginning, she realized. Relatively young, handsome, ambitious, relatively wealthy and on his way to becoming more so. And silver-tongued. Diana would have been doomed to fall from her first day on the job.

She had also been willing to be discreet, keeping knowledge of the affair from even her closest friends. Most of his money stemmed from his wife's family, and the reigning ME back then had been very old-fashioned about things like sleeping with the staff.

'What did you tell her?' Theresa asked. 'That you needed to keep your wife on the hook until your student loans were paid off? That she would become suicidal if you left? That you had to hang in there until the kids were a little older and better able to handle the upheaval?'

He didn't move from the doorway. 'What are you talking about?'

'Why did you keep this, all these years? The evidence that could condemn you.'

'What are you talking about?' But the conviction in his voice slipped a notch. His gaze darted from her to the jar in her hands, as if part of him feared she might drop it and the other part calculated how best to snatch it from her.

'Did you volunteer to act as diener for Dr Reese that day? The eager young doctor, ready to pitch in wherever needed. No one wanted to see their co-worker flayed open like that, best to get it done as quickly as possible. But you were both doctors, so you could both do the work, speed things up a little. You could dissect the organs while he worked on the larynx. That, after all, seemed the relevant area.'

'Can you see Reese delegating work?'

'Any other day of the decade, no. But as zealous as he could be about work, Hubert Reese was a pompous man looking forward to a ceremony acknowledging his stature at no less than Cleveland's premier university. And, as I said, you were both doctors.'

'Let me get this straight. You think I kept Diana Allman's uterus in a jar for the past ten years. That is beyond bizarre.'

'It is. Why didn't you just dissect, discard, then lie about it in your report? Because the autopsy report is false, isn't it? Diana's uterus wasn't "unremarkable". Diana was pregnant with your child.'

'You're crazy,' he stated without inflection, just a regrettable but unmistakable fact. 'The trauma of the past two days has unhinged you – it would affect anyone, so don't feel insulted. I never had an affair with Diana Allman, and I certainly never impregnated her. That specimen is from a different victim.'

'There were no other females autopsied that day, or the two days prior.'

'Then it's mislabeled.'

'The printer emits the labels automatically. Why didn't you just slip it into your pocket to get it out of the room? A small thing, it will fit in the palm of your hand, but how to get rid of it? Someone might notice it in the garbage, and you had Causer and Darryl Johnson hanging around just to get a glimpse of Diana Allman naked. So you slipped into the dispensing cubby for a smoke just to give yourself time to think. Is that what gave you the idea? That a cigarette burn would make a convincing fake cancer? Drop it in a jar and fill with formalin, then leave on the counter with the rest of the specimens. You probably didn't even think about it, just fixed the sticker the way you had a thousand times before. Habits will always out.'

'That's the most ridiculous thing—'

'You went back to the autopsy with nothing left to fear. But you couldn't leave the jar there, of course, or the gals in Histology would section it for Reese and he would see the pregnancy. You had to go back later and get it, but that wasn't difficult. No one ever questioned a doctor popping in and out of autopsy. No one ever questioned a doctor, period.'

'Did you dream all this up when you were locked in the trunk?' he asked. 'Bang your head too hard going over a couple of rumble strips?'

'I identified the strange animal hair on her clothing.' Theresa nodded at the furry rug underneath his guest chairs. 'It's alpaca.'

'Except that rug wasn't in this room ten years ago.'

'No, but it was in your office, where Dr Banachek is now. I remember the other doctors joking about your decorating tastes.'

'Diana dropped off reports and death certificates to my office all the time. You could probably find alpaca fur on all the secretaries then. And now. Animal hair gets everywhere – ask anyone who owns a cat.'

This time Theresa nodded at the framed photos. 'She was going to take up skiing. Was that another plan you made while she was "dropping off reports" on your alpaca rug?'

'This is the snow belt,' he said with an impatient sigh. 'Everyone skis.'

'You know, you're right. I could be way off here, but luckily there's an easy way to resolve this. I'm going to take this specimen down to the autopsy room and do what should have been done ten years ago – examine the interior lining. If I find the beginnings of a child then DNA testing will be completed and the police can formally request a buccal swab from you to do the comparison. If I'm wrong and there's no child present, then you can fire me, chalk my accusations up to PTSD and stick to the official "James killed Diana" story.'

'Just put the jar down and go home.'

'Why? Surely you can't be that attached to a burst subserosal fibroid?'

'I use that for teaching, just like the other samples. Now put it down.'

Instead she held it further from her body. 'Why doesn't it float, by the way? All your other specimens are floating.'

'That depends on the exact formulation of the liquid and the density of the specimen. It means nothing.'

True, but it appeared to mean something to him. 'Where's the harm? Let me have your dead uterus, and we can disprove the entire idea. You know that if I don't, questions will linger forever.'

'A man in my position is no stranger to gossip.'

'A man in your position can't afford to take chances. You took one ten years ago. I see you've learned to hold your temper since then. An affair can be quietly done away with. A murder is a much riskier proposition.'

'So now I not only impregnated Diana, I killed her too?'

'Who else had a motive?'

He took another step forward, closer to her but still blocking the door. It didn't really matter since she'd never make it around him; the office wasn't that big. 'How about her violent, abusive husband who recently murdered three of our staff members and kidnapped a fourth? What did he do to you to create Stockholm Syndrome in only one morning? How did he get you so deep into his corner that you create a fantasy in order to shift blame to the one guy standing between you and your ambition?'

'*My* ambition?'

'You knew I'd never promote you to Leo's position. So, get me out of the way and that sap Banachek becomes ME. You know you can get him to give you whatever you want.'

'That's insane.'

'It is insane, because it will never work. I'm the Medical Examiner. You've only maintained your position because you and your cousin work the system. You probably framed Leo—'

'*What*?'

'—and the trauma of the past few days, added to the traumas of the past few years, have worked upon your delicate little mind until it broke. You've lost it, and no one is going to listen to you.'

She spoke through gritted teeth, determined not to let him get to her. 'You might be surprised. And I am not leaving this office without this jar.'

'Yes, you are. And when you do, it will be for good. You're fired.'

'Where's James' cellphone?'

He blinked. 'What?'

'You got the number from Don's caller ID, when you huddled with him and Shephard, waiting for James to call. When you had a minute alone you called him and arranged a meeting. What did you tell him, that you knew who killed

Diana, that you knew where the ring was? But then your call could be traced from *his* phone, so you had to take his phone with you. Is it here somewhere, too? I would think you would have learned to get rid of the evidence, given your line of work and all.'

'Why would James agree to meet me? He didn't even know me.'

'Because James was about as desperate as a man could be. He wanted answers and knew the window to get them closed by the second. Did you know I was in the trunk?'

'If I were the killer and I had—' he smiled – 'would you be standing here now?'

How could he not know? Theresa flashed back a few hours: James had said, 'I'm *stashing* this woman.' The listeners huddled around the phone had no idea where they were. They could have been in a safe house or a friend's place where James locked her in a room or basement. Stone wouldn't have heard her voice during the phone call. Unless James specifically mentioned her current location – and he hadn't been in a sharing mood – Stone could have missed the possibility altogether.

It all fit. But she held the only possible proof in her hand, with no way out.

Like James, Stone had six inches and a hundred pounds on her, with those ski-pole-strengthened arms. And she had to let him attack first; otherwise he would use it as a sign of her mental instability. But he was also getting angry, frustrated at not getting his way, teetering on the brink of showing that famous temper.

'I'm leaving with this jar,' she said.

'No.'

She started to walk past him. He put one hand on her neck and grabbed the jar with the other one, as if it were going to be that easy. She could smell his aftershave and the remnants of bourbon on his breath.

The movement caused the organ to shift inside its liquid bath. It bumped against the side of the jar, and in their frozen tableau they both heard the tiny, distinctive sound of metal against glass.

Suddenly, she knew. She could feel her eyes widen, and he returned her stare with narrowed lids. A decision had just been made, on both parts.

She hung on to the jar with both hands and kicked him in the groin. The angle wasn't helpful and it wasn't much of a kick, but she wrenched the jar back.

He bent slightly, then punched her in the face. It snapped her head back and put her off-balance. He pulled at the jar. There was no sound in the universe except their assorted puffs of breath and grunts of exertion.

Theresa kicked at his shin as hard as she could, and much more effectively than before, since she had gotten her spare work boots from her office closet. The steel toes came in handy. She tried for the groin again, but he knocked her back across the armchair, cracking her spine in not one but two places.

He leaned over and put his hands around her neck.

He can't kill me, she told herself. He'll never be able to explain it.

But she knew he could. He could take her body out the back, drop it in the park system somewhere and hope she'd be badly decomposed when found. The staff would come up with all sorts of scenarios in which she had gotten connected with James' world and it'd bitten her in the ass.

Or he could hang her from a tree somewhere, or even in her office. Make it look like a suicide – it wouldn't fool a decent pathologist for a second, but when he thoughtfully performed the process himself, sparing the other doctors and especially her pal Dr Banachek, then he could make her death look like anything he wanted. She had been upset. She had been traumatized. It wouldn't look like a stretch to anyone who didn't know her well.

Breathing in became an impossibility. Her throat burned as if it were on fire, and her face probably looked as red as his did, as it contorted with effort and fury and a force beyond reasoning. The back of her neck rested against the thin padding of the wooden arm, so her neck would snap if the suffocation didn't get her first.

She tried to kick his sensitive areas, but her thighs stayed pinned open by his legs. She couldn't attack his face because her hands were full with the jar. No handy letter openers or even a stapler sat within reach on the desk. Her vision began to narrow, the view nothing but stars.

She slid the jar out from between them and raised it over her head, let the other hand join them. Then she brought it down on to his skull as hard as she could. She heard the clunk, but missed the sound of breaking glass – the first indication she had that the jar had shattered were the nicks of small cuts from the broken glass against her fingers and then the stinging pain as wetness found them.

The effect was not immediate. The tension around her larynx eased by only an iota, not enough to let her suck in the oxygen she so desperately needed. But then the formalin coursed over his head and along his scalp. Theresa closed her eyes and turned her head as much as she could, but still she felt the cold drops on her temple and ear.

Then the corrosive formaldehyde mixture reached his eyes, and with a roar of pain he let go of her and straightened up. Theresa slumped to the side and fell to the floor, feeling more stabs to her palms and forearms. But that came as a distant sensation, far secondary to the glorious oxygen that now flooded her lungs. They pumped in and out, frantically, while the rest of her body lacked the energy to do anything else. She could have stayed unmoving for the rest of the night, but the pricks of searing pain in her hands and the burning of her skin and the spastic gruntings of the medical examiner as he lumbered around the room told her that she had to move. *Now*.

She opened her eyes, blinked for focus that didn't want to come. A few inches away sat a smooth pink triangular balloon. Next to it sat a silver ring with a cluster of blue and white stones.

She pushed herself up, forcing slivers of glass further into her fingers.

The blurry figure of the Medical Examiner stumbled out of his office doorway, hands held to his face. A keening wail filled the air, and despite everything it made her want to go help him, to find a sink and a towel to flush out his eyes.

Then she thought of Diana Allman and instead reached for the phone.

She called the police, then scooped up the organ and the ring and went down the front staircase to the deskmen's office.

THIRTY-THREE

The cops found Stone still in the men's room, flushing his eyes with fresh water; a smart thing to do, except that every copious dousing found more formalin in his hair to bring forward, so a complete cleansing took quite a while. He had used the time to formulate a plausible scenario, in which a deranged forensic scientist broke into his office and attacked him, accusing him of multiple homicides to which she had a much closer connection than he had. He was lucky not to have lost either his sight or his life.

It wasn't a bad job, Shephard admitted to Theresa. The man had an ability to think fast when it came to covering up his crimes. But as soon as the officers had gotten a look at the bruises on Theresa's neck, the story abruptly became much less plausible.

Now she sat on a vacant autopsy table while a medic applied ointment to her irritated skin and bandages to the myriad of small cuts on her fingers. Don had brought her coffee, caffeine being her only prop with which to stave off a complete collapse. Zoe held a scale next to Theresa's collarbone to get photos of the purplish handprints. The photographer had to shove Shephard out of the way more than once to get close enough.

'I'm glad you're here,' Theresa said to him.

'I'll drive you home,' he said immediately. 'You've had a horrific day. I just want you to know . . . I'm sure you know that you shouldn't be alone—'

'I meant, for you to be a witness,' she explained. 'To whatever Christina might find in there.'

The pathologist stood at the stainless steel counter, carefully conducting the sectioning and examination of the uterus that should have been done ten years previously. The recovered sapphire ring sat on a clean cutting board under a magnifying lamp.

'Oh,' he said.

'I don't count?' Zoe asked.

Theresa said, 'We need someone who isn't an ME office employee. We could all be conspiring to frame our boss.'

Her back to them, Christina snorted. 'If I thought it would work I would have done the old lech in years ago. Any chance the formaldehyde bath will kill him? It's highly toxic.'

'Nah. He'd have to drink an ounce of close to forty percent solution. The stuff we fix organs in is more like four percent.'

'Darn.'

The medic gave up, and Zoe went to photograph the disrupted interior of the office on the second floor.

Seated on the other vacant table, Don said, 'I can't believe he kept Diana's uterus and her ring in a jar on his shelf for ten years like some sort of sick trophy. How could he be that warped, yet rational enough to run this place?'

'Because Janice actually runs this place,' Theresa said, 'at least, to hear her tell it when she thinks no one can overhear. But I don't think he's warped, not that way – I think he hung on to them out of sheer paranoia. No way of getting rid of them would seem good enough. If he got caught with the ring he'd be sunk. If he took it home his wife might find it. If he threw it out a car window it might land in the lap of the rare honest person who could describe the vehicle. If he tossed it into the biohazard bag with the rest of her organs, the funeral home might find it when raking out the incinerator, and then he'd be worse off than before. We've seen so many ways in which the killer gets caught that, I'll wager, nothing seemed like a sure thing. But he could send a biological specimen out of this room and be sure no one would want to handle or examine it closely. The uterus was a handy disguise. It also contained the only other piece of evidence against him.'

'No maybe about it,' Christina said. She turned to face the rest of the people in the room. 'It's here.'

'She was pregnant?' Theresa clarified.

Christina nodded. 'I'll make a tube for Don to test.'

The room fell silent, reflecting on both the child who never had a chance to be, and its dead mother.

'So he had the stupid ring all along,' Shephard said.

'James was right,' Theresa said. 'The ring was the only

piece of concrete evidence that would support his story. Stone found a moment alone with Diana's body – not hard to do since there would have been hardly anyone else in the building. He removed the bag, took off the ring, put on a fresh bag and closed it with evidence tape, scribbled a passable facsimile of Cousin Casey's initials. No one ever looks at them that closely.'

Don said, 'And I didn't; I just cut them off like I'd done a hundred times before and since. But why did he worry about the ring at all?'

'I don't know. It didn't look wide enough to be engraved. But it was expensive – I didn't say so to James, but those stones were definitely real. Maybe it was custom-made, or at least pricey enough that he thought it could be traced to him. He couldn't be one-hundred-percent sure that Diana hadn't told someone – me, her mother, a second cousin – about the affair, and that ring would be the only physical evidence of it. That and the baby, of course. That the missing ring cemented a case against James became the icing on the cake – just the man I want to see.'

Mitchell Causer had entered the room. He seemed disappointed to find her neither horizontal nor naked.

His expression went from salacious to suspicious. 'Why?'

'You said Stone kept bitching about having to be diener for Diana's autopsy because he had trouble at home. Why did you say that?'

The man's piglike eyes looked blank. 'I dunno.'

'You said you thought he had an argument with his wife. Why? What made you think that?'

'I don't know! It was a hell of a long time ago.'

'But you told me that only yesterday. It must have been stuck in your mind for a reason.'

'Yeah, but—' The smoke in his eyes cleared. 'Yeah – he had a red mark on his cheek. Like somebody smacked him.'

'And you thought his wife had slapped him?'

'No, I thought she laid him out with a right hook.' Causer pondered this further, hand on his chin, thinking so hard that he almost looked intelligent. 'He had, like, a scrape on his jaw and the beginning of a bruise. I ragged him about it for a while, but you know Stone. He don't give nothing up.'

Theresa exchanged a look with Don, who hopped off the opposite table and went to where the ring sat. He pulled on gloves and raised it to the magnifying lamp for a closer look.

'It's got tissue in all the little settings and prongs,' he said. 'But that could all belong to Diana. Having sat in formalin for ten years isn't going to help, either.'

'Don't give up,' she warned.

'Not until I've extracted every last cell.'

'Take this too.' Christina handed him a plastic tube with a screw top. 'I'm giving the rest to Histology.' She left the suite and, since Theresa clearly did not intend to start shedding clothes, Causer followed Christine's bosom right out the door.

Don put the ring in a Petri dish and made to leave also. 'You go home and get some sleep,' he told Theresa. 'I mean it.'

'I will. I—' But she spoke to his disappearing back and let her words trail off.

Then she was left with no one save Sergeant Shephard, who watched her with arms crossed.

'I get it,' he said without preamble. 'He's Just Not That Into You, but you don't want to accept it. We've all been there. It sucks.'

She didn't have the strength to deflect the topic, and she certainly did not have the strength to begin this conversation.

'But I'm here.' He came forward and put his hands, quite deliberately, over hers, letting his palms spill over on to her thighs. His brown eyes were soft and deadly serious. 'I'm right in front of you.'

Very slowly, her cheeks lifted into a smile.

'Yes,' she said. 'So you are.'